Diane Gaston's dream job was always to write romance novels. One day she dared to pursue that dream, and has never looked back. Her books have won romance's highest honours: the RITA® Award, the National Readers' Choice Award, the HOLT Medallion, Golden Quill and Golden Heart®. She lives in Virginia, USA, with her husband and three very ordinary house cats. Diane loves to hear from readers and friends. Visit her website at: dianegaston.com.

A LADY BECOMES A GOVERNESS

Diane Gaston

MILLS & BOON

First published in Great Britain 2018
by Mills & Boon, an imprint of HarperCollins*Publishers*
1 London Bridge Street, London, SE1 9GF

Large Print edition 2018

© 2018 Diane Perkins

ISBN: 978-0-263-07503-8

MIX
Paper from
responsible sources
FSC
www.fsc.org
FSC C007454

This book is produced from independently certified FSC™ paper to ensure responsible forest management. For more information visit www.harpercollins.co.uk/green.

Printed and bound in Great Britain
by CPI Group (UK) Ltd, Croydon, CR0 4YY

To my dear friend Kristine Hughes Patrone,
with whom I've shared the delights
of many a trip to England.

Chapter One

June 1816

Lady Rebecca Pierce trailed behind the seaman carrying her portmanteau on his shoulder and the dour-faced maid who was her companion for this undesired trip sailing across the Irish Sea to England to marry a man she loathed.

The seaman led them across the deck, following other passengers, a woman with children, a gentleman, a tradesman. The seaman took them through the companionway and down the steps to the cabins below.

Rebecca inhaled the scent of brine that permeated the ship's wood. Must she be stuck breathing that sour mockery of fresh sea air for the entire journey? Would Nolan, the maid her half-brother, the Earl of Keneagle, hired to accompany her, at least allow her to spend some time on deck? She loved standing at the bow of a ship, feeling the sea breeze on her face and watching the vessel cut through the inky water.

She slowed her step, simply to annoy the woman. Nolan's duty was to make certain Rebecca fulfilled the nuptials her brother had arranged for her—forced on her—but that did not mean Nolan could control her every move.

Rebecca glanced behind her. But there was no escaping the ship, not when it was anchored in the middle of the harbour. Even if she could swim the distance to shore, her brother had also arranged it that she would have nothing unless she married Lord Stonecroft.

'Lady Rebecca!' a strident voice called. Nolan, of course. 'Hurry. Your cabin is ready.'

Her lips thinned and she simply stopped.

'Lady Rebecca!' Nolan had walked back to get her.

Reluctantly—and slowly—Rebecca followed her to the cabin.

In her cabin, Rebecca sat at the small table and chairs that were securely fastened to the floor. Through a small porthole she watched the ship leave the harbour. There was a good wind. No doubt they would reach England in the morning.

In the open sea, the water grew choppy and the ship heaved and swayed.

'Oh,' Nolan moaned, clasping her stomach. She dropped into the seat across from Rebecca. 'I'm going to be sick.'

Not in her cabin, thought Rebecca. 'Come.' She rose and helped Nolan to her feet. 'I'll take you to your cabin. You can rest there.'

Nolan had a small cabin near Rebecca's, nothing more than a berth and, luckily, a bucket. She helped Nolan into bed.

'Oh,' Nolan moaned again. The older woman had turned pale. She rolled over and faced the wall.

'Can I get you anything?' Rebecca asked. It was hard not to feel sympathy for the woman. 'Eating something will help seasickness.'

Nolan thrashed in the bed. 'No food. No food. Leave me alone.'

Rebecca placed the bucket next to the berth. 'There is a bucket, if you need it. I will check on you later.'

'No,' wailed Nolan. 'Leave me alone.'

With pleasure, thought Rebecca.

But she would check on the maid none the less. She'd never experienced seasickness herself, but in her trips across the Irish Sea during her years in school, she'd witnessed many others who had endured such misery.

She walked into the passageway and could not help feeling as if a weight had been lifted off her shoulders. She was free to do as she wished—within the confines of the ship, at least. It was worth something.

She quickly found her sea legs and easily walked to the companionway. Free of Nolan, this was the perfect time to go on deck and enjoy what she could of the voyage.

The hatch opened and a young woman descended the stairs. She wore a hooded cape that was damp and smelled of the sea.

Rebecca waited. There was only room for one on the stairs.

Head down, the woman passed Rebecca and Rebecca started up the stairs.

'Were you planning to go on deck, miss?' the woman asked. 'The midshipman sent me down.'

Rebecca turned.

The woman pulled the hood of the cloak off her head. 'Rough seas—' Her eyes widened.

Rebecca gasped.

This woman had her same pale hazel eyes, her nose and lips, her nondescript brown hair. She was of a similar height and figure and age. Her cloak was even a similar shade of grey.

Rebecca was looking in a mirror. Except her mirror image wore her hair in a simple style and her dress was a drab brown.

When Rebecca managed to breathe again, she shook her head. 'You look like me!'

Her eyes must be deceiving her. She blinked twice, but her mirror image remained.

The other woman laughed nervously. 'I—I do not know what to say.'

'Neither do I.' What did one say to one's exact likeness?

'It is most unsettling.' The young woman straightened. 'But forgive my manners. Allow me to present myself. I am Miss Tilson. A governess. Nobody you would know.'

Rebecca extended her hand. 'Lady Rebecca Pierce. It is a pleasure to meet you.' She almost laughed. 'To meet me.'

Miss Tilson accepted her handshake.

The hatch opened and a gentleman descended.

They moved to one side so he could walk by them. Miss Tilson turned away from him.

He glanced at them as he passed. 'You ladies should stay in your cabins. The sea is rough. Do not fear. A seaman will bring your meal to you.'

Had he noticed their resemblance to each other?

Rebecca and Miss Tilson did not speak until he disappeared into one of the cabins near the end of the corridor.

'We should do as he says, I suppose.' Miss Tilson

opened a door to a space as tiny as Nolan's. 'My cabin is here.'

'I would like to speak with you more,' Rebecca said hurriedly, before Miss Tilson left her. 'I am quite alone. My maid suffers the *mal de mer* and remains in her cabin.'

The young woman lowered her gaze. 'The sea has never bothered me. I suppose I have a strong constitution that way.'

As did Rebecca.

'Will you talk with me?' Rebecca's pulse quickened with excitement. 'Maybe there is some sense to make of this.' She made a vague gesture in the air between them.

Miss Tilson gazed into her cabin. 'You are welcome to come in, but there is very little room.'

'Come to my cabin, then,' Rebecca said. 'We may be comfortable there.'

The two women settled in Rebecca's cabin, seating themselves across from each other at the small table. Through the small porthole choppy waves spewed white foam.

Rebecca bit her tongue. Instead of blurting out *Why do you look like me?* she asked, 'Where are you bound, Miss Tilson?'

'To a family in the Lake District. Not a family, precisely. Two little girls whose parents were killed in an accident. They are in the care of their uncle now, the new Viscount Brookmore.'

'How sad.' Rebecca had been nearly grown when she lost her parents to illness.

'And you, Lady Rebecca? Where are you bound?' Miss Tilson spoke without the hint of an Irish brogue, Rebecca noticed. As did Rebecca. She'd lost her accent in a Reading boarding school.

'To London,' she replied.

'London!' Miss Tilson smiled. 'How exciting. I was there once. It was so…vital.'

'Vital, indeed.' Except Rebecca had no wish to go there. London would be a prison to her. With Lord Stonecroft.

Miss Tilson's eyes—so like her own—narrowed. 'You sound as if you do not wish to go.'

Rebecca met her gaze. 'I do not. I travel there to be married.'

The young woman's brows rose. 'Married?'

Rebecca waved a hand. 'It is an arranged marriage. My brother's idea.'

'And you do not wish to marry this man?'

'Not at all.' She straightened in her chair. Marrying Stonecroft was the last thing she wished to talk about. 'May I change the subject?'

Miss Tilson blinked. 'Forgive me. I did not mean to pry.'

Rebecca shrugged. 'Perhaps I will tell you the whole story later.' She leaned forward. 'For now I am bursting with questions. Why do we look alike? How can this be? Are we related somehow?'

They traded stories of parentage and lineage, but nothing seemed to connect them. Miss Tilson's family had been gentry. Her mother died giving birth to her and her overwhelmed and grieving father put her in the care of nurses and governesses and finally to school in Bristol when her father died, leaving her to fend for herself. She'd come to Ireland to be a governess and was now on her way to a new position.

Rebecca, on the other hand, was the daughter of an English earl whose estate was in Ireland, but she'd spent much of her life in England, in that boarding school in Reading.

Rebecca blew out an exasperated breath. 'We are no closer to understanding this. We are not related—'

'But we look alike,' Miss Tilson finished for her. 'An unexpected coincidence?'

There was a mirror affixed to the wall. They stood and gazed into it.

'We are not identical,' Miss Tilson observed. 'Look.'

Rebecca's two front teeth were slightly more prominent, her eyebrows more arched, her eyes a bit wider.

'No one would notice unless we were standing next to each other,' Miss Tilson added.

'Our clothes set us apart. That is for certain.' Rebecca swung away from the mirror to face Miss Tilson instead of her image. 'If you wore my clothes, I'd wager anyone would take you for me.'

'I cannot imagine wearing fine clothes like yours.' Her likeness sighed.

'You must wear them then,' Rebecca said impulsively. 'Let us change clothes and impersonate each other for the voyage. It will be a great lark. We will see if anyone notices.'

Miss Tilson shook her head. 'Your clothes are too fine for you to give up. Mine are plain.'

'Precisely. But I believe people pay more attention to dress than to other aspects of one's appearance. Perhaps even more than one's character. In any event, I think there is nothing undesirable about wearing a simple dress.'

The other woman touched the fine vigonia wool of Rebecca's travelling dress. 'I confess, I would love to wear a gown like this.'

'Then you shall!' Rebecca turned her back to her. 'Unbutton me.'

They undressed down to their shifts and traded dresses, acting as each other's maids. Miss Tilson pulled Rebecca's hair into a simple knot at the back of her head. Rebecca placed Miss Tilson's hair—it even felt like her own—high on her head and arranged curling tendrils around her face.

They checked their images in the mirror again and laughed.

There was a rap at the door.

Rebecca grinned. 'Answer the door as me.'

Miss Tilson blanched. 'I could not.'

Rebecca gave her a little shove. 'Of course you can!'

Miss Tilson straightened into a more regal bearing and opened the door. Rebecca returned to her seat at the table.

The seaman who'd warned them to stay in their cabins balanced a tray as the boat continued to pitch. 'Some refreshment, m'lady,' he said to Miss Tilson.

Miss Tilson lifted her chin. 'Thank you.'

Rebecca stole one quick glance at the seaman before averting her face.

Miss Tilson gestured to Rebecca. 'Miss Tilson passes the time with me. Will you bring her food here for her?'

'That I will, miss.' The crewman stepped into the cabin and placed the tray on the table. He returned a moment later with two more trays. 'Your maid, miss?'

Miss Tilson's gaze darted quickly to Rebecca, who

pretended not to notice. The governess finally answered, 'My—my maid is resting. Perhaps you might leave her tray here, as well? We will tend to her.'

The seaman bowed. 'Very good, miss.' He placed both trays on the table.

When he left, Rebecca glanced up and they stared wide-eyed at each other.

'I was afraid he would notice we look alike,' Rebecca said. 'He must have glimpsed me when he left the trays.'

Miss Tilson shook her head. 'A governess is not important enough to notice, my lady.'

Their trays each held two slices of bread, some cheese and a tankard of ale with a cover on it. The two women continued to talk as they ate and Rebecca felt as if they'd known each other for ages.

As if they were sisters, although they clearly were not.

'I believe we should call each other by our given names,' Rebecca said. 'It seems silly to be formal to one's mirror image.'

Miss Tilson fluttered her lashes shyly. 'If you desire it... Rebecca. Then I am Claire to you.'

'Claire!' Rebecca felt as if she were conversing with a sister.

Miss Tilson—Claire—must have felt a similar ease. 'Might you tell me now why you do not wish to be married?' She gave Rebecca a daring look. 'Now that we are no longer formal?'

Rebecca stared into her tankard of ale which she held with both hands to keep it from spilling.

How could she explain?

'A woman gives up everything by marrying,' she said. 'Any wealth or property she might have. Any right to decide for herself what she wishes to do. If I am to give up everything, it should be to a man who loves me and respects me and will not confine me.'

Claire's brows rose. 'And this man?'

Rebecca grimaced. 'I met him only once. He merely wished to ensure himself I could produce an heir.'

Claire did not look the least dismayed by this information. 'But of course he would want an heir. Especially if he has a title and property.'

'He does.' Rebecca tapped her pewter tankard with her fingernail.

'Is the gentleman wealthy enough to provide for you?' Claire asked.

'He is said to be prosperous,' she replied. 'He must be, because he is willing to marry me with a mere pittance for a dowry.'

Claire nodded approvingly. 'Will you tell me who he is?'

Rebecca could see no reason not to. 'Lord Stone-croft.'

Claire gave her an enquiring look.

'Baron Stonecroft of Gillford.'

'Ah.' A look of understanding came over Claire's face. 'You were hoping for a higher title than baron. I mean, you said you are the daughter of an earl.'

Rebecca sniffed. 'I care nothing for that.'

Claire looked surprised. 'Did he seem like a cruel man, then? Is that your objection?'

Not cruel.

Indifferent.

Rebecca sighed. 'I do not believe there is precisely anything to object to in him. I simply do not wish to marry him.'

'Refuse, then.' Claire spoke this like a dare.

Oh, Rebecca would love to refuse. 'My brother— my half-brother—says I am too much of a burden for him to wait for me to find a husband I would like. I've refused every offer he's arranged for me. He has made certain I will be turned out without a penny if I do not marry Lord Stonecroft.' Her face heated at the memory of her brother railing at her. 'I've no doubt he means what he says.' Still, her mind whirled with ways she might avoid this marriage without being turned out into the streets.

None were viable, however.

Claire looked sympathetic. 'How sad. One would hope a brother would understand. Family should understand, should they not?'

Rebecca regarded her curiously. 'Do you have any brothers or sisters? Any family at all?'

Claire shook her head. 'I am alone in the world. Any relations are too distant to be concerned with me.'

More reason to feel a kinship towards her. 'My parents are gone,' Rebecca confided. 'And my brother might as well be dead. He said he never wishes to see me again. Ever. Even if he visits England. He made that very clear.'

Her brother had always resented her. He'd resented her mother, as well. Possibly because their father had loved her mother better than either his son or daughter.

They fell silent.

Claire finally spoke and with a resolved tone. 'I think you are fortunate to marry, Lady Rebecca— Rebecca. You have little money or property, correct? You can only gain by marrying. You'll gain a home of your own to manage. Children of your own. Comfort and security. Even status and a respectable position in society.'

Rebecca glanced away.

All that was true. But Lord Stonecroft had only

cared that she was young and healthy enough to breed and apparently tolerable to look at. He'd made no effort to *know* her. How was she to endure that sort of emotional wasteland? How was she to tolerate life with such a man?

Claire must have sensed Rebecca's desolation. Her expression turned consoling. 'Perhaps it will not be so onerous to be Lady Stonecroft.'

Rebecca managed a polite smile. 'Perhaps not.'

As if by mutual agreement she and Claire began talking of other things. Books. Plays. Art. Music. From time to time Claire, pretending to be Rebecca, checked on Nolan, who never seemed to question who she was, to Rebecca's delight.

Rebecca and Claire talked until night fell, turning the churning sea inky black.

Claire stood. 'I should return to my cabin so you might get some sleep. I'll help you out of your dress, if you help me out of this lovely gown.'

Rebecca rose and let her lookalike untie and loosen the laces at the back of the plain dress she'd worn most of the voyage. What a shame. She'd quite enjoyed not being herself, playing a woman whose life seemed so much simpler, so much within her own control.

She turned to face Claire. 'Let us see how far we can carry this masquerade. You be me tonight. Sleep in my nightclothes, in this bed. And I will continue being you.'

The young woman looked stricken. 'I cannot allow you to be closeted in that tiny berth they gave me!'

'Why not?' Rebecca countered. 'It will be an adventure for me. And you will have the comfort of this cabin as a treat. When Nolan enters in the morning, we shall discover if she still believes you are me.'

Rebecca pulled out her nightdress, made of the softest of muslin. 'Here.'

Miss Tilson fingered the fine cloth of the nightdress. 'Perhaps. If you desire this.'

'I do desire it,' Rebecca insisted, helping Miss Tilson out of her dress. 'I desire it very much.'

In the morning the sea became even more restless. The sky turned even more ominous shades of grey. Rebecca convinced Claire to continue to wear her clothes and impersonate her. Nolan, who remained abed, sick as ever, and the few seamen who attended them still did not guess that Claire masqueraded as Rebecca. Even with the two ladies together, the seamen never seemed to notice how alike they were.

The seamen were rushed and worried, however. There was a storm brewing, the seamen said. The ladies must remain below.

As the day progressed, Rebecca and Claire talked

more about the weather than about their lives. They left the cabin rarely only to check on Nolan, who suffered so much she did not even react when Rebecca, dressed as the governess, attended her.

In the late afternoon, the storm broke, tossing the packet boat even more violently than before.

'We should be nearing the coast,' Rebecca said.

'If the ship can even sail in this.' Claire's face—her identical face—paled in fear.

Suddenly shouts and pounding feet sounded from above them, then a loud crack and a thud that shook the boards over their heads. The two women grasped each other's hands. Their masquerade became unimportant as the wind and sea pitched the ship so constantly that they could not change back into their own clothing.

The gentleman who'd passed them the day before opened the door without knocking. 'Come above,' he demanded in a voice they didn't dare disobey. 'We must abandon ship. Bring nothing.'

Rebecca defied him, grabbing her reticule containing all her money. When they reached the stairs, she shoved the reticule into Claire's hands. 'Here. Take this. I'll be right behind you. I'm going to get Nolan.'

Claire hung the reticule on her wrist.

'Miss!' the gentleman cried. 'We must leave now.'

'I will be right behind you,' she called over her shoulder.

Rebecca rushed to Nolan's cabin. A seaman was at Nolan's door. He turned to Rebecca. 'She refuses to come,' the man shouted. 'Hurry! We must get above.'

Rebecca pushed past him and ran to her maid. 'Nolan! Come with me.'

The older woman recoiled, rolling over and huddling against the wall. 'No. Sick. Leave me alone.'

'Come, miss!' the crewman cried. 'There is no time to waste!'

'I cannot leave her!' she cried.

He dragged her away from Nolan's door, practically carrying her to the steps of the companionway.

On deck, rain poured as if from buckets, obscuring the chaos Rebecca found above. The mast had splintered in two and lay like a fallen tree on the deck, ropes and sails tangled around it.

'To the boats!' the seaman shouted, running ahead.

She followed him, catching sight of Claire and the gentleman at the railing. The ship dipped suddenly and a wave washed over the deck. Rebecca had only a second to grab hold of a rope or be carried in its ebb. When the wave passed and she looked up, Miss Tilson and the gentleman had disappeared.

Her escort seized her arm. 'Come, miss. No time to waste.'

He pulled her along with him to the side of the ship where other passengers and crew were climbing into a rowing boat that had been lowered over the side. Claire was not among them. Rebecca glanced out to sea, but Claire had vanished. Nolan, Claire and the gentleman were lost.

There was no time for emotion. The crew lifted her over the side as the rowing boat bobbed up and down beneath her. Only with luck did her feet connect with the wood of the boat's bottom.

The boat filled quickly. Rebecca huddled next to a woman clutching her two children. Beneath their feet was at least an inch of water and more pouring from the sky. Somehow the sailors rowed the boat away from the packet. Through the darkness and rain, a shadow of coastline was visible. Rebecca kept her eyes riveted on it, watching it come slowly closer. Almost in reach.

From behind her a woman screamed.

Rebecca swivelled around to see the packet boat crash against the rocks. At that same moment the rowing boat hit something and tipped.

Rebecca plunged into icy water.

Chapter Two

Garret Brookmore, the new Viscount Brookmore, received word of the shipwreck off the coast of Moelfre while he waited in an inn in Holyhead. This was the packet he was to meet, the one on which the governess was to arrive. There were survivors of the wreck, he was told, and Garret felt obligated to travel to Moelfre to see if Miss Claire Tilson was one of them.

None of this was remotely within his experience. A year ago he'd been in Brussels with his regiment awaiting what became the Battle of Waterloo. For the past ten years he'd battled the French. Then word came that his brother and his brother's wife had been killed in a carriage accident and he needed to return to England to inherit his brother's title and all the new responsibilities that accompanied it, responsibilities over which he had no preparation. His older brother had been groomed from birth to be the Viscount. John was the family's fair-haired boy, able to do no wrong in their father's eyes, whereas not much was expected of Garret so he'd always been bound for the army.

Now the son from whom the family expected little had an estate to run, Parliament to attend and two little girls, his orphaned nieces, to tend to. Pamela and Ellen, only nine and seven, had been securely in the care of their governess, a long-time retainer of their mother's family, but fate had not finished being cruel. That woman, too, died.

How much could two little girls take? Their mother. Their father. Their governess. Left with a strange uncle whose heart remained with his regiment. Garret had witnessed thousands of deaths, but these seemed the cruellest.

When notified that his nieces' governess had died, Garret had been in London attempting to meet society's expectations of a viscount. He contacted an agency in town to hire a new governess and left his obligations there to travel back to Westmorland to the family's principal estate, to see to his nieces and await the new governess. He'd barely arrived at Brookmore when the agency sent word to expect Miss Tilson to arrive in Holyhead from Ireland.

What if Miss Tilson had drowned in this shipwreck, though? What was Garret to tell the little girls? That another person who was supposed to care for them had died?

He rode to Moelfre and enquired where the ship-wreck survivors might be found. He was directed to the Pheasant Inn, a place bustling with activity.

The innkeeper greeted him. 'Welcome. Do you seek a room?'

'I am looking for a survivor of the shipwreck,' Garret responded.

The man frowned and shook his head. 'Such a tragedy. Almost forty people lost, I'm afraid. Only eleven made it through.'

That did not sound hopeful. 'I am looking for Miss Tilson. Miss Claire Tilson.'

The innkeeper broke into a smile. 'Ah, Miss Tilson! Yes. Yes. She is here.'

Relief washed through Garret. 'May I see her?'

'Of course.' The innkeeper gestured for him to follow. He followed the man up two sets of stairs. 'She's been feverish since the rescue. Some men pulled her from the water, we were told. She seemed better today, our maid said. Might not be awake.'

'I understand.'

The innkeeper knocked and a maid answered. 'Someone to see Miss Tilson.'

The woman smiled and opened the door wider. Neither she nor the innkeeper asked who he was.

He approached the bed and gazed down in surprise. He'd expected an elderly woman like the previous governess. Miss Tilson hardly looked old enough to be out of the schoolroom herself. Her skin was smooth and flawless; her features strong, not delicate. Her hair, the colour of Kentish cobnuts, fell loose over the white pillow. Would her face fulfil the promise of character shown in her repose? He was intrigued.

He looked over at the innkeeper. 'I do need a room.'

'Yes, sir, I can accommodate you,' the man answered. 'Would you like to come with me now? I will show you to the room.'

Now that he'd found Miss Tilson, he was reluctant to leave her. 'I will stay until she wakes up. So she knows I am here.'

She was bound to experience distress, waking in a strange place, after nearly drowning.

The innkeeper reached for Garret's valise. 'I'll take this to the room and come back with your key, if you like.'

Garret nodded his thanks.

The maid spoke up. 'May I leave, sir? I am very hungry. May I get food?'

The innkeeper glanced towards Garret.

'I have no objection.' Far be it from Garret to deny

a hungry girl, so he wound up alone, seated at the bedside of a beauty he did not know, but for whom he was now responsible.

An hour passed, an hour spent with swirling thoughts of all he must remember to do, of all he'd learned needed his attention at the estate and even more demands in London and how much he wished he were simply marching with his men on some foreign road bound for the next battle. He missed his men. Worried about how they were faring. The war was over. Napoleon was on St Helena. Regiments were disbanding.

What was the use of wishing for what could not be? Even if his brother had not died, his army life would have changed drastically.

He had to admit he'd travelled to Holyhead mostly to give himself time away from these duties and regrets. Time to think. He could have easily sent a servant to escort her to the estate.

He rose when the innkeeper brought his key. As he settled back in the chair next to the bed, Miss Tilson's eyes—unexpectedly hazel—fluttered open.

'Where?' she managed, her voice cracking.

He poured her a glass of water from a pitcher on the bed table. 'You are safe, Miss Tilson,' he told her. 'You are at an inn in Moelfre.'

Her brow creased as if she were puzzled. 'Miss Tilson,' she whispered. 'Claire.'

He helped her to sit and held the glass as she drank. 'I am Lord Brookmore.' It still sounded strange on his tongue. In his mind Brookmore was still his brother. 'Your employer.'

She stared at him a long time and it seemed as if he could see a range of emotions flit through her eyes. Puzzlement, horror, grief and, finally, understanding.

Rebecca's heart pounded in her chest. This was not another fever-filled vision, but a real man touching her, helping her drink. Once she quenched her considerable thirst, she became acutely aware that she wore only a thin nightdress. From where? From whom? Had even the clothes she'd worn—Claire Tilson's clothes—been lost? Her throat tightened again, but this time from grief. Claire. Nolan. All those poor people.

She shrank away from the man and he sat back in his chair, placing the glass on the side table.

He was Claire's new employer, he'd said, and he thought she was the poor governess who'd been swept away by that killing wave. He did not look like a man who would hire a governess. His rugged face and muscular frame made him look untamed. His piercing blue eyes seemed a thin shield against painful remembrances. Dark hair, longer than fashionable, was as windswept as a man who'd galloped over fields on a wild stallion. The shadow of a beard covering a strong jaw gave him a rakish air.

Her eyes darted around the room. Why was such a man alone with her? She certainly had never before been alone with a man in her bedchamber, in her night clothes.

'Why—?' Her throat closed again and she swallowed. 'Why are you here?'

His blue eyes fixed on her. 'I waited at Holyhead. News came of the shipwreck so I rode here to see if you'd…survived.'

The shipwreck. Again she watched the wave consume Claire. Again she felt the rowing boat smash against rocks and plunge her into the water.

She shivered with the memory and he rose again, this time to wrap a blanket around her shoulders. Her skin heated at his touch.

She looked up into his face. 'How many? How many survived?'

'Eleven, the innkeeper said,' he replied.

Only ten others? What about the woman and her two children? Were they swept out to sea like Claire and the gentleman with her? Her eyes stung with tears.

'My God.' She dropped her face into her hands and sobbed.

She could feel him staring at her, even though he was still and silent. How humiliating to become so discomposed in front of this stranger. It was so unlike her.

She wrested some control, finally lifting her head and taking deep breaths.

Without speaking, he pulled a handkerchief from his breast pocket and handed it to her. She wiped her tear-soaked face.

The handkerchief was still warm from his body.

'Thank you.' She took another deep breath and started to return the now soaked handkerchief. She pulled it back, laughing drily. 'I—I will have it laundered.'

What a silly thing to say. She had no means of getting it laundered. She had no money. No clothes. Nothing.

She, of course, could identify herself. Send word to London of her predicament. To Lord Stonecroft. Who else was there to help her in London? But why would she want to ask for his help when she wanted to escape him? Being his brood mare seemed even worse than drowning.

Lord Brookmore sat back in his chair again, his face averted.

She should tell him she wasn't Claire Tilson, that she saw Claire washed overboard.

Oh, why had Claire drowned and not her? Claire had independence. She had work for which she earned her own money and she also had the hope of finding a man to love her some day. Claire would have fared so much better than Rebecca, who had nothing to look forward to but a prison of a marriage. Why could fate not have let them trade places in death as easily as they'd worn each other's clothes?

She stole another glance at Lord Brookmore and her heart quickened.

He thought she was Claire. Perhaps she was the only one who knew she was really Lady Rebecca Pierce, doomed to marry Lord Stonecroft.

She could not die in the watery depths instead of Claire. She'd have been willing to do so. But she could trade places with Claire now. She could live Claire's life for her.

Escape her own life.

Lord Stonecroft would not mourn her; he'd merely be annoyed that he must search for another brood mare to marry. Her brother would not mourn her. He'd get to keep her dowry. She could not sacrifice her life instead of Claire's, but she could become Claire.

Guilt pricked at her. She'd be deceiving this very handsome man. What a way to repay his kindness.

He did need a governess, though, did he not? She could be a governess. How hard could that be? It would help him, would it not?

'I—I had a fever, I think,' she said. 'I don't remember much except—' Except plunging into churning, cold water and thinking she would die. 'Except the wreck.'

His eyes fixed on her again. 'I know nothing more than you were saved and you were ill.'

'Am I still to be your nieces' governess?' Will he accept her as Claire? she meant.

'If you feel up to the task, yes.' His voice was stiff and formal and so deep she felt the timbre of it as well as hearing it. 'If you need a long recuperation—'

'I am well enough.' She sat up straighter as if to prove it. 'I am quite recuperated.'

'Good.' He stood. 'I will send for the maid and some food, if you are hungry.'

She didn't really know if she was hungry, but the mention of food made her stomach growl. 'Thank you, sir.'

He nodded. 'We can travel to Brookmore House as early as tomorrow, if you are able.'

Better to leave soon, although, out of ten other survivors, who was likely to know she was not Claire? Someone must have already identified her as such. 'I will be ready for travel tomorrow. I am certain.'

He nodded. 'Very good. Anything you need, Miss Tilson, just ask for it. I will see that it is provided to you.'

She glanced down at herself. She needed everything! Lady Rebecca would not hesitate to enumerate each necessary item, but she could not imagine Claire doing so.

'Thank you, sir,' she murmured instead.

'I will take my leave, then.' He inclined his head. 'Miss Tilson.'

'My lord,' she responded.

After he walked out the door she threw off the covers and climbed out of bed, suddenly restless. The wood floor was cold beneath her bare feet and her legs were weak. She made her way to the window and looked down upon a village street, its whitewashed buildings glowing in the waning light of early evening. Wagons and carriages rumbled by and villagers hurried here and there as if this day was like any other.

Her days would never be the same, though. A *frisson* of trepidation rushed up her spine. She was about to become a whole new person.

She rubbed her arms and smelled the faint scent

of the sea on her skin. She did not want to smell the sea! She wanted to banish the memory of plunging into the water where so many others died.

There was a rap at the door and a maid entered, carrying a tray. The scent of stew and cheese and ale seemed to affirm her choice of life. A new life.

'Oh, you are up, miss,' the maid said. 'Are you feeling better? The gentleman gave me some coins and said to bring you food and whatever you need.'

Rebecca seated herself at a chair next to a small table. 'I am much better. I am afraid I was too feverish—what is your name?'

'I'm Betty, miss.' The maid put the tray of food on the table. 'What else might I bring you?'

Dare she ask? She did dare, because she needed to feel renewed. 'I would love a bath, Betty.'

The maid smiled. 'A bath you shall have then, miss.'

'And I will need some clothes.'

By the next morning, Rebecca was not only clean and well fed, but also clothed.

The maid, Betty, brought her undergarments and a dress. 'His lordship said to find you clothes and so I did,' she'd said. 'The ones you wore before were ruined.'

Claire's clothes.

Betty helped her into the simple shift, a corset that fit tolerably well and a plain dress, not unlike the one Betty herself wore. The stockings looked newly purchased and the shoes, well-worn half-boots, were only slightly too big. Included in the bundle of clothes had been a new brush and comb, as well as a set of hairpins. Betty helped pull her hair back, as Claire had done.

Rebecca looked at herself in the mirror, but in her reflection she could only see Claire Tilson. Her eyes again filled with tears.

She blinked them away.

'I'll tell his lordship you are dressed,' Betty said, hurriedly making up the bed. The maid left and a moment later Lord Brookmore entered.

'Good morning, sir.' Rebecca remembered to curtsy deferentially. This was her employer, after all. His presence made her a bit breathless, but that must be only nerves. She was lying to him, after all. It was not because he was very tall and very masculine.

'Miss Tilson.' He nodded. He handed her a bundle wrapped in paper. 'I took the liberty of purchasing items you will no doubt need on the journey to Brookmore.'

She untied the string around the bundle and unfolded the paper to reveal a paisley shawl, a silk bonnet and lavender kid gloves.

'These are lovely,' she whispered. Every bit as fine as she'd once owned.

He nodded in response. 'How are you today? We need not travel if you are not sufficiently recovered.'

'I am well!' she assured him. She was eager to start her new life.

Claire's life.

She looked up from the items. 'Thank you for these. Thank you for the clothing, as well.'

He shrugged. 'You needed something to wear.'

Everything that had belonged to Rebecca Pierce was gone.

He stood just inside the door. Her impulse was to invite him to sit, to order tea, just as she might have done at home in Ireland. How foolish! She had no means to order tea and did a governess even invite a viscount to be seated?

It would take a little work to rid herself of Lady Rebecca.

He looked uncertain, his blue eyes finding hers only fleetingly. 'I will arrange for a carriage, then. If you are certain you are ready.'

'Quite ready,' she replied.

She crossed the room to retrieve his handkerchief, which she had washed with the soap and water provided for her and dried in front of the fire. It was not pressed, but this had been the best she could do with no means to hire someone for the task.

She handed the handkerchief to him. 'It is clean, sir.'

As he reached for it, his gaze lingered on her. Their fingers brushed and she felt a flush warm her skin. She stepped back.

He cleared his throat. 'I will see to the carriage.'

He turned and left.

Chapter Three

The carriage Lord Brookmore arranged was a small two-horse landaulet with two coachmen on the box. It was comfortable enough, but if she'd had to share it with the Viscount, it would have seated them so close their bodies would have touched. Luckily he rode on horseback, so she did not have to face being in such intimate quarters with him. Unfortunately it also meant she had no company at all.

For half the day, the road skirted the sea whose sight and scent made it impossible to forget the terror and loss she'd endured from its violence. There was nothing to divert her thoughts away from those memories. With every glimpse of waves outside her window, she relived the shipwreck.

She tried to look away, out the window that did not face the sea. Occasionally Lord Brookmore rode next to the carriage and asked her how she fared. She always replied that she did very well. The truth could not be easily explained. Other than that, she was silent, even saying little during their brief contacts when they stopped only long enough to change horses and procure food which she ate in the coach.

Eventually the sea disappeared from view, replaced by farms and fields and small villages. Rebecca's nostrils filled with the odour of growing things. Of life instead of watery death, but still, being alone, her thoughts drifted back to the sea.

Lord Brookmore, who looked even more imposing on horseback, again appeared beside the carriage. 'We are nearing Chester. We will spend the night there.'

At the inn in Chester, Garret dismounted and handed his horse off to the waiting ostler. The carriage pulled in behind him and one of the coachmen jumped down to help Miss Tilson descend the steps. Garret stood nearby, his valise in hand.

Miss Tilson carried only a small bag with those few items he had purchased for her.

In the waning sun, she looked even paler than when they'd started the journey. He'd suspected then that she was not recovered enough. Now he kicked himself for not insisting she rest in Moelfre at least one more day. He'd been impatient to return to Brookmore House, though, eager to see her settled and his nieces comfortable, and matters set to rights. Brookmore House still felt like his brother's house, not his, even though he'd grown up there. Of course, when he'd been a child he'd been constantly reminded that his brother was the heir, the eventual owner of the estate.

He needed to return to London, although he was not as eager as he ought to be. He'd been swept up in events in London. It had been like watching another person negotiating that society and its expectations. Not him. Not at all him.

But it had been what he must do. Colleagues of his brother and father guided him through the ceremony, customs and politics of the House of Lords and of what was expected of a viscount there.

He needed to secure the inheritance, they'd insisted. His family would lose everything to some distant relation if he did not beget an heir. He'd seen the logic in that and so had done his duty. Attended the marriage mart. Became betrothed.

Lady Agnes was the perfect choice, his advisors assured him. He agreed. She was the daughter of the Earl of Trowbridge. She was polished, pleasant, accomplished and beautiful. She'd be the perfect hostess. There was absolutely nothing to object to in Lady Agnes.

Except Miss Tilson pulled more emotion from him than Lady Agnes ever had.

He stepped towards the governess and reached for her small bag. 'You look fatigued. I will arrange a room for you and have a meal sent up to you.'

She gave him a stricken look that he did not understand, but he took her bag and she fell in step with him to the door of the inn.

When they entered the hall, the innkeeper's eyes darted between them. 'Welcome. A room for you, sir?' His tone was uncertain.

'Two rooms,' Garret replied. 'The lady will require a maid and a meal in her room.'

'Very good, sir.' The innkeeper bowed.

'No!' Miss Tilson broke in, her voice sharp. She immediately modified it. 'No, please. I would prefer to eat my meal in the tavern.'

The innkeeper's brows rose, as did Garret's. She wished to expose herself in a public tavern? What sort of governess was she?

Garret frowned. 'As you wish.'

The innkeeper cleared his throat. 'Let me show you to your rooms.'

Garret followed behind the man and Miss Tilson as he led them up two flights of stairs and down a long hallway.

'These two.' The innkeeper gestured to two rooms

across the hallway from each other. He opened each of the rooms and handed them their keys. 'Shall I send a maid up now, ma'am?' he asked Miss Tilson.

'Not now,' she replied. 'Later. Perhaps nine or ten?'

'Very good, ma'am.' He bowed and left.

Garret placed his valise inside his room and his hat and gloves on a table, but he did not move from the doorway.

Neither did Miss Tilson.

She lifted her chin. 'Lord Brookmore, I am of a mind you disapprove of my not eating in my room. If you wish it, I will do so.'

He folded his arms across his chest. 'A public room can be a rowdy place, Miss Tilson. Not suitable for an unaccompanied woman.' Not suitable for his nieces' governess, he meant.

She lowered her gaze. 'I did not think of that. I thought only to have people around me. To not be alone.' Her voice cracked on her last word.

His insides twisted at her emotion.

She raised her eyes again. 'When I am alone, the shipwreck comes back to me.'

The shipwreck. Of course she would be reliving the shipwreck. Before yesterday she'd been too feverish to become accustomed to the memories.

'Would you accompany me to the tavern, then?' she asked. 'I would not require you to make conversation. Simply being among people—even rowdy people—would—would—distract me.'

How often after a battle did he seek the companionship of his fellow officers? To be alone with one's thoughts simply repeated the agony. Companionship, drink and carousing kept memories at bay. He ought to have realised this young woman would feel such a need, as well.

Truth be told, he was trying not to think of her that deeply.

Her lips thinned. 'Forgive me. It was wrong of me to ask.' She turned to enter her room. 'Have my dinner sent up. That will suffice.'

He crossed the hallway and seized her arm, dropping it as soon as she turned back, looking alarmed.

He straightened. 'If you do not wish to dine alone, I will not compel you to do so. I will request a private dining room and you will be my guest.'

Her expression relaxed into a relieved smile. 'Oh, thank you, my lord.'

He closed his door. 'I will arrange it immediately.'

She touched his arm this time. 'May I go with you?'

Her need for company was that strong? He nodded. 'In that case,' he said, 'allow me a few minutes to rid myself of the dust of the road and we can seek a meal right away.'

Her smile grew. 'Thank you, my lord.'

He washed his face and hands and brushed off his clothes. A glance in the mirror made him rub his chin, debating whether to take the time to shave. He decided against it. This was not a London drawing room and Miss Tilson was eager to be free of her solitude.

When he opened his door, she awaited him in the hallway. They walked together down the stairs through the hall to the tavern room.

The tavern room was everything Garret feared it would be. Loud voices, talking, laughing mingled with the clatter of dishes, tankards and cutlery. The air reeked of hops, cooked meat and male sweat. Men of all classes gulped from tankards of ale. Some enjoyed the company of the few women who shared booths with them. Serving girls threaded their way through the crowd.

Garret sought out the publican. 'We seek a private dining room,' he yelled over the din of the crowd.

The man's bald pate gleamed with perspiration. His white apron covered a swelled girth. 'This way, sir!'

Garret held Miss Tilson's arm as he followed the publican through the room. Men definitely glanced her way, their expressions curious, appreciative or licentious. He pulled her a little closer, feeling protective. Had he ever felt protective of Agnes?

Unfair comparison. He'd never walked Lady Agnes through a rowdy tavern and he could not imagine ever doing so.

Miss Tilson trembled beneath his touch.

He released her as soon as they reached the private room, hoping she had not thought his actions too forward. He'd felt protective. Nothing more.

The private dining room was simply furnished with a table, four chairs and a sideboard. There was a window with brown curtains and a small fireplace with a few pieces of coal glowing on the grate. The walls were bare.

'What drink do you desire?' the publican asked as he lit two lamps from a taper. 'I'll have the serving girl bring them directly.'

'Ale for me,' Garret said. Not a drink for a viscount, but he was parched. 'Miss Tilson?'

She gave him a sideways glance. 'Claret?'

He turned to the publican. 'A decanter of claret for the lady.'

The man rubbed his hands. 'And food? We have char fish and a mutton stew and pigeon…'

'Not fish!' Miss Tilson cried.

The publican eyed her with a surprised look.

Garret turned to her. 'Stew, then?'

She nodded.

He addressed the publican again. 'We will both have the stew. And bring some bread and cheese, as well.'

'Very good, sir.' The man bowed and left the room.

When he closed the door behind him, Miss Tilson lowered herself into a chair at the table. She expelled a nervous breath.

Garret inclined his head towards the door. 'You see why you could not come alone.'

She took another breath, pressing her hand against her chest. 'It was so odd. The voices. All the men. Walking through that room I thought I was on the deck of the ship again. I actually saw it.' She looked up at him, her forehead creased. 'Now you will think me mad.' She pressed her temples. 'I think myself mad.'

He settled in the chair adjacent to her. 'Some soldiers relive a battle after it is all done. As if they were there.'

She frowned. 'I don't understand.'

'They hear the sounds of the battle again. Even think they see the battle.'

Her puzzled eyes turned hopeful. 'Do you think it could be the same?'

'It could be.' He looked away and drummed his fingers on the table.

Seated this close, under the lamplight, her eyes—their irises thin brown rims circled in green—had captivated him, created a yearning inside him. Perhaps it was the changing emotion he saw in those eyes. Perhaps he was drawn to her because she'd suffered and she knew what it was like to survive when so many others died.

But he could not desire her. How could he desire her? She was a governess. In his employ. And he was a viscount now. A governess was beneath him.

What was he thinking? He could not desire her. He was betrothed.

He pressed his lips together, feeling as confined as if the walls were closing in on him.

She shifted in her chair. 'Have I annoyed you?'

She had no idea that annoyance was not his problem. His problem would be forgetting who he was now and thinking he was a soldier again.

'Not at all,' he responded perfunctorily.

She folded her hands in her lap and kept her gaze averted. It felt to him as if she held herself in check and he wondered what he would see if she set herself free. He laughed inwardly. Apparently they were both confined, both unable to be who they were inside.

But he did not need this sense of kinship with her, fuelling that inexplicable yearning inside him.

It was not physical desire—or, more accurately, not only that.

How odd that her looks should captivate him when she did not meet society's ideal of beauty.

Lady Agnes certainly did.

Miss Tilson was too tall, too strong-featured, but somehow not plain. It was difficult for his gaze not to be riveted upon her face and her changing expressions.

She took a breath, as if trying to clear away whatever had been in her mind. 'So you were in the army?'

He shrugged. 'I was a younger son, until my brother died.' He blinked away his own intrusive memory.

The polite smile she'd pasted on her face faltered a bit. 'What regiment?'

She seemed determined to make conversation. 'The 28th.'

His father had purchased a lieutenancy for him when he turned eighteen. And why not? He'd not been suited for anything else, or so he'd always been told. As part of the 28th, he'd been in nearly every major battle of the war with Napoleon, from Egypt to Toulouse.

'Were you at Waterloo?' she asked.

He gritted his teeth for a moment. 'No.'

He could have stayed in Belgium with his regiment, when he inherited the title, but battles were unpredictable matters and he dared not risk being killed and leaving his nieces to the mercy of relatives so distant as to have no care for them.

He'd grieved not being a part of the Waterloo battle almost as much as he'd grieved his brother's death. Many of his men died at Waterloo. He should have been leading them. Protecting them.

'On the Peninsula, then?' she persisted.

'Yes. On the Peninsula. And in France.' His regiment had been a part of that bloody pursuit of the French as they retreated from the Pyrenees into France.

Her brow furrowed. 'And some soldiers relive battles afterwards, the way I relived the shipwreck?'

Apparently the shipwreck was never far from her mind. 'Yes. Many. I expect if I heard cannon right now, it would put me right back into battle.'

'It would?'

There was a rap on the door and a serving girl entered with their drinks and food. After she left, Garret took a generous gulp of ale and plunged his spoon into the stew.

Miss Tilson nibbled on a piece of bread, a pained expression on her face.

It tugged at his sympathy. 'Talk about it.'

She glanced up. 'About what?'

'About the shipwreck,' he explained. 'It helps.'

Although it might be more help to him to keep his distance from this young woman—his nieces' governess.

Rebecca glanced away. She wanted desperately to talk about the events crowding her head and overwhelming her senses, but ought she to do so?

Claire Tilson would have declined this invitation, she was sure. Indeed, Claire Tilson would not have fished for this conversation at all. She would have remained in her place. She would have gone to her room as the Viscount requested, even if spending more hours alone would have been unendurable.

Well, she would be Claire Tilson later. Right now she needed to be Rebecca Pierce, on an equal footing with this gentleman and with a great need to talk.

She faced him. 'Shortly after we woke that morning, the storm began and we were told to remain in our cabins.'

'We?' His brows rose.

She must be careful how she spoke. 'I—I befriended another young lady. We spent most of the voyage in each other's company.' And in each other's clothes.

She described how the storm grew and how their

alarm escalated. And how the gentleman came to take them on deck. She told him of the wave that washed Miss Tilson and the man off the deck.

She did not tell him of being pulled away from Nolan, her poor sick maid. Could she ever forgive herself for that?

She saw an image in her head of Nolan in her bed as the water rose around her. Rebecca covered her eyes.

'Go on,' his voice demanded.

'I was dropped into a rowing boat. There was a mother and her children next to me, but then we saw the ship crash against the rocks and the rowing boat tossed us into the sea.' She remembered the cold water all around her, not knowing which way was up, not being able to breathe. 'I don't remember anything else very clearly until waking up in the inn.'

What had happened to the mother and those dear little children? She could not bear thinking of them under the water. Could not bear thinking of their dead bodies floating to shore.

She glanced at Lord Brookmore, whose gaze did not waver.

She took a breath. 'That is it. That is all.'

Did his eyes turn sceptical? She could not tell. 'A harrowing experience,' he said, more factually than sympathetically.

That was a good thing, though. Had he offered her comfort she might have broken down and turned into a watering pot the way she'd been yesterday.

He dipped his spoon into the bowl of stew, making her realise he'd refrained from eating while she told her story.

She ate a few bites, as well. 'I don't know why I was saved. Why me over so many others?'

She downed her glass of claret.

Lord Brookmore took a more leisurely sip of his ale. 'There is no making sense of those matters, you know. In battle, good men die. And yet men like me live. There is no making sense of it.'

Of course. He must know more about death than she could ever know. 'What do you mean "men like me"? Are you so bad, then?' She tried for a light-hearted tone.

He faced her, a sad smile on his face. 'There were times in my youth that my father was convinced of it.' He poured her another glass of claret.

She took a sip. 'I cannot believe it. You have been nothing but kind to me.'

He laughed drily. 'I need a governess for my nieces.'

She pursed her lips. 'I do not think a governess is so difficult to find. You could have sent for someone else and never have come looking for me.'

He met her gaze. 'And how could I have explained to my nieces that, after losing their parents and their old governess, I could not be bothered to discover if their new governess survived a shipwreck?'

She lifted her chin. 'A bad man would not have cared. I'll not hear you speak of yourself so.'

He averted his gaze.

She finished the claret left in her glass. 'Did it ever occur to you that you survived all those battles so that your nieces would still have you to care for them?'

His expression turned bleak. 'How much better it would have been for my brother and his wife to live and me die.'

His words knocked the breath from her.

Because it would have made so much more sense for Claire to have survived instead of Rebecca. Claire had everything to gain by living. Rebecca, instead, had been facing a dismal future in a loveless marriage.

At least she knew there was another good reason she had decided to live Claire's life for her. So Lord Brookmore would not have to tell his nieces that their new governess had died. He'd travelled all the way to Moelfre in the hopes that he would not have to tell them such news. She wasn't going to let his efforts be for naught.

She just needed to learn to act a little like Claire and less like Rebecca. 'Tell me about your nieces,' she asked.

He shrugged. 'They are aged seven and nine, but you probably know that.'

She knew nothing. 'Their names?'

He peered at her. 'Were you not provided their names?'

Oh, dear. She must be careful if this deception was to work.

'It was in the letter—' There must have been a letter. 'But I fear, with all that happened, I've lost my memory for the details. I do apologise.'

He seemed to accept that—to her great relief. 'Pamela is the elder. Ellen, the younger.'

Pamela and Ellen. She repeated to herself over and over.

He frowned. 'I have not been present in their lives. I can tell you little else of them.'

She returned to her stew, even though she could no longer taste it.

They fell into a silence, broken only by the clink of spoons against the bowls. Her heartbeat accelerated. How was a governess supposed to handle this?

A governess, she suspected, would sit quietly, no matter how oppressive the silence, no matter how compelling the gentleman. But Rebecca was inclined to be outspoken, even when it was better to keep her mouth shut. Silence was torture to her.

The sounds of their eating grew louder and louder in this vacuum. She'd go mad if this continued much longer.

She knew how to end this. She'd received the training. After her brother discovered that her boarding school had educated her too liberally, he'd sent her back to England to a finishing school in Bath, so she knew very well how to engage a gentleman in conversation, even though it might be quite un-governess-like to use the skill now.

'Do tell, my lord, about the house where your nieces live. Is it in a lovely part of the Lake District?'

'All parts of the Lake District are lovely.' He looked up from his stew. 'Have you not been there?'

When his gaze reached her eyes, it made her insides flutter. She glanced away. 'I never had the pleasure.'

He cocked his head as if in apology. 'Of course. Why would you?'

She forced herself to meet his gaze again. 'Tell me. What will I see?'

This time he glanced away and took a sip of ale before he spoke. 'You will see mountains. They are green this time of year, but they'll turn all shades of orange in autumn and white when winter comes.

The lakes change colour, too, with the sky. From silver to blue to purple.' He looked as if he were gazing at the landscape right now. 'I have been to many places in the world, but none is as fine.'

She was moved by the suppressed emotion in his words. 'I shall be eager to see it.'

He finished his ale and his voice turned flat. 'You will not like the house.'

She felt a niggle of alarm. 'Why not?'

He shrugged. 'It is old.'

What family seat possessed a new house? She laughed softly. 'I am in no position to complain. An old house. A new house. As long as I have a roof over my head.'

He did not seem to appreciate her attempt at levity. 'I am hopeful you will find it tolerable. I do not want my nieces to lose another governess.'

And Rebecca needed a place to stay. A different life to live. Somehow she must make this work for everyone.

She'd figure it out in time.

She forced herself to smile. 'Let us not worry at the moment, my lord.' She gestured down at herself. 'As I own nothing and have nowhere else to go, let us assume I will be happy as your nieces' governess and that you will be happy with my services.'

She lifted her glass of claret as if in a toast.

* * *

Garret raised his empty tankard, more affected than he wanted to admit at the emotions flitting over her face.

He knew loss. His parents. His brother. Sister-in-law. And countless friends and fellow soldiers on the battlefield. But for him there was always something left, even if it was merely a title and property he'd never desired and never deserved. How might it be to have nothing left? Not even the clothes on one's back?

He admired her for not giving in to the raw emotions grief could cause.

He must see to replacing her wardrobe and other essentials a lady must need. There ought to be some reparation he could provide for not giving her more time to recover. He should have known that more than the body needed to heal.

He pushed the plate of bread and cheese towards her. 'Please help yourself, Miss Tilson.'

She more dutifully than hungrily cut herself a piece of bread and cheese before looking up at him. 'Shall I slice some for you?'

He nodded. 'Thank you.'

He was, perhaps, even less desirous of more food than she, but he accepted the tray, selected the bread and raised it to his mouth.

'Have you any family, Miss Tilson? I ought to have asked before now.' One more way he was remiss. 'Is there anyone you would wish to contact?'

She paused before answering. 'There is no one. No family.'

The bread tasted dry in his mouth. She *had* lost everything.

She finished the bread and cheese and folded her hands in her lap. She was thinking too much. He'd seen such a look on his soldiers' faces. Social conversation was not a skill he excelled in, but he wanted desperately to distract her from those thoughts.

'Is there anything else you desire?' he asked her.

She gave a wan smile. 'I am quite sated. The portions were generous, were they not?'

'They were indeed,' he agreed.

He did not know what else to say. Should he ask if she was ready to be alone again? How could he leave her alone after knowing how alone she truly was?

He drummed his fingers on the table. 'Have you been a governess long, Miss Tilson?'

What a foolish question. She could not be more than twenty or twenty-one, but he did not know what else to ask except about the one thing he knew about her—that she was a governess.

A look of distress flashed over her face. 'Um. No, not long, sir.'

Why the distress? He was trying to distract her.

'Then your last position was your first as a governess?' He seemed to remember that from the letters from the agency he and his housekeeper had used to fill the position.

Her eyes darted. 'Yes.' She took a breath. 'My first of any consequence, that is.'

'And…' This was not going well at all. 'Why did you leave?'

She blinked rapidly. 'Not for any bad reason, sir. I was not discharged, if that is what you are asking.'

That was not what he meant. 'No. I was merely curious.' Though it was not curiosity, just his clumsy attempt at conversation. He took another gulp of his ale. 'No other reason. I wondered what your life was like before. What the previous family was like. How many children were in your charge. That is all.'

She leaned forward with an earnest expression. 'Are you having second thoughts about hiring me? Because I would hope you would not judge me by these past two days. Or by my—my forward behaviour at this meal—'

Forward behaviour?

'Please give me the chance to show—to show what I can do,' she pleaded.

He gripped his tankard of ale. 'Miss Tilson, I am not having second thoughts. Rest easy on that matter.

You remain distressed about the shipwreck. I understand that. Distraction helps at such times.'

She sat back. 'Oh.'

He attempted a smile. 'Shall we talk about something else?'

She shifted in her chair. 'Perhaps I ought to retire to my room.'

'As you wish.' He felt as if he'd driven her away, which was not at all what he'd intended.

Another reason he should have remained a soldier. Conversing with his fellow soldiers was not so fraught with peril.

He stood and helped her out of her chair.

When they walked through the tavern again, it was no less full of life. There were still men and women laughing and drinking away whatever their cares might be. He envied them. He had not imbibed nearly enough drink to drown his emotions this night.

The innkeeper greeted them when they walked back into the hall. 'I hope your meal was satisfactory.'

Miss Tilson replied before Garret opened his mouth. 'Thank you, sir. It was very satisfying.' Then she shifted her gaze to him as if he might object to her speaking.

As they approached the stairway, Garret remembered the innkeeper's offer of a maid. 'Would you like the maid to attend you now?'

'Oh, yes,' she replied. 'A maid now. Or as soon as it is convenient.' She glanced back at the innkeeper.

The man spoke up. 'I will send someone directly, miss.'

Garret followed her up the stairs and escorted her to her door. She took a key from her pocket and he opened his hand. She gave him the key and he unlocked the door. In the open doorway she turned to face him.

He was quite aware of how close he stood to her and how the soft light of the hall lamps made her skin glow and her eyes darken.

'I'll arrange for the maid to wake you in time to leave tomorrow,' he managed to say.

Her voice turned raspy. 'Thank you, sir. For eating your meal with me.'

He lowered his voice, too. 'I hope it eased matters for you.'

Her eyes softened. 'Much better than being alone.'

That seemed faint praise.

She affected him more than he wished to admit. His arms itched to hold her.

To comfort her, that was all. Merely comfort her. He had no business acting upon any other temptation, although it struck him how easily it could be done. She could not refuse him, could she? She had nothing but the position of governess that was entirely in his control.

No. He would not touch her.

Oh. And he was betrothed. He'd forgotten about that.

He stepped back. 'My room is across the hall. Knock on the door if you need me—if you need anything. Otherwise, sleep well, Miss Tilson.'

She lowered her head and curtsied. 'You, as well, sir,' she replied dutifully.

She turned and entered the room, closing the door behind her. The key sounded in the lock.

Garret stared at the closed door for a moment before heading back to the stairway and returning to the tavern for something stronger than ale.

Chapter Four

The next day Garret rose early, ignoring the pounding in his head from too many glasses of a rather bad brandy. He sought out the innkeeper and arranged for a man to ride ahead to Preston on a specific errand.

When Miss Tilson was ready, he arranged for breakfast in the private dining parlour. The sun shone through the parlour window, lighting her face with its dark circles under the eyes. Her skin was nearly as pale as his first sight of her abed in Moelfre.

He frowned. 'I fear you did not sleep well, Miss Tilson.'

She blushed, which at least gave her some colour. 'Not very well.'

'Were you troubled by dreams?' Nightmares followed battles. Why not shipwrecks?

She glanced at him in surprise. 'I was. I dreamed of the water.'

Poor girl.

'You won't always have the dreams,' he reassured her.

She nibbled on toasted bread and jam. He ate a piece of ham and racked his throbbing brain for some way to make this trip less unpleasant for her.

'I could hire a larger carriage, if you like. Ride with you.' There was really no need for her to be alone.

Although how comfortable would it be to be so close to her for so many hours?

She looked alarmed. 'I would not so inconvenience you, my lord. I will manage well enough in the landaulet. You must not give up the pleasure of riding horseback.'

He was most comfortable on a horse, that was true. On the Peninsula, he and his horse moved as one and in battle his horse never failed him.

He glanced out the window. 'It does look to be a fine day for riding.'

Her voice turned wistful. 'A lovely day for riding.'

He heard her take another bite of her toast. He gazed out the window, but his mind was working.

Finally he turned back to her. 'Do you ride, Miss Tilson?'

To his surprise, her hazel eyes kindled with pleasure—a captivating sight.

'Once upon a time I rode every chance I could,' she said dreamily. 'So I well understand what a joy it is to view the countryside from the back of a horse.'

He nodded. 'If we can procure a riding habit for you and a ladies' saddle, would you like to ride today?'

He could pay off the coachmen. They certainly would not mind receiving the same pay for a trip they did not have to take.

Her eyes widened. 'Surely you cannot arrange such a thing.'

He lifted a shoulder. 'I can try. We shall see what can be done.'

Her eyes brightened. 'I would love to ride.'

It took some effort—and a generous output of coin—but Garret managed to provide Miss Tilson with a decent and well-fitting riding habit, riding boots, gloves, hat, riding crop and a side saddle that suited her almost as well as if made for her. He paid enough for the owner of the items to purchase three replacements and ones of finer quality, too.

But he would not tell Miss Tilson the cost. It exceeded her yearly salary, which would seem a fortune to her, but to him, now that he'd inherited wealth, it was a mere trifle.

The stable provided them both with horses, which

they would change periodically at other coaching inns on the road.

The air was crisp and the sky so vivid a blue it almost hurt the eyes. Rolls of white clouds added to the day's grandeur. What finer day could there be for a ride?

In Chester the road was busy with farm wagons, mail coaches, carriages of all kinds, from the simplest gig to elegant landaus to a lumbering post chaise, but as they rode further away from the town there were times they were alone on the road and could ride side by side.

'How are you faring?' he asked. 'I can always hire a carriage if riding is too taxing.'

She was as game as he'd hoped, though. 'It is not too taxing.' She smiled at him. 'It is wonderful!'

Garret was pleased. He'd brought her some happiness after all she'd been through.

'You ride well,' he said.

She grinned. 'It is one of my favourite pastimes, I must say. When I was a little girl I rode astride and bareback on my beloved pony. When I was sent to school, my father provided a horse and I learned how to ride properly.'

'Where was your school?' he asked.

Her smile faded and she took a moment to answer. 'Bristol,' she finally said.

Whenever he asked her a question, her demeanour changed. It kept him from asking more.

But as they rode in silence for a while, he felt compelled to say something. 'You must have the use of the stables at Brookmore. There are a couple of mares there—my sister-in-law's horses—that you would find pleasant to ride.'

Her face lit up. 'I might ride? How very wonderful!'

Changing horses at the inns gave them both a chance to stretch their muscles and ease any soreness from the time in the saddle. Garret was used to long hours on horseback, but Miss Tilson could not be as seasoned, even if she loved riding.

When they took refreshment at the inns, their conversation was more comfortable than the night before, but, then, any questions he asked her were about the inn, the food, the fresh horses they were given. Apparently questions about the present were not difficult for her to answer.

He liked being in her company. She was neither too chatty nor deadly silent.

When the sun dipped low in the sky, they reached the outskirts of Preston. Preston was a large and busy town and the traffic on the road was almost as bustling as London. Many a male rider would have found it daunting to guide a horse through such busy streets. Miss Tilson still rode confidently.

He led her to the inn. In the yard, ostlers ran up to hold the horses. Garret dismounted and turned to see Miss Tilson expertly slip off hers. Their gazes caught briefly and, for a moment, he was lost in the depths of her hazel eyes.

He quickly glanced away.

For a multitude of reasons—her position, his fiancée—he must not allow any physical attraction to her, yet at unexpected moments like this desire coursed through him.

The ostler handed him his valise and Miss Tilson gathered the small bag carrying the few items she could now call her own.

She took a step and winced.

He stepped towards her and put his arm around her. 'Are you able to walk?'

She let him support her. 'I am stiff, of course. I'm sure it will pass.'

He was more than happy to have her lean against him, although this was precisely the sort of contact he should avoid.

When they entered the inn and Garret gave the innkeeper his name, the innkeeper's eyes lit up.

'Lord Brookmore, sir. Welcome.' The man bowed. 'Let me assure you your rooms are ready and the items you requested have been placed in the lady's room.'

Miss Tilson looked at him quizzically.

He did not enlighten her.

Their rooms were on the first floor, next to each other, too close to make defying temptation easy. Better he were on the other side of the building.

The innkeeper grinned as he opened Miss Tilson's door.

Obviously the man Garret had sent ahead had managed his task very well. Across the bed were items of clothing and rolls of cloth, everything he could think of that would be of use to her.

Rebecca gasped. 'What have you done?'

The bed was laden with rolls of cloth, but there were also three dresses, shifts, petticoats, gloves and hats.

She stepped into the room as the innkeeper withdrew.

Lord Brookmore stood in the doorway, leaning against the door jamb. 'Preston is known for its cloth. I simply took advantage of this fact. I sent a man ahead.'

'The cloth is beautiful.' She gestured to the pile. 'But there is clothing here, as well.'

The innkeeper spoke up. 'My wife took up the

challenge, miss. She found a dressmaker who had dresses the buyers never collected. I will send my wife to assist you whenever you wish. She has a seamstress on hand to address any alterations.'

Rebecca could not find her voice. Lord Brookmore had gone to a great deal of trouble and expense for her, so unlike how other men had treated her of late. Her brother begrudged any expense and had only arranged the marriage in order to be rid of her.

Lord Brookmore spoke. 'You must select what you like, Miss Tilson. As many pieces as you like. When we get to Brookmore House a local seamstress can make whatever you need.'

She smiled at him in wonder. 'This is so generous.'

His face stiffened. 'I am clothing my nieces' governess. You need clothing and I am well able to provide it.'

She walked back to his side. 'I am so very grateful.' She touched his arm and it seemed as if the warmth of his kindness spread all through her.

The innkeeper broke in. 'Shall I ask my wife to attend you?'

Rebecca lifted her hand away. 'Yes. Please have her come at her convenience. I will just wash off the dirt of the road.'

Lord Brookmore stepped away from the doorway. 'I will leave you now. Send word when you wish to dine.' He turned to the innkeeper. 'May we have a private room for dining?'

'I'll see to it, m'lord.' The man bowed again and left them.

Rebecca did not wish for Lord Brookmore to leave. 'What time would you wish to dine, sir?'

'Whenever you wish.' His tone softened. 'I need to clean up, as well.'

But neither of them moved. His blue eyes seemed to pierce her, reaching parts of her that felt vulnerable and raw. Perhaps he really could see inside her. He certainly was able to anticipate her needs and discern her emotions. When had a man ever been able to do that? She'd been used to demanding what she needed.

Lord Brookmore averted his gaze and took another step back. 'I will leave you now.'

She watched him enter his room and close the door behind him. Only then did she do the same.

By the time Rebecca had stripped off her riding habit and washed off the dirt of the road, the innkeeper's wife and the seamstress knocked on her door.

'I am Mrs Bell, dear.' The woman was small and round, with a kind face and warm voice. 'This is Miss Cox. We were told of your misfortune. You poor creature!' She put her hands on her hips. 'Well, well. Let us see what we can do about providing you with some clothes to wear.'

The two women helped Rebecca out of the corset and shift she'd been given in Moelfre and into the undergarments that Mrs Bell had brought her. Two of the shifts fit her very well and one of the corsets was near perfect and so much more comfortable than the one from before. There was a nightdress that would be heaven to sleep in and two day dresses that fit her well enough.

One needed only minor alterations, which were accomplished on the spot. The other, the seamstress promised to have ready by the morning. With the help of the two women, Rebecca chose a length of wool for a winter dress and another for a cape. She picked out some plain white cotton for some aprons and caps and a print for another dress.

The ship had carried two trunks full of her clothing. She'd packed walking dresses, morning dresses, carriage dresses, dinner dresses, nightdresses and ball gowns. She had hats for all occasions and several pairs of shoes and gloves. Her undergarments had been made of soft linen. The wardrobe had been worthy of an earl's daughter and soon-to-be wife of a baron.

These makeshift clothes were—serviceable. But

they were also more dear to her than all of her lost dresses. Because of the thoughtfulness behind them.

Her father had indulged her with the finest clothes and jewels—all lost now—but he'd been unable to stand the sight of his daughter after her mother died. She'd reminded him too much of his beloved wife.

When Mrs Bell and Miss Cox left her, Rebecca took the pins from her hair and brushed it out with the brush Lord Brookmore had purchased for her. She rearranged it into a simple coil at the back of her head, as Claire had done. She wore the dress that the seamstress fixed for her, a dress of plain grey.

She glanced at herself in the full-length mirror that had been provided for her.

Her breath caught.

She saw Claire Tilson.

Donning the lavender gloves Lord Brookmore had purchased for her in Moelfre and the paisley shawl, she glanced at her image again and felt a little more like herself.

She left the room and knocked on Lord Brookmore's door.

He answered it in his shirtsleeves and looked even more handsome than when wearing his well-tailored coat, waistcoat and neckcloth.

'Miss Tilson,' he said in some surprise.

Oh, dear. This was a bit improper of her. 'You said I should let you know when I was ready to dine.'

'I assumed you would send word.'

Yes, but it had seemed silly to send someone else with the message when she was right next door. Besides, she had seen her father and brother in shirt-sleeves on occasion—but they did not look at all like Lord Brookmore.

He quickly donned his waistcoat and buttoned it.

She averted her gaze. 'I can return to my room, if you would prefer to eat later.'

'No. No. I am quite ready.' He put on his coat, pulling at the lapels and the cuffs to straighten its fit. He threw a neckcloth around his neck and managed to tie it into a reasonably neat mathematical.

He paused, his eyes scanning her. 'That is one of the new dresses? It looks well on you.'

Her face flushed at the compliment. Why should she react so to such mild praise when most men's flattery left her cold? Who had ever complimented her when wearing such a plain garment?

Their dinner was a lovely relaxed affair and Rebecca marvelled that there were long moments when she did not think of the shipwreck and when she quite forgot she was supposed to be a governess.

When Lord Brookmore's eyes lit upon her, it

seemed as if her insides would melt. She'd met other handsome men, but he was so much more than any man she had ever met.

How ironic that she should meet him as his lowly employee and not as a suitor. As Lady Rebecca she would have been acceptably eligible to him.

Not that he would have desired such an impulsive, wilful female, who'd defied her brother until he'd put her in a corner from which she could not escape.

Except she had escaped. All it had taken was the loss of Claire's life.

That thought brought a stab of pain.

But during the dinner with Lord Brookmore she tried very hard to push thoughts like that away and instead simply enjoyed his company.

After dinner they climbed the stairs to their rooms.

'Do you wish to ride again tomorrow?' he asked.

She glanced up at him. 'I would love to ride.' Riding had made the trip a pleasure.

'We should reach Brookmore House tomorrow.'

He walked her to her door where she would have to take on the role of governess completely and leave Lady Rebecca behind. A companionable night like this would be impossible then. A viscount simply did not become friends with a lowly governess.

Like the night before, he held his hand out for her

key. She took it from her pocket and placed it in his palm, very aware of her fingers brushing his skin.

He unlocked the door and returned the key to her.

She gazed up into his face. 'My lord, this was a lovely day. How can I ever thank you for all the kindness and generosity you've shown me?'

He stared at her, not speaking. They stood close, no more than a foot apart. His scent filled her nostrils, the faint odour of horse, of lime and something very male. It was more intoxicating than the wine she'd consumed at the meal.

Once when a man stood so close to her, he had forced her into a kiss. Even Lord Stonecroft had placed his wet, pulpous lips upon hers before he'd left to return to London. She'd wanted to retch. Somehow, though, if Lord Brookmore did the same, she would not mind.

What a brazen thought!

If she were herself—Lady Rebecca—instead of pretending to be Claire, could she, this moment, invite a kiss? All she needed to do was rise up on tiptoe.

Perhaps it would not hurt to be Lady Rebecca for a few minutes longer.

Garret gazed down at her face, so close to his. His heart thundered in his chest as her words echoed.

How can I ever thank you?

A kiss would be more than thanks.

The hall lamp shone on her, making her skin glow, bathing them both in light. The darkness cocooned them. Nothing else existed but the two of them, so close.

She rose, bringing her tantalising lips a whisper closer. It was enough to undo him. Garret seized her arms and lowered his lips to hers.

She tasted of claret and raspberries, her lips whetting an appetite he'd tried hard to deny. Her mouth opened to him and she placed her palms on his cheeks, holding his kiss.

It was all the encouragement he needed. He deepened the kiss and pressed her against him, against where the need for her had escalated. Her arms wrapped around his neck and her fingers buried themselves in his hair. She returned his kisses with an ardour matching his own.

What might it be like to make love to her? Would she match his passion making love?

'Lord Brookmore,' she murmured in a voice tinged with both passion and anxiety.

It woke him up.

He was Lord Brookmore. Her employer.

He pushed her away. 'Miss Tilson, I—' Words

failed. What could he say to her about what he'd done? And almost done?

He turned on his heel and strode away, back down the corridor and stairs.

Chapter Five

What had she done?

Had she risen on her toes or had he leaned down?

She'd wanted to kiss him, of that she was certain. Once his lips touched hers, she had not wanted him to stop.

She'd enticed him. How could she think otherwise? And he recoiled from her. She'd acted the hoyden and had created a disgust in him.

What her schoolteachers warned had been true— she was too forward. Too impulsive. She must take care lest she unleash the carnal impulses of a man. The man who once forced his kiss upon her blamed her for it. She had been too alluring, he'd said. But she'd been reasonably certain she'd not been too forward then and her impulse had definitely not been to kiss him.

But with Lord Brookmore? She might have enticed

that kiss from Lord Brookmore. How foolish she'd been to want that kiss.

There was a knock on the door and Rebecca jumped up and rushed to the door. She hesitated. Had he returned?

She cleared her throat. 'Who is it?'

'The maid, miss.' Not Lord Brookmore.

Rebecca opened the door, unsure if she were relieved or disappointed.

The young woman helped her take off her dress and assisted her with donning her new nightdress. When the maid left, Rebecca crawled into bed and buried herself under the covers.

She had very likely ruined her respite as a governess. Brookmore would discharge her; his nieces would endure another loss and she would be forced to tell him who she really was and beg for enough money to travel to London.

Worst of all, she would have to find another way to avoid marrying Lord Stonecroft and enduring his wet, disgusting kisses.

But how could she ever kiss another man after being kissed by Lord Brookmore?

The next morning Lord Brookmore had sent her breakfast to her room to avoid her, no doubt.

After she dressed again in her riding habit, she

dismissed the maid and tried to eat the cooked egg, bread and cheese Lord Brookmore provided for her. Giving up on finishing the food, she picked up her new bag packed with the new dresses and fabrics with which he'd surprised and delighted her. She left the room, fearful he might have already abandoned her.

When she entered the yard, though, he stood by his horse. An ostler held the reins of another horse wearing her side saddle. As she approached Lord Brookmore mounted his horse and avoided looking at her.

The ostler helped her into her saddle and fixed her bag behind her. Lord Brookmore handed the man a coin and started for the gate. Rebecca called a quick thank you to the ostler and hurried to catch up.

She could tell already that the horse she rode was more spirited than the horses provided for her the day before, but the enjoyment of riding such a horse was dampened by the fact that Lord Brookmore acted as if he were riding alone. He said not one word to her.

Rebecca, too, stayed silent, concentrating on keeping her horse steady and keeping up with him on the busy streets of Preston. They rode past Horrock's Mill and eventually reached the countryside.

Rebecca began this journey feeling shame about her behaviour and fear that she had lost any good opinion Lord Brookmore might have had of her. By the time the roads cleared, she felt angry. How dare he not even address what happened between them, not even acknowledge her presence? That kiss had not solely been her fault. She might have acted like a hoyden, but Lord Brookmore had not behaved as a gentleman, had he?

In any event, this silence was intolerable.

Her father might have blocked her out of his life and treated her as if she did not exist, but Rebecca would not take such treatment from anyone else.

She quickened her horse's pace until she reached his side. 'You must speak to me some time, sir.'

He darted a glance at her, but said nothing.

'I did not know you would kiss me,' she snapped.

His gaze was again fixed on the road. 'It will not happen again.'

He spoke this like an order, in a tone he might have used with his soldiers. He did not have to order her not to kiss him again. As if she would! Her anger was escalating and she was not sure if its source was his icy treatment of her or if it was her disappointment that he'd turned out to be just as thoughtless and cruel as other men in her life.

'It is unfair to blame me for it,' she retorted. 'You kissed me, after all.'

He actually looked at her. 'Blame you?'

She lifted her chin. 'I fear you are trying to discharge me. Or perhaps you have already discharged me by giving me the cut direct.'

A day ago she would not have believed him capable of such thoughtlessness.

He gaped at her. 'I am not discharging you.'

Her voice rose again. 'Then why pretend I do not exist? Why refuse to speak to me? I am left to guess you wish me gone.' As her father had done.

He stopped his horse. His jaw flexed. 'Is that what you think?'

'What else am I to think?'

He turned his horse and came directly next to her, leaning towards her. The space between them was only a few inches more than when they'd kissed. 'Think that I behaved abominably towards you. Think that I do not know what to say to you.'

He thought he'd behaved abominably? She almost softened towards him. 'Did you also think boorishness was preferable to a simple apology?'

'A simple apology seemed inadequate.' He frowned.

He turned his horse and rode on. This time she held back a little.

He had not discharged her! She could still pretend to be Claire.

Her cheeks burned with shame. She had called him a boor and here she was, nothing but an imposter.

* * *

Garret had even more reason to chastise himself. He'd assumed she would know he regretted what he'd done to her—and what he'd almost done. He'd simply made matters worse by not speaking of it.

They stopped at an inn to change horses.

He dismounted and turned to assist her. 'Let us get some refreshment.'

She looked down at him with a haughty expression. 'As you wish.'

She slid off the saddle, landing nearly as close as when he'd kissed her the night before. He must keep more distance.

The ostlers took charge of the horses and Garret escorted Miss Tilson into the tavern. At this morning hour, the public room was nearly empty and Garret thought better of a private room. Best not to be private with her.

He chose a table some distance away from the other diners, helped her sit and chose the chair across from hers. He ordered tea and biscuits for them which came quickly, accommodating those patrons who needed to be quickly on their way.

She poured the tea for him.

He knew they must discuss what had transpired between them. He searched for a way to begin.

She spoke first. 'I want you to know that I did not

intentionally entice you, sir. I have been accused of such wiles before, but, I assure you, I do not know precisely what one does to entice.'

Who was it who'd accused her? he wondered in a surge of jealousy.

Jealousy? He had not the right.

He leaned towards her and spoke quietly. 'What transpired last night was entirely my fault.'

She raised her eyes to his. 'I must have seemed too willing. That is what disgusted you, I am sure.'

She had been willing, he remembered. She'd kissed him back and resisted nothing. She'd kissed him back with a fervour matching his own.

'You did not disgust me,' he told her.

She persisted. 'But you left so angrily.'

'Anger at me, not you.' Let her be clear about that. 'It was wrong of me to kiss you.'

Her gaze did not waver. 'Then why did you?'

Why? Because she was a fascinating combination of vulnerability and strength. Because her animated features fascinated him. Because she'd been game enough to ride a whole day and never complained. He admired courage, even in small matters. She'd even been courageous enough to talk to him about the kiss when he could not think of a word to say. Because she was the first woman he'd truly wanted to kiss in a long, long time.

'You were enticing,' he admitted.

'I did not mean to be!' she cried.

He placed his hands on the table. 'I know, Miss Tilson. I placed you in an intolerable position.'

She straightened in her chair. 'I refuse to allow you to take all the blame.' She touched his hand.

It made him remember her eager response to him. The attraction was strong between them, which only made it more difficult for him.

He withdrew his hand. 'You are in my employ. A governess is at the mercy of her employer. I will not take advantage of you again.'

Something akin to self-reproach crossed her face. 'Then how are we to go along?' she asked, her voice nearly a whisper.

'I will behave correctly from now on.' He took a sip of his tea, lukewarm now. 'And I will not stay at Brookmore for very long.'

She looked more disappointed than relieved. Even more reason why he should only stay long enough to be certain his nieces accepted this enticing governess.

They finished their tea and walked out to mount fresh horses. This steed was not as spirited as Rebecca's previous one, but her mind was too preoccupied by her conversation with Lord Brookmore to care. The joy of the day before had disappeared and she was left with regret and disappointment. Regret that she'd not shown more restraint when he'd kissed her and disappointment that he did not intend to do so again. Instead he planned to leave.

They passed a house with a model of a ship above the door, reminding her that things could be so much worse for her—had been so much worse for Claire.

On the road the ease with Lord Brookmore that made the previous day so pleasurable was lacking. He kept a distance that was appropriate for a titled lord and a lowly governess.

The countryside they rode through was not unlike that around Reading where she'd attended school. Rolling hills, grazing sheep, planted fields. Gradually, though, it changed. The hills rose into mountains of brilliant green, glimpses of grey rock peeking through. In the valleys were lakes of deep blue water. The sheep that dotted the hills were a dusty brown, so unlike those in Berkshire. The houses, churches and other buildings were made of grey slate. From the mountains, no doubt. The countryside was lined with walls made with pieces of slate stacked one on the other.

The road led them up a mountain and when they were near the top, Rebecca stopped her horse and gasped.

'It is lovely,' she exclaimed, gazing down at the scene. 'The mountains and lake.' So green and blue.

He turned his horse to amble next to hers. 'We call the valleys *dales*. The mountains with grazing land are *fells* and the lakes are *waters* or *meres*. Several of our words like these are from the Vikings who once settled here.'

'It looks like a foreign land.' She made a small laugh. 'Not that I've seen any foreign lands. It looks unlike any place I've ever been.'

He moved his horse back on to the road. 'It is unlike any other place.'

It was the sort of place that could change a person, Rebecca thought. Her grim outlook lifted a bit. This land offered hope.

They stopped in a village to change horses. These buildings, too, were constructed with the grey slate, contrasted with a few that were whitewashed. The lack of colour in the buildings merely set off the green of the *fells* and the blue of the *waters*.

See? She was already speaking in this new foreign tongue.

Their road skirted a long lake.

Lord Brookmore inclined his head towards the lake. 'Windermere,' he said. 'The largest lake in England.'

It did seem to stretch for ever.

When the lake was no longer in sight they reached another village with the lovely name of Ambleside. Ambleside had the same stone buildings built on the rises, twists and turns of the land.

He pointed to a little house built on a bridge over a small river. 'See the Bridge House? It is a cobbler's house and has been here over one hundred years.'

He seemed to relax in these surroundings, places that must be as familiar to him as the landscape and villages around her father's estate and those around her school in Reading. She welcomed his ease of manner.

They left the village behind and entered a lane lined with ferns and shrubbery and trees so tall that the mountains disappeared from view. Their horses' hooves clip-clopped over a stone bridge spanning a stream, its water creating music as it tumbled over rocks.

Lord Brookmore quickened the pace. 'We are almost there.'

The wooded lane opened into fields again where cattle grazed. In the distance appeared a great house, built, of course, with the grey stone she'd seen everywhere this day. The house had a tower in front, crenelated like the castles of old, and another on the wing of the house.

'Brookmore House?' she asked as they approached, knowing it could be nothing else.

'Brookmore House,' he repeated with pride.

They passed through a wrought-iron gate and followed the road to a circular courtyard. There was no grand entrance to the house, merely a large carved wooden door. As they neared, the door opened and two footmen and a female servant emerged.

'Good day, m'lord,' the woman called. She eyed Rebecca with a puzzled expression.

'Mrs Dodd. I hope you are in good health.' Lord Brookmore dismounted.

'I am, sir,' she responded. Mrs Dodd was at least forty, a sturdy woman with a crisp apron and cap and an efficient air about her.

The footmen each took hold of a horse.

Lord Brookmore turned to Rebecca. The look he gave her set her heart to skittering.

She slid from the saddle.

Lord Brookmore addressed the footmen. 'We will need our bags. Tell Mr Lloyd to return the horses to the coaching inn.' His tone was matter of fact, even friendly. Her brother would have sneered at the men and barked out orders.

The footman holding Rebecca's horse handed the reins to the other and started unfastening her bag from the saddle.

Brookmore gestured for Rebecca to step forward, which she did.

He presented her to the female servant. 'Mrs Dodd,' he said. 'This is Miss Tilson, the new governess.'

'The governess!' Mrs Dodd exclaimed, looking her over again.

He turned to Rebecca. 'Mrs Dodd is the housekeeper.'

The woman in charge of the maids, the cook and the kitchen staff. But not the governess. A governess was not a servant, but was answerable only to who hired her.

Mrs Dodd nodded to her. 'How do you do, Miss Tilson.'

Rebecca smiled at her. 'I am a little fatigued, but quite in awe of this lovely place.'

The door opened and out dashed two little girls followed by a tall, thin, impeccably dressed man who Rebecca would wager was the butler.

'Mr Glover!' said Mrs Dodd disapprovingly.

'There was no stopping them.' The man panted.

Rebecca felt as though reality struck her full in the chest. She would be the governess to these girls. And she did not know how to be a governess!

She took in a deep breath. How hard could it be?

The two girls looked less like sisters than she and

Claire had. The older girl seemed all legs and arms and was as dark-haired and serious as her uncle. The younger girl was tiny, sturdy and blonde and seemed bursting with excitement.

She remembered their names. Pamela and Ellen.

Pamela, the older girl, faced her. 'Are you our new governess?'

Why be nervous? This was a little girl.

Rebecca made herself smile. 'I am. And you must be Miss Pamela.'

The girl assessed her carefully.

The younger one bounced forward. 'I am Ellen!'

'Are you?' Rebecca squatted down to her level. 'I am—Miss Tilson.' She'd almost said Lady Rebecca.

'We saw you riding,' Ellen added.

'Where is the maid?' Mrs Dodd asked Mr Glover. 'Mary was supposed to be watching them.'

'I do not know,' the butler replied. 'The children dashed through the hall. I followed them out.' He gazed apologetically at Lord Brookmore. 'My lord.' He bowed.

'Good to see you, Glover.' Lord Brookmore nodded to the man.

Rebecca stood.

Little Pamela pulled her sister behind her as if protecting the child from her uncle.

Brookmore gestured to Rebecca. 'Mr Glover, this is Miss Tilson, the new governess.'

Mr Glover's brows rose. Undoubtedly the household expected someone different.

'How do you do, Mr Glover.' Rebecca smiled.

'Miss.' He bowed.

Lord Brookmore moved impatiently. 'Let us go in the house. Miss Tilson and I have been riding all day. I am certain she needs a rest.'

Mr Glover hurried to open the door and scooted the children inside. Rebecca followed them in to a huge oak-panelled hall. The ceiling had an ornate white plasterwork design of interlocking circles unlike anything she'd seen before. Dominating the room was a huge fireplace, like a castle might have.

A maid rushed into the room. 'Miss Pamela. Miss Ellen. You must come back to the schoolroom.' She looked fearfully at Mrs Dodd, then Lord Brookmore. 'I told them to wait. I am sorry, my lord.'

'No harm in it,' he told her. 'Perhaps you can show Miss Tilson to her room and attend her?'

'Oh, yes, sir.' The maid curtsied to Rebecca. 'This way, miss.'

As they headed for a large carved oak doorway, Rebecca heard Mrs Dodd say to Lord Brookmore, 'Mr Evans wants to see you. Something about the crops…'

The maid led them to an oak stairway, its newel post and balusters ornately carved. Little Ellen scampered up the stairs. Pamela followed, walking very correctly. They climbed to the second floor and walked down a long hall past several closed doors. At the end of the hall was another hall off to the side with more doors.

'This is the children's wing,' the maid said.

Ellen pulled on the maid's dress. 'Mary, are you sending us to the schoolroom?'

'I am,' the maid admitted.

'But I want to stay,' Ellen wailed. 'We can help Miss Tilson.'

'I don't think so, Ellen,' her sister said. 'I think we aren't allowed. It is for servants to do.'

The maid gave Ellen an affectionate hug. 'You will be with Miss Tilson soon enough.'

'Come on.' Pamela took the little girl's hand. 'I will read to you from *Aesop's Fables*.'

Reading, thought Rebecca. *I can have them do a lot of reading.*

'Miss?' the maid said. 'I will show you to your room.'

The room was a comfortable size. Its oak walls made it a bit dark, but there was a nice window overlooking other buildings. She could see one of the footmen leading the two horses to what must be the stables. Would she still be welcome to ride? she wondered. Lord Brookmore's invitation had come before he'd cooled towards her.

The maid bustled around the room, straightening things that did not look as if they needed straightening. 'I will fetch some water directly. We did not know you would arrive today. Someone will light the fire, as well.'

The other footman appeared in the doorway. 'Your bag, miss.'

The maid ran to take it from his hands and he left quickly.

Rebecca removed her gloves and her hat and placed them on a table. She felt all dusty and dirty from the ride. The maid held the bag.

'Just place it on the floor.' She stepped towards the maid and extended her hand. 'I should introduce myself properly. I am Miss Tilson, as you have already guessed.'

The maid shook her hand limply and pulled away to drop into a curtsy. 'I am Mary Beale, miss.' She backed towards the door. 'I'll run and get your water.'

When the maid was gone. Rebecca pressed her hand against her abdomen and breathed deeply. Could she truly perform this masquerade?

She'd had a governess when she was about Ellen's age. Before that her mother had taught her. She remembered her mother reading books to her and showing her numbers and letters on a slate. Her governess lasted only a year. After that she'd been sent to school in Reading.

All she remembered about her governess was that the woman never smiled and often scolded. Rebecca might know nothing about being a governess, but she would be one who would smile.

Chapter Six

Garret retreated to his room right after Miss Tilson and the children disappeared above stairs. He'd not taken over the room that had once been his father's and then his brother's. He'd not wanted the memories…the ill feelings.

He'd kept the room given to him after he'd gone to school, although even that room had never entirely felt like his. He'd only stayed there on school holidays. It was on the second floor, the same floor as the children's wing, but closer to the top of the stairway.

Inside the room was his valet, the valet who had served his father and brother and was now old enough to be pensioned off. When Garret suggested it, tears filled the elderly man's eyes. 'Where would I go, m'lord?'

Garret hadn't the heart to send him away, then,

even though the job occasionally seemed too much for the man.

'Good day to you, m'lord,' the valet said.

'To you as well, Brant.'

Brant helped him off with his coat, brushing it with his hand. The footman appeared with Garret's bag and it took two hands for Brant to carry it into the small dressing room off the bedchamber.

Brant had known Garret since his boyhood. Knew everything about him. Garret could not help but wonder if the old man compared the ne'er-do-well second son with his father and sainted brother.

'So you have brought the new governess,' Brant said when he returned to the bedchamber.

'Yes.' Garret unbuttoned his waistcoat. 'I will stay long enough to make certain she is well established.' And long enough to make certain all was well on the estate. He still needed to hear why Ben Evans needed to speak with him about the crops. 'After that I might return to London.'

So not much would be required of the valet. He could rest easy.

'Indeed?' Brant took his waistcoat. 'London is hot in summer.'

Not that Brant had ever spent a summer there. He'd come to London with Garret's father and brother, but that was one accommodation Garret had insisted upon. Brant would remain at Brookmore House and Garret's old batman would act as his valet in London or elsewhere. If Garret needed him, that is. He'd happily forgone a valet on his trip to collect Miss Tilson.

Perhaps if he'd sent for his batman, Garret would not have acted so abominably towards her. Or have forgotten he was betrothed.

The memory of how Miss Tilson's lips had tasted, how she'd felt in his arms, flashed through him, more vivid than any kiss or embrace with Lady Agnes. If only he could have remained a second son. Lady Agnes would never have looked at him and he might have courted Miss Tilson.

What was the use of thinking of what could never be?

Garret stripped down, washed and donned fresh clothes, and at least felt…cleaner. Mrs Dodd had told him dinner could be ready in two hours. Garret was much too restless to sit and wait. Or to sit and consume brandy until mealtime.

It was early enough to call upon the estate manager and find out what the man wished to speak with him about. Garret left the house and strode to the manager's office and rapped on the door.

'Ben!' Garret cried. 'Are you there?'

The door opened.

'Garret. You are back.' His manager thrust out his hand to shake.

Garret accepted it warmly. Ben Evans was the son of his father's manager and he and Garret had grown up together as boys. Some of Garret's happiest memories at Brookmore House were the adventures he and Ben shared.

Garret was glad that Ben moved into the job of estate manager when his father could no longer perform it. He trusted Ben. Best of all, he could just be Garret with Ben. Not Viscount Brookmore.

'I brought the girls' governess finally.' Perhaps one day he'd tell Ben about Miss Tilson's shipwreck. He certainly would not tell him about the kiss.

Ben gestured for Garret to sit. He opened a drawer and pulled out a bottle, offering it. Garret nodded.

Ben poured a glass for Garret. 'I know you said you were not staying here long, but I want to persuade you to change your mind.'

Garret took a sip. 'Whisky?'

Ben grinned. 'Do not ask.'

Importing whisky was illegal, but smuggling the liquor was not unheard of.

Ben's expression sobered. 'Stay. Through the harvest season, at least.'

He had no intention of staying. This was his father's house, his brother's house; memories lurked around every corner. And now there was the additional temptation of Miss Tilson. 'Why?'

Ben poured a glass of whisky for himself. 'I need you here.'

'Me?' Surely not. 'You know more about managing the estate than I could ever know. Father never bothered to teach me a thing. He thought he needed only the heir, not the spare.' The spare was merely good for cannon fodder.

'I do not need you to run the estate,' Ben said. 'I need your authority.'

Garret waved his hand. 'You have it. You have my full authority.'

Ben leaned forward. 'Heed me, Garret. The workers are slacking. No matter what I say or do, they are not working as hard as they should. The farm, the quarry, it is all going to suffer because of it and, let me tell you, you cannot afford for that to happen.'

'Not afford?' Garret's brows rose. 'Are we in financial difficulty? Our men of business in London led me to believe otherwise.'

'Not yet, but it would not take much to tip the scales. A poor harvest. An outbreak of gid. Bad weather.' Ben sat back, shaking his head. 'Things have been slacking since your father died. Your brother made terrible decisions.'

'My brother?' Garret could not believe his ears. 'He was taught to run the estate like my father.'

'I know,' Ben said. 'I remember how it was, but I am telling you, John ignored all sense. His way of caring for the estate was ruinous.'

'I cannot believe this.' The fair-haired boy ruinous?

Ben downed his drink. 'He neglected the tenants and the workers. No matter what I said, he'd never authorise me to make necessary repairs to the houses or the equipment. The workers were convinced he cared nothing for the estate and for them and they've assumed you to feel the same. You've spent no time at all here.'

That was true. He had travelled straight to London upon receiving word of his brother's death. He'd avoided the estate until his nieces' governess had died.

He rubbed his face. 'What's to be done?'

Ben gave him an earnest look. 'For a start, stay through the harvest. Show yourself in the field, the stables, the barns and the quarry. Show them you value the estate and them.'

Garret and his brother John had known the people on the estate their whole lives. If the estate failed, what would become of those people? He hated thinking that they'd be forced to leave this beautiful land to work in one of the big factories being built near the larger towns. They might find work, but they'd lose the mountains and lakes and fresh air.

'You want me to act the Viscount,' he said cheerlessly.

Ben held his gaze again. 'You are the Viscount, Garret.'

He drained his glass and let the brown liquid burn down his throat. He placed the glass loudly on the table.

'Very well, I will stay.'

Garret walked back to the house, then sat in the drawing room, sipping brandy. Glover soon announced dinner. Garret entered the dining room. His place was set at the head of the long table in the seat that really belonged to his father and brother. The thought of eating alone in this cavernous room, in that seat, made his appetite flee.

He'd much prefer a simple private room in a tavern. The last two dinners he'd shared with Miss Tilson had been more pleasant than many he could remember.

He thought of that first night when she'd been so desperate not to be alone. Who would keep her company tonight? The girls would eat separately. The maid would eat with the servants.

He turned to Glover. 'Do you know if Miss Tilson has dined?'

'I believe not, sir,' the butler responded. 'We would serve you first.'

'Set another place here and send word for her to join me. She should dine with me. Tell her she does not have to dress for dinner. She may come in her day clothes.'

'As you wish, m'lord.' Glover signalled to a footman to do what Garret requested.

If Garret were completely honest, she was not the only one with a dread of eating alone. At least tonight.

A few minutes later Rebecca followed a footman to the dining room, which was located off the hall.

This room had the same plasterwork ceiling as the hall, but its walls were covered in leather. All these brown walls made it feel as if she were in a box and yet the feeling was a comfortable one, warm and protected. The dining room contained a long table. Lord Brookmore sat at the far end. He rose when she walked into the room.

'Miss Tilson,' he said formally. 'Thank you for coming so promptly.'

She had not dared to refuse.

He gestured to a chair adjacent to his. Glover pulled out the chair for her and held it while she sat.

'You may serve us now,' Lord Brookmore said to the butler.

When the soup was served, Brookmore spoke to her. 'Is your room comfortable, Miss Tilson?'

He was acting as if they'd merely met an hour ago.

'It is quite comfortable,' she replied in the same tone. 'As is the schoolroom and the girls' bedroom.'

'You must let me know if you need anything.' He sounded sad, she thought, and her heart went out to him.

'I think all is sufficient,' she replied, suddenly more concerned about his mood than her own worries. She made a try at conversation. 'What did you do, my lord, before it was time for dinner?'

He took a drink of his wine. 'I visited the estate manager.'

Was that what had depressed him?

She glanced at the butler and footman, who remained in the room. Not likely he would say much in the presence of servants, but he must have invited her to dine with him for a reason. So as not to be alone? They both knew she'd understand that.

No matter the strain between them earlier in the day, Rebecca wanted to distract him from whatever thoughts plagued him, like hers had done two days before.

'Your nieces are lovely little girls,' she began. Talking of the children seemed a safe enough topic.

'Yes.' He finished his wine.

'As different as night and day, are they not?' she went on.

He nodded.

This conversation was going nowhere.

'Tell me about the estate,' she tried.

He looked up at her. 'What would you like to know?'

She took a breath. 'Well…what crops do you grow? What livestock? That sort of thing.'

'Sheep and beef,' he said.

'Those funny brown sheep we saw on the ride here?'

'Herdwick sheep. Yes, we raise them. Mostly for eating. Their wool is too coarse for weaving.'

'And crops?' she asked.

The main course was served—a lamb roast.

'Hay and oats for the livestock and what you'd expect in a kitchen garden,' he replied. 'We brew our own beer so we also grow barley and hops.'

She was impressed. Her brother's estate was not so diverse. 'It is a large estate, then.' It must be for so much industry.

He shrugged. 'I suppose.' He glanced at her sideways and a smile tugged at the corner of his mouth. 'We have a quarry, as well.'

She laughed. 'A large estate, indeed! And I will wager your quarry produces this grey slate I see everywhere.'

He nodded. 'The house was built of it. Most of this house is Elizabethan with some modernisation in the 1700s. The family has been here since the fourteenth century, though.'

That explained all the oak panelling and plasterwork. 'The hall must be Elizabethan, then. And the tower in the front of the house?'

'That remains from the original house, built in the 1300s. The matching tower on the same wing as the children's rooms is a later copy.'

She smiled. 'You've good reason to be proud of all this.'

He looked sad again. 'I never expected it to be mine.'

By the time she had finished the cake for dessert, the day finally caught up with her. Her legs ached and her arms felt like lead.

'May I have your leave to retire?' she asked him. 'I am suddenly very fatigued.'

He nodded. 'It has been a long day. Of course you may retire. I will walk up with you.'

She gave him a plaintive look. 'Are you certain that is wise?'

He averted his gaze. 'I will walk you to the top of the stairs.'

Glover pulled out her chair and Lord Brookmore rose. He followed her as she walked the length of the long room. The footman opened the door for them. When they crossed the hall, they were out of earshot of any servants.

He fell in step next to her. 'I hope you approved of my asking you to dine with me.'

Her approval was hardly necessary.

'I was surprised,' she admitted. 'But glad. I still have a dread of too much time alone and there was no one else with whom to share dinner.'

His sadness made her ache for him. A governess had no business asking him about it, but she could not help herself. 'Did something happen, my lord? Something to upset you? Besides this morning, I mean.'

A look of surprise flashed across his face. They took several steps before he finally responded. 'My estate manager requires my presence here for longer than I'd hoped. It seems I will not be returning to London as I'd planned.'

He would not leave soon? She could not help being glad.

'Is there a problem somewhere? Perhaps I could help.' She'd grown up on a farm. Not as grand as this one, but she'd learned something of farm life when home for school holidays.

He glanced directly into her eyes and seemed about to confide in her. His gaze made her remember their kiss.

Instead he said, 'Share breakfast and dinner with me. The servants should not have to serve us separately and…' he paused '…I would appreciate the company.'

See him twice a day? She should refuse. She was still too affected by the kiss. More time with him also meant more time to discover she was an imposter.

She should keep her distance.

'It would be my pleasure, my lord.' Against all good judgement, she simply wanted to spend time with him.

She could be careful.

Besides, offering her company at meals seemed a small way to repay him for the very clothes on her back.

And an escape from a marriage she could not want.

As they climbed the long stairway, he asked, 'How did you fare with my nieces?'

Rebecca certainly was not going to tell him she felt daunted by them. 'I did not see much of them. The maid took me on a tour of the children's wing. The girls tagged along. They should be in bed by now.'

The clock had struck eight as they'd finished their meal.

'You should have a tour of the house, as well,' he said. 'Tomorrow, perhaps.'

'That would be lovely.' She imagined the housekeeper would act as tour guide. She'd not made a good first impression on Mrs Dodd, she feared, and a tour would give her an opportunity to do better.

At the top of the stairs, he halted, just as he said he would. 'I will bid you goodnight here.' He stepped away from her. 'Breakfast at half-past eight? I prefer to rise early.'

She curtsied. 'As do I.'

She started down the hallway, but turned around at the children's wing and saw him walking back down the stairs.

She continued on to her room. There was a fire in the fireplace and the room was comfortably warm. Rebecca looked for her bag, but discovered the maid had unpacked it and stowed it away in a cupboard where her few dresses were neatly folded. Mary had said earlier that she would come and assist Rebecca to get ready for bed, but, for the first time in days, Rebecca just wanted to be alone.

She was able to untie the laces of her dress and pull it over her head. She lay it carefully over a chair, intending to wear it the following day. Her stays were a bit trickier, but she managed to remove them and soon she was in the nightdress Lord Brookmore had purchased for her.

Light still shone in through the window and, tired as she was, Rebecca's mind was too full for sleep. After combing out her hair and tying it back with a ribbon, she sat cross-legged on the bed, visions of Lord Brookmore's face coming back to her. His stony expressions of the morning and the melancholy ones of this evening. What would it be like to see him each day, to share meals with him, like the equals they really were? Would he ever kiss her again?

The memory of his kiss made her senses sing.

She forced herself to think of more practical matters. How to be a governess. Should she be preparing lessons, as her teachers at school had done? What was she expected to teach? Reading and writing, certainly. Mathematics. Would she need to teach Latin? French? Or needlework, drawing, comportment?

The door opened and Rebecca jumped.

Little Pamela walked in, dressed in a long white nightdress with lace at the collar and sleeves.

'Pamela! What is it?' Rebecca cried, her heart still thumping at the surprise.

The little girl walked halfway to Rebecca's bed. 'Miss Cooper died in that bed, you know.'

A chill went through Rebecca, but she did not want this child to realise that. 'Was Miss Cooper your governess?'

Pamela nodded. 'She was always our governess.'

'And she died.' Rebecca's voice caught.

Their new governess died, too. Claire.

'She died,' another voice parroted. Ellen stood in the doorway.

Rebecca gestured for her to come closer.

Ellen scampered in and climbed on the bed. 'Mary said they brought in a new mattress, so it is not so bad, is it?' She looked uncertain.

'Not so bad.' A big difference, really.

'I liked Miss Cooper,' Pamela stated in an emphatic tone.

What to say to this child? 'So you are very sad that she died, are you not?'

Pamela did not answer, but her eyes looked huge in her little face and they glistened with tears. Rebecca's throat tightened.

Ellen nestled against her. 'I miss Miss Cooper, too!'

Rebecca put an arm around her.

Ellen looked up at her with her big brown eyes and bouncing blonde curls. 'Will you die, too, Miss Tilson?'

Oh, her heart was breaking for the little girl. 'Well, I am quite young, so I do not expect to die for a very long time.' As long as storms at sea didn't cause ships to wreck and plunge her into a watery grave.

Like Claire.

And all the others.

Pamela's voice rose. 'Sometimes people die young!'

Of course they do. These children knew that. Their parents died young.

'You are right,' Rebecca told her. 'But mostly they don't. Mostly they live for a long time.'

'Like Miss Cooper?' Ellen piped up. 'She was very old. Fifty, maybe.' She lifted her hands, but could not figure out how to show fifty.

Pamela walked to the side of the bed. 'Mrs Dodd says you are too young. She says you will be trouble.'

'Because you rode the horse!' Ellen added.

Obviously the girls had not remained in the children's wing. And obviously Mrs Dodd disapproved of her riding a horse instead of arriving in a carriage.

'I like riding horses,' Rebecca said, jostling the

little girl. She turned her gaze on Pamela. 'Do you like riding horses?'

'We were never allowed to. Miss Cooper did not like horses.' Pamela looked affronted.

'I like horses!' Ellen cried.

The clock on Rebecca's mantel chimed nine and the sky outside had darkened to a soft grey.

'Goodness! It is late. We must get some sleep, mustn't we?' Rebecca slipped off the bed and picked up Ellen, who clung to her. 'Come, girls. Let me tuck you in.'

Rebecca remembered her mother tucking her in. This was a task she was certain she could do.

Pamela ran ahead to the girls' bedchamber and she climbed into bed. Rebecca followed, carrying Ellen. She placed Ellen in the other bed in the room and covered her with the blankets, the ribbon in her hair coming undone and her hair falling around her shoulders.

'There you are, Miss Ellen. All tucked in.' She wrapped her ribbon around her hand and brushed the little girl's hair off her forehead.

She turned to Pamela, who had done a good job of tucking herself in.

'Miss Pamela, how efficient you are.' Might as well praise the child for it. 'I'll just smooth your covers a little.'

Rebecca smoothed the already smoothed covers, but stopped herself from touching Pamela. Something told her Pamela would not yet welcome it.

'There. You are both tucked in.' She straightened. 'Goodnight. I will see you in the morning.'

'Goodnight, Miss Tilson,' Ellen cried.

Pamela rolled on her side, facing away from Rebecca.

'Goodnight,' Rebecca repeated.

She closed the door behind her and walked back to her room, which was the first room on the children's wing. As she opened her door, she heard a sound. Thinking Mary might be coming from downstairs, she stepped into the hallway.

Lord Brookmore stood at a door and glanced her way, his gaze settling on her and not moving.

Rebecca was in her nightdress. And nothing else.

Her skin heated and she feared it was not from embarrassment.

'The children woke up,' she said, her voice higher than usual. 'I took them back to bed.'

Why was she explaining?

He nodded and turned to enter the room.

Was his bedchamber really so close to hers?

She groaned and ran back to her room.

Chapter Seven

Garret rose early the next morning when the golden sun was only peeking over the horizon. He'd not slept well, although he did not know if the prospect of tackling the problems of the estate was disturbing him or the fact that Miss Tilson's bedchamber was only a few steps away.

He'd known, of course, that the governess slept in that room on the children's wing. Years ago his governess had slept in the same room, but seeing Miss Tilson framed in the hallway wearing her nightclothes, her hair unbound, somewhat altered his perception.

He washed and dressed himself, trying to be quiet enough not to wake Brant, whose snores he could hear from the valet's room. Carrying his boots with him, he hurried down the stairs, stopping at the bottom to pull them on his feet. He walked to the back door and crossed the park to the stables.

His valiant horse would be there, the horse who'd brought him through battle after battle.

Garret entered the stable.

'Good morning, m'lord.' Jeb, one of the stable workers, was up early as well, tending the horses. Jeb was another worker Garret had known since boyhood. Jeb's father had worked in the stables and Jeb had grown up around the horses.

'Good morning, Jeb. Good to see you. Think I'll ride Skiddaw this morning.'

Garret had named Skiddaw after one of the nearby mountains. At Garret's voice, the horse whinnied and grew restless in his stall.

Jeb laughed. 'He'll be glad to see you. And glad for a good run.'

'As will I,' Garret said, stroking the horse's neck.

At least on the back of Skiddaw Garret could feel at home. It seemed like everywhere else he'd been these days had felt wrong. He belonged with the army. With his regiment where his skills held him in good stead. He knew how to prepare men for battle and how to lead them when the time came.

After the horse was saddled, Garret led him out of the stable and mounted him. When they reached the fields, he gave Skiddaw his head and tried to forget everything but the exhilaration of the ride.

* * *

Rebecca woke from a nightmare. She'd been under the water again until a man's hand pulled her out. In the dream it had been Lord Brookmore's hand, but he'd released her again and a wave swept her away.

It took several seconds before she realised she'd been dreaming and could remember where she was. In his house, a corridor away from him.

Even though the room only showed the barest hint of dawn, she climbed out of bed. Her bare feet touching the cool wooden floor helped reassure her the water was far, far away.

She padded over to the window and opened it, smelling the fresh mountain air. The merest hint of gold shone behind the mountains, now black in the distance. From below she spied a figure crossing the park. Lord Brookmore.

He disappeared into the stable.

What a lovely morning for a ride. So crisp and cool.

She watched until the sky grew brighter, infusing the landscape with colour. He emerged again, riding a magnificent black horse, giving it its head.

She envied him. Perhaps one morning she, too, could gallop over the green fields beneath the grandeur of the mountains.

She closed the window again, remembering she

was employed to educate two little girls. A flock of butterflies seemed to flutter in her stomach. Today she would really have to be a governess.

Girding herself mentally, Rebecca turned to dress.

She'd managed to wash and was struggling with her stays when the door opened.

'Oh, miss!' It was Mary carrying a coal scuttle, broom and a bucket. 'I did not expect you to be awake so early. I am here to tend the fire.'

How early had Mary risen? 'Thank you, Mary.'

Mary swept the ashes from the fireplace and placed them in the bucket. She put some new pieces of coal on the fire and turned to Rebecca, who was still fussing with her stays.

'I'll help you with that, miss.' Mary washed and dried her hands and pulled the laces of the corset tight. She helped Rebecca put on her dress.

'In the mornings I first tend to the fires in the children's wing,' Mary said while she tied the dress's laces. 'But after that I will come and help you dress. If you know a certain time you would prefer, I will come at that time.'

'I doubt I will always be awake this early,' Rebecca assured her. 'What time do the children rise?'

'I wake them at eight, miss, but Miss Ellen is often up before then.' She rolled her eyes.

Rebecca smiled. 'I am not surprised. And Pamela always stays abed until you come, I suppose.'

'Yes, indeed!' Mary laughed. 'What else might I do for you, miss?'

'Nothing I cannot do for myself.' Rebecca could fix her own hair. 'I do not wish to disrupt your duties.'

'I am here to serve you, miss. And the little girls.' She retrieved her bucket and scuttle.

'I believe I will look at the schoolroom before Miss Ellen and Miss Pamela wake up. Prepare for the day, you know.' Try to figure out how to be a governess, she meant.

'Very good, miss.' Mary curtsied and left.

It was not half past six when Rebecca entered the schoolroom. She lit candles from the fireplace that Mary had obviously already tended.

The room was neat and tidy. Books in bookcases along the wall. Boxes stored on shelves underneath. There was a long table in the centre of the room with two slates in front of two chairs and sticks of chalk and folded cloths to wipe the slates clean.

Rebecca pulled out books, one by one. She nearly whooped in pleasure. One book was titled *The Governess or The Little Female Academy*. Surely she could discover what a governess must do from this book. She sat near a candle and read, with increasing dismay. The book was about a school where the students all tell their own stories. The teacher provides the moral to be learned, but the book was hardly a model for how to be a governess.

Unless she was to provide moral lessons for everything. She'd spent her school days and afterward bucking what she was supposed to do.

Rebecca searched through other books.

A voice startled her. 'What are you doing, Miss Tilson?'

Ellen had entered the room.

Rebecca placed a hand over her fast-beating heart. 'I wanted to see what books you have.' She peered at the girl. 'Are you not supposed to be in bed?'

Ellen sauntered closer. 'I woke up. Are you going to read one of the books to us?'

Goodness. Rebecca did not know. 'I am not certain. What did Miss Cooper do?'

Ellen made a face. 'She made us read them.'

Rebecca nodded to herself. 'What else did she do?'

'Made us do sums.'

Rebecca did not mind sums. 'Anything else?'

'Needlework.' Ellen spat out the word as if it were rancid.

Rebecca concurred. Most of the female arts held little interest to her.

Ellen stood right next to Rebecca's chair and looked up to her. 'Will you eat breakfast with us?'

She'd promised to breakfast with Lord Brookmore. 'Did Miss Cooper eat breakfast with you?'

Ellen nodded, still staring into Rebecca's eyes.

What could she say? 'Of course I will!'

She brushed the hair from Ellen's forehead.

'Now I am guessing that you should go back to bed and wait for Mary to rouse you.' Rebecca stood.

She took the little girl by the hand and walked back to her room with her. If Pamela was awake, she could not tell, but she tiptoed in and quietly tucked Ellen back in bed.

When it was nearing eight o'clock Rebecca waited for Mary in the hallway outside the children's room.

The maid looked puzzled to see her. 'Miss?'

Rebecca caught her before she reached the door. 'Did Miss Cooper eat breakfast with the girls?'

'Yes, miss,' Mary responded uncertainly. 'Why do you ask?'

'Do you know why she did so?' Was this part of being a good governess or did Miss Cooper simply want some company for the meal?

'I think she used the time to teach them manners,' Mary replied.

Manners. Was teaching manners of a priority over

risking offending the man who employed her? And with whom she could not help wanting to spend time?

'Miss Cooper got them talking to her at breakfast,' Mary added. 'That was the only time I ever heard them talk about their parents. About them dying, you know.'

Talking helped, Lord Brookmore had said.

'Do you think I should eat breakfast with them?' Rebecca asked.

Mary's brows rose. 'Oh, miss. I would not presume to tell a governess what to do.'

She had no one else to ask. Except maybe little Ellen.

'Where is breakfast for them?' Rebecca asked.

'In the tower sitting room. Lots of sunlight there.' Mary started for the girls' door.

'I will eat with them,' Rebecca called after her.

She hurried to the schoolroom and found paper and ink. She wrote a note for Lord Brookmore, explaining why she would not be at breakfast. She started to fold the paper, but opened it again and added another sentence.

If you so desire, you would be very welcome to share this breakfast in the Tower Room.

He would not come, of course. What man would? Certainly not her father. Nor her brother. At least he would know that she was not avoiding his company.

She blotted the ink dry and folded the note and went downstairs. As she hoped, a footman was attending the hall.

She handed him the note. 'Would you please see that Lord Brookmore receives this note before he breakfasts?'

'Yes, miss,' the footman said.

She returned to her room and waited until Mary finished helping the girls dress.

Garret came in from his ride, feeling marginally more settled.

If Ben thought it important he help solve the problems on the estate, he'd do that. Perhaps if he kept busy, his mind would not wander to Miss Tilson so frequently.

He'd merely felt sympathy for her, because of the shipwreck, he decided. He must put her solely in the role of governess and that would be that.

He bounded up the back stairs to his bedchamber where Brant awaited him.

'Good morning, my lord.' Brant stood ready to help him with his coat.

He changed out of his riding clothes into buckskin

breeches and boots and one of his more comfortable waistcoats and coats. He kept an eye on the time.

It was eight-thirty already before he descended the stairs.

When he entered the hall the footman stepped up to him. 'Beg pardon, m'lord.'

'What is it, Mason?' He tried to disguise his impatience. He'd told Miss Tilson that breakfast was at eight-thirty and now he was late.

'A note for you, m'lord.' Mason handed him the folded piece of paper. 'From the new governess.'

She was not coming. What else could it be? He unfolded the paper and read that she intended to eat breakfast with his nieces and that he was welcome to join them.

He expelled a relieved breath. A part of him feared she was writing a letter of resignation.

Breakfast with his nieces.

He could understand Miss Tilson's desire to eat with Pamela and Ellen, but why would he be included?

It would be ridiculous for him to attend, would it not? On the other hand, he would have the opportunity to see Miss Tilson with the children. Make certain all was as it should be. It would give him an opportunity to see Miss Tilson...

'May I assist you, m'lord?' the footman asked.

'Hmm?' Garret was still lost in thought. 'Oh. Yes, Mason. Tell Glover that I will have breakfast in the Tower Room with the children. Have the food brought up there.'

'The Tower Room, sir?'

It did seem unbelievable.

'Yes, Mason,' Garret repeated. 'The Tower Room.'

The Tower Room was back upstairs where the main hallway met the children's wing. Unlike the medieval tower at the front of the house, the tower that had been part of the original house, this was only eighty years old or so. Unlike the medieval tower, the rooms on each floor of the tower had large windows facing east. Sunshine poured in in the mornings.

When he'd been a boy, he and his brother breakfasted in that room with his governess. His parents often joined them. His father never tired of hearing about his brother's achievements.

So it made sense Garret had been invited. He was the children's guardian.

He opened the door.

A table was placed in the centre of the room, just as it had when he'd been a child. Miss Tilson and the children all looked over at him in surprise. The children and Miss Tilson each had bowls of porridge, just as it had been in his youth.

She rose to her feet. 'Lord Brookmore. How lovely of you to come. Are you staying to dine?'

'I am staying,' he responded. 'Glover will bring my breakfast up here.'

'How very nice!'

She sounded happy he'd come. His two nieces, though, merely gaped at him.

Miss Tilson gestured to the fourth chair. 'Do sit, my lord. I'll pour you some tea.'

He pulled the chair up to the table, but did not sit. 'I should have coffee soon.' He waited until she sat down before seating himself.

Sure enough, the footmen arrived with the food from the dining-room sideboard and a welcome pot of coffee. When they left, Garret filled his plate with ham and cheese and cold veal pie. He brought the basket of bread to the table as well as the butter, honey and blackberry jam, which he suspected the girls would like.

They went from staring at him to staring at the bread and jam.

'You may have some,' he told them. 'As much as you like.'

They seemed very hesitant.

'Show your uncle how you spread the butter and jam on the bread and do so like ladies,' Miss Tilson suggested.

Only then did they accept the treat, little Ellen taking a gob of jam for her piece of bread. Miss Tilson gave him an amused smile over that. It was endearing, but should she not correct Ellen? It was not the best of manners to pile on so much jam.

If Miss Tilson did not scold the child, Garret certainly wouldn't.

The room felt very quiet, filled only with the sounds of chewing. Garret had supposed he would merely observe the breakfast, but now he felt as if they were all waiting for him to direct the conversation.

He addressed the girls. 'Did you fare well while I was away?' he asked. 'Did Mary take good care of you?'

'Yes, Uncle Garret,' they said in unison.

He tried again. 'Have you become acquainted with Miss Tilson? Shown her a welcome?'

'Yes, Uncle Garret,' they parroted again.

He glanced at Miss Tilson for help, but she shrugged her shoulders.

'You are so very quiet,' he remarked. 'Were you quiet when other people visited you at breakfast?'

This time they merely stared.

Finally Pamela spoke in a very quiet voice. 'No one visited, Uncle Garret.'

'Surely your parents—' he began, but stopped himself. He did not wish to remind them of their loss.

'No,' Pamela quickly cried.

Ellen piped up. 'Mama came to our classroom sometimes. And we visited her in her sitting room every afternoon.'

'And your papa?' he asked.

This time Pamela answered. 'Papa did not like us,' she said in a scathing tone. 'I heard him once. He yelled at Mama for having girls instead of boys. He wanted boys.'

Ellen's eyes grew very serious. 'He made Mama cry.'

Garret felt pain deep in his gut, an old familiar pain. This one filled him with rage, as well. His damned brother. So they were little girls. They were his children.

He glanced at Miss Tilson and saw compassion in her face.

This was more pain than he'd thought his nieces had endured.

He leaned forward. 'Your papa was my brother. He did not like me very much either.' They had that in common.

The girls gaped at him again, hungry for something besides bread and jam. He probably could not give it to them, but he'd give them something.

He turned to Miss Tilson. 'Miss Tilson, do you like boys above girls? I confess I like them both.'

Miss Tilson responded as if this point was the most important in life. 'I'm a bit partial to girls.'

He almost smiled at that. He glanced back at Pamela and Ellen. 'You may have something there. Little girls are charming.'

His nieces visibly relaxed. He had not realised how stiffly they were holding themselves, as if bracing for more hurt.

Never had he thought he had any importance to them. He'd seen them only fleetingly, spoken only two or three words to them. Now, however, he'd inserted himself into their lives and if he withdrew too soon they would conclude that his brother was right.

Another reason to stay for a while. He must compose a letter to London this day, explain the reasons for his delayed return. Surely Lady Agnes would find enough to entertain her without his presence.

The conversation did not go any more smoothly after that. After more failed attempts at engaging the children, Garret finally asked, 'What will you do after this?'

Pamela and Ellen glanced directly at Miss Tilson.

'Um.' She looked uncertain, but a light came into her eyes. 'You promised me a tour of the house. We could all do that.'

Shouldn't she have them do their lessons first? That's what his governess would have done.

She turned to the girls. 'Would you like that?'

'Yes, Miss Tilson,' they said in unison again, but at least this time they sounded a little pleased.

Chapter Eight

Rebecca followed Lord Brookmore down the stairs. Behind them both trailed the little girls, who were not nearly as thrilled at touring the house as Rebecca thought they would be.

'We will start in the hall,' Lord Brookmore said, leading them into the first room Rebecca had seen in the house.

Rebecca hesitated. He was conducting the tour? Not Mrs Dodd? She quickened her step. The children stood in the doorway to the room.

'This is the oldest part of the house,' he began. 'It used to be the central part of the house in the 1300s.' He pointed to the crest above the huge stone fireplace, so large Rebecca could have walked inside it without ducking. 'Queen Elizabeth's crest was added later, but she never visited here.'

The room was panelled in oak in parquetry

squares, which indeed made it seem as old as the Middle Ages.

He proceeded to the drawing room, another oak-panelled room, but with decorative carving on the oak, especially above a smaller stone fireplace. 'This drawing room was also part of the original house.'

The chairs, tables and sofas looked at least one hundred years old, although undoubtedly the red-damask upholstery was more recent.

Lord Brookmore gestured to a huge desk in the middle of the room. 'The desk was my great-grandfather's, made by Gillows of Lancaster.'

This meant nothing to Rebecca, except that the most modern piece of furniture in the room must have been over half a century old.

Lord Brookmore spoke of the portraits on the walls, ancestors whose names Rebecca instantly forgot.

During this discourse, Pamela remained very still, just inside the door, but little Ellen traversed the room, looking at whatever captured her eye, and there were certainly several porcelain decorative items at her eye level on the various tables. She stopped by the terrestrial globe when Lord Brookmore pointed it out. As he went on to another piece in the room, Ellen spun the globe.

She laughed and spun it again. The third time she swung her arm back to give it a really hard spin and knocked over an Oriental porcelain ginger jar. It careened off the table and smashed on to the wooden floor.

'Ellen!' Pamela cried in a panicked voice.

Ellen burst into tears and tried to pick up the shattered pieces.

Rebecca rushed over to the little girl, worried that she would cut herself. She took the pieces from Ellen's hands and took over picking up the rest while Ellen continued to wail.

'Leave it,' boomed Lord Brookmore, crossing over to them.

Pamela stood where she was, trembling.

'Leave it.' His voice softened. He took little Ellen's arms and guided her away. He turned to Rebecca. 'The maids will clean it up.'

She placed the pieces she'd collected neatly on the floor. Why had she insisted the children come on this tour? Why had she not watched them more carefully? This was not going well at all.

'No need to cry,' he said, crouching down to Ellen's level. 'Things break sometimes.'

Rebecca gaped at him. He was not angry? The jar had obviously been valuable.

Pamela continued to look shocked and Ellen's

whole body still shook with her sobs. He guided Ellen over to a sofa and walked over to take Pamela by the hand to join her sister.

He sat between them and pointed to a pyramid-shaped blue and white Delft tulip vase that sat next to the fireplace.

'See that tulip vase? Two hundred years ago our ancestor collected Dutch tulips. There was no price too high for him to pay for tulip bulbs. Tulip Madness it was called later.' The two girls looked at him as if he were speaking Greek. 'Anyway,' he continued. 'when I was a boy, there were ten of those tulip vases lined up. My father's pride. He'd often tell the story of his ancestor's tulip collection. One day, I was playing chase with your father, which we were not allowed to do.' The girls' interest seemed to increase with mention of their father. 'I knocked into one of the vases and it fell against the next one and they all fell, one after the other. Only one—' he pointed '—this one—survived.'

Ellen was rapt by this time. 'Did your papa beat you?'

Her uncle nodded. 'I had a proper whipping and a scolding, as well.'

Pamela cringed.

'But I learned an important lesson that day,' he went on.

'Don't break things?' Ellen offered.

'No.' His arm around her tightened. 'I learned that no vase or any item was worth so much as to deserve a whipping or even as big a scolding as I received.' He looked from Ellen to Pamela. 'Accidents can happen, but I know I can trust both of you to be careful, now you know what can happen.'

Rebecca gazed at him in wonder. What sort of man was this who thought a little girl's feelings were more valuable than a priceless piece of porcelain? Her heart swelled.

Lord Brookmore looked up at her. 'Is there anything you wish to say to Ellen, Miss Tilson?'

She was surprised to be included, but then she remembered she was the governess. 'Yes.' She cleared her throat. 'Miss Ellen, you must be more careful.'

Lord Brookmore looked less than satisfied at her response. She was unsatisfied herself. A proper governess would have known the right way to handle this, but all she could think of was how upset Ellen had been.

The tour continued through the rest of the first floor, the library, the game room, and the bedrooms that had been the children's parents'.

Rebecca hesitated on them visiting those rooms with the girls, but she did not intervene.

It seemed like the girls had never seen their father's bedroom, but Ellen blurted out one or two memories about her mother. Pamela stood silent as a stone.

Ellen touched her mother's comb and hairbrush, still resting on the dressing table. 'Mama let me brush her hair sometimes,' the little girl said. 'Her hair was the colour of mine.'

'Would you like her brush for your very own?' her uncle asked.

Ellen's eyes grew wide. 'Am I allowed?'

Lord Brookmore smiled. 'I am the one who says and I say you may have it.' He turned to Pamela. 'You must choose something of your mother's, as well, Pamela. Something to keep for your own.'

Rebecca's heart was melting.

Pamela stared at him for a long time. She eventually crossed the room to a chest of drawers. She opened one and pulled out a miniature.

'Ah.' Lord Brookmore nodded. 'A miniature of your mother. Good choice.'

Rebecca's throat tightened with emotion, but she managed to say, 'Perhaps you should take your treasures up to your room before we continue the tour.'

They exited the bedchamber and the girls immediately turned to their right and disappeared up a back stairway.

* * *

Garret called after the girls, 'Meet us back in the hall.' He turned to Miss Tilson. 'That stairway leads to the room where you had breakfast. You might find it more convenient at times.'

He walked with her back to the hall.

He was surprised he could keep his demeanour so matter of fact. This entire episode with the children had shaken him.

They had never been in his brother's room. Of course, what Pamela said of his brother should have made that no surprise. Their visit to their mother's room had touched him deeply. He was glad he'd let them take something from the room. Some time, before he returned to London, perhaps, he ought to tend to her other belongings. Surely there was jewellery of hers that should be kept for them. Other personal items, as well.

Then there was the broken ginger jar. He'd never entered the drawing room that he did not think of breaking the tulip vases. He'd been about Ellen's age. His father's scolding had been a thousand times worse than the welts on his buttocks. He had concluded that his father would have preferred Garret die rather than the vases be destroyed.

Garret would not have his little niece feel the

same, but he'd been shocked when Miss Tilson did not chastise Ellen. Weren't governesses supposed to?

He turned to Miss Tilson. 'I was surprised you did not scold Ellen for the broken vase. My governess certainly never missed a chance to scold me.'

She looked chastised. 'I suppose I ought to have said something, but at the moment I was too afraid she'd cut herself on the pieces.' Her expression turned curious. 'For what did your governess scold you?'

He thought it a curious question. 'Well, breaking things, for one.'

The scolding did have the effect of making him careful not to be reckless around his father's possessions, but his father's reaction had the opposite effect of what he might have supposed. From that moment on Garret placed very little value on things and more in people's emotions.

Miss Tilson broke into his thoughts. 'Those poor little girls.' She sighed. 'I thought I would weep when Ellen spoke of her mother.'

At least she had compassion for the girls.

'Or when Pamela said nothing,' he added.

'You were marvellous with them, you know,' she said.

His face grew warm from her praise.

She added, 'I was quite in awe of you.'

'I'm their guardian,' he said stiffly. 'I am supposed to treat them well.'

She laughed. 'My brother was my guardian and he never treated me well.'

He stopped at the entrance to the hall. 'I thought you said you had no relations.'

She paled. 'I—I—he was my half-brother and—and—I do not credit him as a relation.'

That made sense. 'After today, I am not certain I want to credit my brother as a relation either.'

She looked relieved. Was she that worried about his opinion of her?

'It is not so unusual for a father to want sons, you know,' she said.

Not all sons, just the heir. 'I do not begrudge him the desire to have sons. God knows I wish he'd had a son, so the son could inherit.' Garret frowned. 'What I do not accept is his not wanting his daughters.'

'Well, it is obvious you value them,' she remarked as she examined a suit of armour on display.

Another compliment? He was not doing anything special that he could see.

He gazed at her as she moved from the armour to a Rubens painting. She was a puzzle, sometimes so very unlike what he expected a governess to be.

When faced with a puzzle, who would not wish to solve it? The enigma she was only drew him in more.

He ought to be maintaining his distance. Instead, what had he done? He'd invited her to share dinners with him. He ate breakfast with her and, instead of giving the task to Mrs Dodd or Glover, he made himself her guide.

At least his nieces served as chaperons.

The clatter of little feet approached. The girls running. Why did Miss Tilson not tell them not to run, like any governess would? Not that Garret minded them running. Let them run through the house. He'd done so only when his father and the servants were not looking.

'We are here, Uncle!' cried Ellen.

'So I have guessed,' he quipped. 'Shall we show Miss Tilson the gardens?'

'The gardens!' Ellen took his hand and pulled him towards the door.

Pamela and Miss Tilson followed.

He led them out the front door and through an archway, the entrance to a stone-walled garden.

When Miss Tilson walked through the entrance and saw the other side, she clapped her hands. 'It is a topiary!' She ran into the garden, laughing. 'Look, Pamela and Ellen. Look at all the fanciful shapes!'

Her delight was too charming.

Ellen skipped after her and even Pamela walked briskly. Miss Tilson dashed from one sculpted bush to the other.

'Look! An archway. Very like the stone one. Look! These look like silly hats.'

She dropped to her knees when she came upon the elephant which was quite a bit smaller than many of the others. 'How clever. How very clever.'

Garret had always liked the topiary. He'd pretend some of the trees and bushes were soldiers and that the whole garden was a battlefield. That had been before he learned what a real battle was like.

'Come!' Miss Tilson took Ellen by the hand and gestured to Pamela. 'Let's run to the end of the garden!'

Ellen joined in eagerly. Pamela ran a few steps, then slowed to a walk.

Garret walked over to the gardener working in one of the squares with the cone-shaped topiary.

'Phibbs!' he called. 'Good day to you.'

The man beamed. 'Garret, my boy.' He stood and doffed his hat. 'I mean, my lord.'

Garret extended his hand. Phibbs had been tending the garden since he was a boy. 'It is good to see you. You look unchanged.'

Phibbs rubbed his hip. 'Some aches and pains, you know, but I cannot complain.'

Garret glanced towards Miss Tilson. 'Your garden has a new admirer in the new governess.'

'Governess, you say?' The older man inclined his head towards her. 'She looks a game one for the poor bab'es.'

A game one. An apt description.

'She is indeed,' Garret agreed. And very unlike what he'd expected for them.

Next Garret showed Miss Tilson the orchard, the kitchen garden and the fountain garden. On their own, without Miss Tilson's leading them, the girls ran through the gardens.

Then Garret took them to the stables. The horses were in the paddocks and, as soon as Skiddaw saw him, he cantered up to the fence.

'Oh!' he heard Pamela exclaim. Her eyes were glowing.

'Would you like to meet the horses?' Garret asked her.

She nodded enthusiastically.

Ellen was not so certain. She hid behind Miss Tilson's skirts.

Garret lifted Pamela on to the fence.

'This is Skiddaw.' Skiddaw came up to him for attention.

One of the mares approached Pamela and nudged her.

'She wants you to pet her,' Miss Tilson told the girl. She demonstrated. 'Stroke her gently on the shoulder. She will love that.'

Pamela reached over the fence and stroked the horse just as Miss Tilson showed her. 'Nice horse,' she repeated soothingly.

When it came time to leave, Pamela had to be dragged away with the promise of a biscuit and milk when they visited the kitchens. The girls ran ahead and Miss Tilson fell into step next to him.

'You need to buy them ponies,' she said.

'Ponies?'

She nodded. 'Pamela, because nothing else has turned her into a normal little girl. And Ellen so she learns not to be afraid.'

Ponies.

'We shall see,' he responded, but he liked the idea.

'They are old enough to learn to ride,' she pressed on.

He turned to her. 'Miss Tilson, you've convinced me.'

The smile she returned to him was as golden as this fine day.

* * *

By the time they reached the kitchen and Cook had given Pamela and Ellen a biscuit and milk, Rebecca was filled with energy and optimism. She knew it was because of the man beside her.

She marvelled at how he apparently attuned himself to others' feelings. He always seemed to know the right question to ask, the right support to give. Of course, he'd been a bit cruel to her that third day on the road when he would not speak to her, but that was because of the kiss and the fault had been hers as much as his.

That lovely, thrilling kiss.

Rebecca stopped that thought. She must remember she was the governess and not Lady Rebecca.

She'd made a terrible slip, mentioning her brother. She must not do that again.

Mrs Dodd appeared in the kitchen while they were waiting for the children to finish their *petit repas*.

'Good day to you, sir.' Mrs Dodd curtsied to Lord Brookmore.

He smiled at the housekeeper. 'How are you faring, Mrs Dodd? Are things running smoothly in the house? Any problems?'

The housekeeper spoke at length about the workings of the house and the needs of the servants. While she spoke, she gave Rebecca black looks.

How was Rebecca to get on Mrs Dodd's good side? The woman had taken a severe dislike to her.

After Mrs Dodd finished and Lord Brookmore promised to look into some improvements she'd suggested, she and the kitchen servants went back to their work.

Rebecca approached Lord Brookmore. 'Do we proceed with the tour?' She hoped so. It was lovely to spend the day with him.

He darted a glance to the little girls. 'Another time, perhaps. I think your charges are too fatigued.'

Her charges.

She should have realised. The little girls could hardly keep their heads up to finish their biscuits. 'Yes, perhaps a rest is due. I suppose I should take them back to the children's wing when they've finished eating.'

'I'll not wait,' he said. 'As long as I am on this wing, I want to stop by the dairy and the brewery. See how they are faring.'

He walked over to the girls to say goodbye to them. Their faces had lost that panicked look when he came near. He'd charmed them, as he'd charmed her.

She regretted losing his company.

She approached Mrs Dodd. 'The house looks marvellously well kept, Mrs Dodd. It must take a great deal of co-ordination on your part.'

The compliment did not soften her. 'I do my job.'

Rebecca became more direct. 'Forgive me for saying so, but you seem unhappy with me. May I know why so I might make amends?'

Mrs Dodd looked her up and down. 'You don't seem like a proper governess to me. Riding next to the Viscount. Eating meals with him. He's not for the likes of you, you know. People should remain in their stations.'

Her insinuation raised Rebecca's hackles, perhaps because it was too near the truth. 'I disagree, Mrs Dodd. I believe people—men and women—should rise as high as their talent, ambition and hard work take them. I do assure you, though, that I am here as governess for Miss Pamela and Miss Ellen. No other reason.'

'Hmmph!' Mrs Dodd exclaimed. 'You'd better not have any other designs.'

'I do not,' Rebecca repeated.

Mrs Dodd turned and marched away.

Cook came up to her, drying her hands on a towel. 'Do not pay her any mind, miss,' she said. 'She's a stickler, she is.' Cook inclined her head towards the doorway by which Lord Brookmore left. 'What a fine man our Master Garret turned into. He was a rackety charver in his day, eh.'

'Charver?' she asked.

Cook seemed to search for a translation. 'A rackety boy. Full of mischief.'

Rebecca nodded, repeating the word *charver* in her head so she would remember it.

She would also remember that Mrs Dodd thought her not a proper governess.

Back in the schoolroom, Rebecca was at a loss what to ask of the children, who immediately sat at what she suspected were their usual seats.

'What would Miss Cooper have you do at this time of day?' she asked them.

'Different things,' Pamela said unhelpfully.

'Like what things?' Rebecca asked.

The little girl shrugged.

'We could play!' Ellen suggested.

Somehow Rebecca did not think that was what Miss Cooper would have done.

She found paper and pencils and put them in front of each girl. 'Why not write about what we did this morning?'

They looked at her blankly.

'Why?' Pamela asked in a suspicious tone.

'Well.' How to explain it was the only idea she'd come up with? 'To remember it. Like in a journal. You write down what you did so you remember it.'

'What is a journal?' Ellen asked.

'It is a book of blank pages that you write in about your day.' Rebecca had kept a journal, but hers were now at the bottom of the Irish Sea.

'But we do not have books with blank pages,' Pamela said.

This child was too concerned with things being just so. 'If you like doing this, I'll buy you one, so you can keep a journal.' She'd have to ask Lord Brookmore, she meant, but he would say yes.

'Why would we keep a journal?' Pamela asked.

'To remember what you did,' Rebecca replied. 'But not only what you did, but how you felt about your experiences. Because, you may not realise it, but what you do and think and feel is important.'

Pamela's eyes widened. 'May I write about the horses?'

This was progress. 'Of course you may. You may write about anything. You get to decide.'

'I didn't like the horses,' Ellen said.

'Well, then, write about something else.'

'What?' Ellen looked at Rebecca as if this was the hardest task ever asked of her.

'Anything.' Somehow Rebecca suspected Miss Cooper had never had this sort of problem when she gave the girls work.

Ellen just stared at her. Where was her imagination? At age seven, Rebecca was always making up stories.

'Write about your favourite room in the house,' Rebecca came up with. 'What you saw in there.'

'I'm not good at writing and spelling,' Ellen complained.

'I'll help you.' Rebecca pulled up a chair next to her.

Ellen wrote about her mother's room, but every word she wanted to write she had to ask how to spell, making the task tedious for Rebecca, who at least kept a semblance of good humour. At least Ellen knew her letters. What would Rebecca do if Ellen had not known her letters?

Pamela apparently had a lot to say. She'd filled one page and was starting on another.

Rebecca breathed a sigh of relief that would be short-lived. After this task, what would they do next?

'After this we'll draw pictures of what we saw,' she blurted out.

That would take up a little more time.

Chapter Nine

Later that day Garret stopped by the estate manager's office. Ben was seated behind his desk, the desk his father used before him.

'Garret.' Ben rose to his feet and gestured to a chair. 'Come in. Sit.'

'I came to tell you that I've started what you suggested.' Garret lowered himself into the chair. 'I rode the property this morning.' Because he could not sleep. 'I saw some of the workers. Spoke to them.'

Ben nodded approvingly.

'I've also talked to one of the gardeners, the stable workers, the house servants, the dairy and the brewery.'

'All that?' Ben blew out a good-humoured breath. 'I did not mean for you to accomplish everything in one day.'

'It was convenient to do so.' Because he'd given

Rebecca the tour, it had pushed him to be out among those who worked on the estate.

Ben's expression turned to one of concern. 'I hope you are not trying to cram this into a few days.'

Garret held up a hand. 'I know. You want more than an appearance by me.'

'It is not what I want,' Ben stated. 'It is what the estate needs. It needs your leadership.'

'I'm not certain of that,' Garret said. 'But I want the estate to prosper. There are many people depending upon it.'

'Precisely,' Ben agreed.

Garret left Ben and returned to the house. When he climbed the stairs to his room, he had half a notion to take himself into the children's wing to see how Miss Tilson was faring.

He'd see her soon enough at dinner.

He entered his bedchamber and let Brant help him change out of the clothes he'd worn all day. A clean change of clothes for dinner made him feel presentable. In his father's and brother's days, one dressed formally for dinner, but he'd feel foolish doing so to eat alone or with Miss Tilson, who did not have enough clothes to dress for dinner.

He was eager to see her, to hear what she thought about the house, the children, the horses.

But he should not be eager to see her.

In fact, he needed to write a letter. He must do so before dinner so he could send it in tomorrow's post.

'Thank you, Brant,' he said to the valet who was brushing off his coat as if putting the finishing touches on one's creation.

'Very good, m'lord.' Brant limped away.

Garret peered at him. 'Are you in some difficulty, Brant?'

The valet looked puzzled. 'Difficulty, sir?'

Garret pointed. 'You are favouring one leg.'

Brant limped across the room to pick up Garret's discarded clothes. 'Just a touch of the rheumatism, my lord.'

'Perhaps you should rest. I can forgo your services for one night,' he offered.

Brant shook his head. 'I would not think of it, sir.'

He worried about this man. 'Very well, but you must tell me when you do need rest.'

Garret left the valet and went down to the drawing room. He took paper, pen and ink from the desk and sat to compose a letter to Lady Agnes, explaining he would be remaining at the estate for unforeseen weeks.

While he put pen to paper he tried to remember what she looked like exactly. He knew she was blonde-haired and blue-eyed and that his father's friends and advisors had enthusiastically supported a match between them, but she did not come alive in his memory.

Not like Miss Tilson.

He should limit his time with Miss Tilson. Not share breakfast with her and the children again. Rescind his invitation for her to dine with him. Keep his distance.

But if he did withdraw from her company, it would mean distancing himself from his nieces, too. He could not do that. Not now. Not when he'd made himself more important to them. Not when he learned of his brother's treatment of them.

And he did not want to eat dinner alone.

He turned back to the pen and paper, managing a short note, suggesting Lady Agnes spend the summer at Brighton as she'd planned and where he was to have joined her, although Brighton held no appeal to him.

He sealed the letter and gave it to one of the footmen to see that it reached the post by tomorrow.

Glover announced dinner.

Garret entered the dining room, wondering if there was not a smaller room in which they might dine. This was the most convenient to the kitchen, though, and he was not about to inconvenience the servants any more than he had done by breakfasting with the children.

Miss Tilson was not yet there.

'Was dinner announced to Miss Tilson?' he asked Glover.

The man opened his mouth to answer when she came rushing in the door. 'Yes, dinner was announced to me. I hope you haven't been waiting long.'

'Just arrived,' he said.

She took the seat adjacent to his, where she'd sat the night before. Garret forgot all his self-warnings and simply enjoyed her company. They talked of what they each had done after the tour and she told him about the journals. He supposed journal writing was a good day's lesson for them, but an unusual one. In any event, the time went swiftly and felt very companionable.

Dinner came to an end, and he again escorted her out of the room, but did not feel like ending the time with her.

When they were out of earshot of the footmen, she said, 'I enjoyed today so very much, my lord, and the dinner. I thank you for both.'

He should bid her goodnight.

'Come to the drawing room with me,' he said instead.

They entered the room where Ellen had broken the vase earlier that day. He walked directly to a cabinet against the wall.

'I am having brandy, if you do not mind.' Although he was unsure why he was asking the governess for permission.

'I do not mind at all.' She took a seat on one of the sofas. 'Might I have a glass, as well? It has been a long time since I've tasted brandy.'

His brows rose in surprise. Most unlike a governess.

But appealing in its boldness.

He poured her a glass and one for himself and joined her, choosing a nearby chair.

In the candlelight her skin glowed and her features softened and he felt intimate with her, even though he vowed he would not touch her.

She took a sip. 'I think it so beneficial that you spend time with Pamela and Ellen. You saw what marvels you created today. You saved a little girl's pride and you sparked some life into one who dares not stray off the path of what is expected of her.' She smiled. 'And you introduced her to horses!'

'I think you make too much of nothing.' He'd done what anyone would do, surely.

Except perhaps his brother. Curse him.

'I think not.' Miss Tilson's eyes shone with admiration.

Do not look at me like that, he thought. *It is too dangerous for both of us.*

She took another sip of her brandy and appeared unrepentant for enjoying it. 'Tell me more about your tour of the estate.' He had spoken of it at dinner. 'Was all well?'

Had he betrayed his worry when speaking of it at dinner? He ought to merely say yes, all was well, but there were no servants listening and he was grateful she'd changed the subject.

'The estate manager says matters are not good. My brother apparently neglected the estate and the workers are unhappy. They are not as productive as the estate needs and my brother spent so lavishly that there are not many reserves to offset any future problems.' Saying this out loud somehow made him feel the worry more acutely.

'Your brother neglected the estate?' she responded. 'How?'

He took a sip of his brandy. 'He neglected the buildings, including the tenants' houses, which are apparently in some disrepair. I am uncertain how bad things are in that area.'

'No wonder the workers are unhappy,' she said.

'The repairs must be made, obviously, but that will

take time and something must be done to encourage the men to work hard enough for the estate to produce enough revenue.' He downed the rest of his brandy and stood to pour himself another. 'That is why I must stay. At least until after harvest, Ben, the manager says.'

'Of course you must stay.' Her voice was sympathetic. 'The workers need you.'

He laughed drily. 'That is what Ben says, but I am at a loss as to what I can do. They are reluctant to talk to me.'

'Make it impossible not to.' She made it sound so simple.

'And how am I to do that?' He sat again. 'I was not bred for this. My brother was the one who was to inherit. I was merely sent to the army.'

She sipped her drink and seemed lost in thought. Finally she spoke. 'You commanded men in the army, did you not?'

'Yes, I commanded men.' And sometimes sent them to their deaths.

'There must have been something you did to make your men follow you into battle,' she went on.

'What has that to do with running an estate?' he snapped.

She finished her brandy and rose. 'Forgive me, my lord.' Her voice lost all its sparkle. 'I simply thought that commanding soldiers and commanding workers might be similar, but I see I spoke out of turn. I should retire.' She started for the door.

He caught her arm before she entered the hall, putting himself dangerously near to her, breaking his vow not to touch her.

'I did not mean to speak sharply, Miss Tilson.' Her lips were too tantalisingly close and her muscles melted in his grasp.

She held his gaze and it felt as if energy was sparking between them.

He released her. 'Yes, it is probably best you retire for the night.'

She nodded and her voice softened. 'I hope you sleep well. I am certain you can solve these problems, Lord Brookmore. I'm of a mind there is nothing you cannot do.'

She turned and left.

He walked back to his brandy and swirled the liquid in the glass, his body humming for her and his mind turning.

Was it so very different commanding workers and commanding soldiers? Was she correct? Could he do this?

Garret stayed awake half the night thinking of how he commanded his regiment in those last years and how he'd dealt with his company before his rise in rank. He'd never given it much thought, had merely done whatever he felt needed to be done, said what needed to be said. He realised finally that, before everything else, he ensured his men's needs were met. Whenever humanly possible, he made certain they had adequate food, shelter, clothing, medical care, if needed. He kept them in muskets, ammunition and powder. They rewarded him by following his orders and fighting bravely in battle.

There was no reason he could not do the same for his workers. He'd incur whatever expense necessary to repair their houses and equipment and to keep them in necessary supplies. No one on the estate should go hungry or suffer cold or endanger themselves by working with faulty equipment. This was his obligation to them, his duty, just as it had been with his soldiers.

How had his brother not seen this?

The next morning at breakfast, Pamela jabbered about horses and journals and Ellen complained about both. Ellen again asked Garret to tell the story about breaking the tulip vases. Finally as they were leaving the Tower Room, Garret had a chance to say something privately to Miss Tilson.

'I am going to speak to the workers,' he told her

as they entered the corridor. 'I now know what I need to do.'

She smiled at him. 'I knew you would sort it out.'

'What you said helped,' he added.

She looked about to ask him what he meant when the children pulled her away to the schoolroom.

He'd tell her more tonight after dinner. He expected to have a lot more to tell her.

Garret hurried from the breakfast room to Ben's office, eager to put his plan into effect.

Over the next few days Rebecca was pleased to hear Lord Brookmore speak about his efforts on behalf of his workers. He'd taken command, just as she'd suggested, but the best thing of all was he'd spent time meeting with as many workers as possible, hearing their concerns and promising to address them.

He also rode into Grasmere to purchase journals for the girls and he sent a seamstress from Ambleside to sew more garments for her.

He still ate breakfast with her and his nieces, so he was practically the first person she saw each day. In the evening they ate dinner together and talked over the day's events. Her esteem of him continued to grow.

She encouraged him to do most of the talking,

lest he ask her about her lessons with the children. She was an abominable governess. Oh, she managed to fill the time with the girls, but she had no idea if what she was doing was anything like she ought to be doing. She skipped from one sort of lesson to another, usually finding some excuse to explore the gardens with the girls or visit the horses.

This morning, though, Rebecca was as restless as a stormy sea, and no wonder. She'd dreamed of the sea, of the shipwreck, of the mother clutching her children to her. Only she was the mother and the children were Pamela and Ellen.

She'd woken in terror and could not return to sleep.

The walls confined her this day, even more so because the day was as beautiful as any she'd ever seen. The sky was vivid turquoise with puffs of white clouds as decoration. The mountains sparkled with green and the flowers in the garden danced in the breeze. The air was brisk, chillier than a normal summer, but, still, she could not bear to stay inside.

'I thought to take the girls on a walk today,' she told Lord Brookmore, although she'd merely thought of it that minute. 'Where can we go? Somewhere we can see something new or unexpected.'

He thought for a moment. 'Rydal Water is near. An easy walk from here. You can make your way around the lake and see birds and fowl. It is not difficult to find. You won't get lost.'

She turned to the girls. 'What say you, young ladies? Shall we walk to Rydal Water?'

'Yes!' Ellen shouted exuberantly.

Pamela said nothing.

Lord Brookmore gave her the direction to the lake and shortly after they finished breakfast she and the girls donned their hats, half-boots, walking dresses and jackets and started off.

Being outside in the fresh air and sunshine helped Rebecca's restlessness a bit and the children did not demand much of her. Ellen skipped ahead, stopping to examine every flower and insect, and kept up a constant narrative on what she saw. Pamela, like Rebecca, seemed lost in her own thoughts.

How much better it was to inhale the scent of elderflower and wild garlic than the chalk dust and paper of the schoolroom.

They walked over a hill—or rather Ellen ran—and finally they could see the lake below, mimicking the blue of the sky even down to the reflections of the clouds in the water.

With a laugh, Ellen ran down the hill and Rebecca and Pamela quickened their pace. The water's edge was not accessible at the hill's bottom, but they found a path that seemed to circle the lake. Rydal Water had an island in the middle, a green spot amidst the blue water.

As they walked around the lake, it was easy to stay close to the water, although occasionally rocks or shrubbery separated them.

'What is that?' Ellen pointed to a bird that just took flight.

'A heron!' Rebecca told her. 'See its long legs and beak?'

They spied a red squirrel and an otter, and Ellen was beside herself with excitement. Pamela seemed to relax, as well, stopping to examine leaves and flowers and picking up stones to take home with her. Rebecca cleared her mind and let the peacefulness of the day calm her.

'Think of all you will be able to write in your journals,' she said to the girls. 'And to tell your uncle.'

He would listen interestedly, as if each word his nieces uttered was very important. What sort of man cared what little girls said?

A fine man.

Rebecca imagined the expression on his face as he listened attentively to her, too, when they conversed at dinner. *He'd* become important to her.

'Look! Look!' cried Ellen. 'A swan!'

The elegant creature, so white it shimmered, swam

at the water's edge, which was down the slope from the path where they walked.

Ellen raced towards it. 'A swan! A swan!'

'Slow down!' Rebecca shouted. She raced after her.

'Stop, Ellen!' her sister cried.

But the child ran too fast to stop. Ellen tripped when her feet hit the stones at the water's edge and, as she struggled to keep her balance, she stumbled into the water.

She fell in with a splash, crying out. In her effort to stand, she pushed herself further into the lake and soon was flailing into deeper and deeper water.

Pamela screamed.

Rebecca ran into the water, reaching for Ellen, who floated further away. Reeds beneath the water tangled in Rebecca's feet and she fell beneath the water's surface.

Suddenly she was back in the Irish Sea, the sounds of splintering wood and human screams muffled under the water. Her feet gained purchase on the bottom and she pushed herself out of the water, now up to her chest.

Ellen clung to a thin branch that protruded from the water. Just a step or two further into the water and Rebecca could reach her.

But Ellen's cries turned into the cries of the children in the ship's rowboat. Pamela's screams rang in her ears like those of panicked men and women facing death. The water was cold. Like that day. Cold.

'Miss Tilson! Help her! Help her!' Pamela cried.

Rebecca shook her head and the thunder of pounding horse hooves sounded in her ears. The mountains and the lake came in to focus. Ellen's hand was slipping off the branch.

Rebecca cried out and surged forward. She grabbed Ellen, but they both sank beneath the water. Ellen thrashed about, but Rebecca would not let go of her. Rebecca's feet slipped on the bottom as she struggled to lift Ellen out of the water.

Her mind's eye saw lifeless bodies of children floating under water. Her panic rose.

Suddenly she was seized from behind by strong arms that pulled her and Ellen towards the shore. Their faces broke through the water and Rebecca took gulps of air.

When she could stand again, Ellen was scooped from her arms and carried out of the water. Only then did she see their rescuer.

Lord Brookmore.

He placed the coughing and spluttering child on dry ground. Her sister ran to her and hugged her tightly.

Rebecca was afraid to move from the water, afraid

of falling under again, but, no matter, Ellen was safe. Lord Brookmore charged into the lake again, took her in his arms and carried her to shore. When he released her to stand, he held her for a brief moment in a tight embrace before they both hurried to Ellen's side.

Ellen's teeth chattered and her lips were blue. Rebecca's chest hurt from the cold water and she could barely feel her legs.

Lord Brookmore's coat lay on the rocks nearby. He picked it up and wrapped it around Ellen. He lifted the child into his arms. 'We have to get her warm as quickly as possible.'

Rebecca could only nod.

He carried Ellen to his horse. 'I can't take you both. Can you walk, Miss Tilson?'

'I'll m-m-manage.' She was not at all sure she could walk, but she didn't want him to waste time with her. Ellen must be taken home immediately.

Lord Brookmore turned to Pamela. 'You must walk Miss Tilson home. Do you understand, Pamela? Do not allow her to stop. Come all the way home.'

Pamela nodded. The girl took Rebecca's hand and pulled her until she got to her feet, still numb from the cold water.

Brookmore mounted his horse and placed Ellen before him on the saddle. He turned to Pamela again. 'Make sure you do not stop. All the way home.'

Pamela held Rebecca's hand and pulled Rebecca on. 'Come, Miss Tilson. We have to walk home.'

It was a huge responsibility Lord Brookmore had given this little girl, the responsibility of Rebecca's welfare. Rebecca could not bear it if she were to keep Pamela from completing her task.

Rebecca walked.

Rebecca heard the sounds of the shipwreck while she struggled to keep the pace little Pamela set for her. She could not always tell where she was. One minute she'd be drifting at sea and the next on a road with mountains surrounding her and a little girl telling her to keep walking.

Gradually the cold left her, but her skirts were heavy with water and her feet chafed against the wet leather of her shoes. She felt close to collapsing, but pushed on, so as not to become too big a burden for a little girl.

Just when it seemed she could not take another step, a gig appeared in the distance.

It pulled up beside them, driven by one of Lord Brookmore's coachmen. 'His lordship said to come pick you up.'

Chapter Ten

Garret's horse had made the trip to Brookmore House at great speed. He'd shouted for help and Glover and a footman ran from the house to assist him. Ellen had been swiftly placed in the arms of one of the maids who hurried her up the stairs to change her out of her wet clothes and wrap her in warm blankets.

Only then had Garret realised he was also cold and dripping water on the floor of the hall.

Brant belied his age and quickly helped Garret change out of his wet clothing and into dry ones. As soon as Garret was dressed again, he hurried to the children's room to see Ellen.

She was sitting up in bed, a shawl wrapped around her shoulders. Mary, the girls' maid, fed her some hot liquid on a spoon.

'Uncle!' Her face tensed. 'I did not mean to chase the swan! I did not mean to fall in the water!'

He hurried to her bedside and crouched down to speak to her. 'There now.' He tried to sound soothing. 'You did not know what would happen. Never worry. It was an accident.'

Tears welled up in her eyes. 'I am very sorry.'

He held her tiny hand in his. 'I know you are.' He looked her over. 'Are you hurt in any way?' She looked unharmed, except for damp hair and a pale face.

She shook her head. 'I'm cold, though.'

'That is why you must let Mary feed you—whatever it is.' He glanced at Mary.

'Camomile tea with honey,' Mary offered.

'There you go. That will warm you,' he said.

Mary offered a spoonful and Ellen dutifully swallowed it.

'Where is Pamela?' she asked. 'And Miss Tilson?'

He was asking himself the same question. As soon as he'd arrived with Ellen on the horse, he'd shouted instructions to send the gig for them. They should have been here by now.

'I am sure they will be here any minute,' he said. 'In the meantime, rest and finish your tea.'

'Yes, Uncle Garret,' she replied.

He straightened. 'I will check on you later, so don't let me hear you've given Mary any trouble.'

'Yes, Uncle Garret.'

He walked out of the room and down the back stairs, trying to decide if he should set off towards Rydal Water to find Miss Tilson and Pamela himself. He was not at all confident Miss Tilson could walk the whole distance. If the gig could not find her, she might succumb to the cold. Garret had seen soldiers die of the cold in the mountains in Spain. The men who'd kept walking stayed alive.

Garret tried to quell his worry. When had he before felt this frantic? Or cared this intensely? In the army he'd learned not to become too close to anyone; too many were killed. When a child, he'd learned not to care so much; it hurt when caring was not returned. But Pamela and Ellen—and Miss Tilson—somehow had made their way into his heart.

He was going after the gig.

Garret was in the doorway to the hall when he heard a carriage and shouting voices. The door opened and Pamela dashed in and ran for the stairs. Miss Tilson was helped in by one of the maids. Mrs Dodd followed behind, muttering, 'You've caused a great deal of trouble.'

Garret's impulse was to snap at Mrs Dodd for her cruel remark and take Miss Tilson in his arms and carry her to her room, like he carried Ellen. He did not do either, though. Instead he held back, remaining in the doorway, watching the maid help her up the stairs.

He closed his eyes and said a prayer of thanks that he'd ridden to the lake instead of the quarry where he'd been bound. Even as he'd turned his horse on to the road to Rydal Water, he'd told himself he should go to the quarry.

Then he'd heard the screams.

He reached them seconds before seeing Miss Tilson disappear under the water trying to reach Ellen. It was easy to become tangled in the reeds and be unable to rise again, even in shallow water. But she had risen again to grab Ellen at the same moment Ellen's fingers slipped from the twig she'd grasped. Then both of them went under again.

By that time he'd jumped off his horse and torn off his coat and sprinted into the water after them.

How easy it would have been for them both to drown. What if he'd not been there to save them?

He turned away and made his way out to the garden, even though the chill still penetrated through him.

What if the water triggered another spell in her? It stood to reason she might experience visions of the shipwreck. He'd never told anyone about the shipwreck. Had she? Even if she had, would they know how to help her if the visions returned?

* * *

Rebecca woke to a warm but darkened room. She must have slept the day away. Neglected even more of her duties.

She closed her eyes again and saw Ellen clinging to the branch, crying for her help. She rolled on her side and curled into a ball. What sort of person fails to save a child? That precious child!

There was a knock on the door. The maid or Mary come to check on her, no doubt.

She sat up and wiped her eyes. 'Come in.'

The silhouette in the opening door was not a maid. She drew the covers over her. 'Lord Brookmore!'

He stepped inside the room and closed the door. 'I came to see how you fared.'

She turned away from him. 'Better than I ought.'

He came closer. How could he bear to even look at her?

'She cried for me and I could not move. How awful is that?' She faced him again. 'Me, who knows what drowning is like.'

He stood next to her bed. 'I did not see you hesitate.'

She blinked. 'She would have drowned!' She twisted away again. 'I am the very worst of creatures! How could I do that? She was crying for me!'

He touched her face, turning it back to look at

him. 'You did not hesitate. She did not drown. She is unharmed.'

She pulled out of his grasp. 'I am supposed to take care of the children! Mrs Dodd is right. I am nothing but trouble.'

She'd been trouble for everyone. Her father. Her brother. Even at school. Now she'd almost let a child drown. Not merely any child. Ellen. Dear Ellen.

'Never mind Mrs Dodd for the moment.' His voice turned low and soothing. 'You had a vision of the shipwreck, did you not?'

She nodded. 'But that is no excuse.'

This time when he touched her face it was like a caress. 'It was brave of you to rush into the water—'

'I was not brave. I froze,' she insisted.

'You might think you froze, but it must have only been for a second or two,' he countered.

He brushed the hair from her forehead and pulled his hand away, holding it behind his back.

She rose to her knees, forgetting to cover herself. 'It was like at the inn! I was there again. I was there and I heard the sounds. I smelled and tasted the sea. I felt the boat capsize.'

He nodded. 'Like the soldiers after a battle. You could not help the memories that came to you. But they must have lasted only seconds, because, I tell you, you didn't hesitate.'

She searched his face to see if he was telling the truth or just trying to make her feel better.

He put his arms around her and held her close. 'Do not torture yourself. You could not help but be caught in the vision. Even so, you did everything you could do.'

Her cheek pressed against his and the roughness of his beard scraped her skin. It felt so good to be held by him.

Just as quickly she pushed away. She did not deserve comfort.

They stared at each other and she did not know what to read in his eyes. Pain? Regret?

She felt angry at herself and ashamed and regretful that she could not remain encircled by his arms.

The door opened suddenly and Lord Brookmore stepped back.

'Miss Tilson!' Ellen ran in and climbed on the bed, giving her a hug. 'We heard talking. We wanted to see you.'

'Ellen wanted to see you,' Pamela clarified. 'I told her we must let you rest, like Mary said.'

Ellen turned to her sister. 'But we heard her talking, so she wasn't resting any more.' She seemed to notice Lord Brookmore. 'You were talking to her, weren't you, Uncle Garret?'

'That I was,' he said stiffly. 'Talking.'

Rebecca extended her arm. 'Come here, Pamela.'

Pamela approached the bed.

Rebecca reached over and took the girl's hand. 'This is the brave one! How can I ever thank you for bringing me home?'

Pamela reddened. 'Uncle Garret told me to.'

He touched her shoulder. 'You did a fine job, Pamela. Just as I knew you would.'

The girl glanced up at him with worshipful eyes. Rebecca knew exactly how she felt.

She hugged both girls. In these mere few days they'd become as dear to her as she could imagine her own children to be. 'I am so glad we are here safe and sound.' She released them and directed her gaze at Ellen. 'I am so sorry I did not pull you out. I am so very sorry!'

'But you caught her and Uncle Garret pulled you both out,' Pamela said.

Lord Brookmore spoke. 'Do you know why it was especially brave of Miss Tilson to go in the water after Ellen?'

Both little girls looked up at him. 'Why?' they asked in unison.

'Miss Tilson was in a shipwreck and she almost drowned. The lake water made her afraid all over again. It brought back the memories as if it was all happening again, but she still grabbed hold of Ellen.'

'A shipwreck!' cried Ellen. She glanced from Rebecca to Lord Brookmore. 'What is a shipwreck?'

'When a ship sinks in the ocean.' Pamela turned to Rebecca. 'What memories did the water make you have?'

'Of being under the water...' She paused. The children did not need to hear about the screams. About Claire and the gentleman washed overboard. About the mother and children in the rowboat. 'When I sailed from Ireland to come here, there was a storm and the ship crashed into rocks. But it was close to shore so, even though I was tossed under the water, I did not drown. Somebody saved me.'

'That is why Miss Tilson does not have more dresses,' Lord Brookmore added. 'They were all lost at sea.'

'You lost your dresses?' Pamela asked.

Rebecca nodded. 'I lost everything. What I have now is what your uncle kindly bought for me.'

'Mama had lots of dresses,' Ellen piped up. 'She even had new dresses that came after—after—you know.'

'After she died,' Pamela added helpfully.

'The dressmaker will make Miss Tilson more dresses, too,' Lord Brookmore said.

The girls knew that the dressmaker had come to

measure her and collect the cloth Lord Brookmore purchased.

'But!' Rebecca pushed away this focus on her. She still must act like a governess. 'You girls should be in bed! It is late and I am sure Mary does not know you are still awake.'

'We crept out after she left us,' Ellen explained.

'Well, then, let's get you back to bed before Mary comes to check on you.' Lord Brookmore gestured for them to move out of the room.

Rebecca climbed out of bed. 'I'll tuck them in.' She wrapped herself in her shawl.

'I want Uncle Garret to tuck me in!' Ellen demanded.

'Very well.' He laughed softly. 'I'll come, too.'

Garret should have begged off, but he was charmed by his little nieces and, after the day they'd had, he did not wish to deny them anything.

Besides, he was loathe to leave Miss Tilson, although he knew he ought to.

He accompanied his nieces and Miss Tilson, wearing only her nightdress and shawl, to the girls' bedroom and tucked them both into bed and kissed them each on the forehead.

His heart filled with emotion. They were securely lodged there in his heart, all three of them. To almost lose them was taking a slice out of him. What a shock to need these three people, to need to keep them safe, healthy and happy.

Not even the woman he would marry mustered that much emotion in him.

He felt a pang of guilt.

'Now go to sleep,' Miss Tilson ordered the girls. 'Tomorrow we go back to our lessons.'

'May we start by writing about today in our journals?' Pamela asked.

'You may,' her governess said. 'If you stay in bed until morning and get some sleep.'

The girls made a show of shutting their eyes. Garret and Miss Tilson left the room and closed the door.

They walked side by side to the door of her bedchamber.

'Are you hungry, Miss Tilson?' To his knowledge, she had not eaten since breakfast.

She nodded. 'But it is of no consequence.'

'You must eat,' he insisted. 'Shall I have food sent up to you?'

'No,' she responded. 'I do not want to cause Mrs Dodd any more trouble.'

He frowned. 'Perhaps I must talk to Mrs Dodd.'

She put a hand on his arm. 'No, please do not. Let it be.' She dropped her hand. 'I will go down to the kitchen and beg for food.'

'I'll come with you,' he said.

Why ever had he said that? He ought to bid her goodnight. At every turn he did the opposite of what he should. All afternoon and evening he'd told himself to stay away from her, that his servants were checking on her, that he should wait until morning when everyone was accustomed to him sharing breakfast with her and the children.

But when the sky turned dark and the house quieted, he could no longer bear the wait. He needed to see for himself that she was unharmed. He'd intended only to peek in at her, but she'd answered his knock and he'd become like a moth to a flame after that.

And he was still flying around her, unwilling to lose her light.

Rebecca wrapped her shawl around her. She ought to feel undressed around him, but it always felt right to be with him even in her nightclothes.

How scandalous was that?

Truth was, she wanted him to stay with her. He took the edge off her wretchedness. She still felt responsible for Ellen almost drowning.

Lord Brookmore stopped near the stairs. 'I have an idea. Wait for me in the breakfast room. I will go to the kitchen and tell Cook I am hungry and want to carry food up to my room. She will not question that. I'll bring the food to you.'

She shook her head. 'Have you wait on me? That cannot be right.'

'No one will complain that I am causing them trouble and you will not be seen walking with me in your nightdress.'

The truth was she did not want to encounter anyone else.

'If you insist, my lord.' She parted from him. If no one knew they were together, there would be no harm done.

And in her desolation she could not resist his kindness.

Their clandestine repast was healing for Rebecca, a moment in time where she pretended they were merely Garret and Rebecca, even though she could never call him anything but Lord Brookmore and he could only call her Miss Tilson. She did not have to think of children drowning or of pretending to be Claire. She could simply enjoy being in his company.

She could enjoy loving him.

But now the candles were wearing to nubs and the clock had passed midnight.

'We should retire,' she said.

'It is late,' he agreed. She stacked the dishes, but

he put a stilling hand on hers. 'I will take them to my room later.'

And keep the secret of their lovely meal. Bread, cheese, wine and blueberry tarts.

He stood and extended his hand to help her up. His hand so strong and warm in hers. She remembered his arms around her pulling her out of the water. She remembered the feel of his body against hers when she wrapped her arms around him in that grateful embrace.

She threaded her arm through his as they sauntered down the hallway, slowing the walk to her bedroom as much as possible.

Once there she leaned against the door, looking up at him, at the face that had become so dear to her. 'How am I to thank you, my lord? I seem to ask this once again.'

She remembered the last time she asked this of him. In the inn. When he kissed her. That night had also been an idyll, but then she did not know the half of how wonderful he was. Surely it would do no harm to kiss again. Just once more, to keep the fantasy of this night a bit longer, that it was right to love him, just this once.

He looked down at her, his eyes darkening, his features softening. He placed his hands against the door, caging her between them. That time at the inn, she could not be certain if she or he initiated the kiss. This time there would be no question.

She rose on her tiptoes, slid her arms around his neck and reached for his lips.

Desire exploded inside Garret when her lips touched his. He lifted her in his arms to deepen the kiss and feel the soft curves of her body against his.

He'd longed to hold her again, to taste of her, to share with her the passion that simmered between them from that first moment when she'd opened her eyes to him after the shipwreck. He needed her forthrightness, her daring, her admiration of him. He needed her lips against his, a joining, that, forbidden as it was between them, he could not resist.

He yearned for more, however. His passion flamed, urging him to ask for more. God help him, he wanted more from her. He wanted that completeness between man and woman, that shared ecstasy that would bind them as one.

She moaned beneath his lips and opened her mouth to him. He lifted her higher, wrapping her legs around him. He opened the door and carried her through, closing it behind him with his foot. He brought her to the bed, kicking his shoes off as he went. Her shawl fell to the floor. Once he placed her on the bed she pulled him with her. He rose over her, rubbing his hands over her breasts, sliding his hands down until he could reach beneath her skirt.

'Garret,' she murmured, her voice as urgent as his senses. 'Yes. Yes.'

She pulled him down for another kiss.

This was the sort of drowning from which he wanted no rescue, drowning in the pleasure of her warmth, her skin, their shared need.

The clock on her mantel chimed once and jolted him awake from his reverie.

'No,' he said more to himself than to her. 'We cannot do this.'

He pushed himself off her and off the bed.

She covered herself with her nightdress and sat up, her expression panicked. 'Sir?'

He turned back to her and stroked her hair. 'Do not fear. I am not angry with you and I do not blame you. I put us in this position of intimacy.'

'You have to know I wanted it,' she said quietly.

He did know, but had he not nurtured that desire in her? Had he not brought her to this very place where she would want to make love so urgently that she would abandon all good sense?

'I knew how to make you want it,' he admitted.

She slid off the bed, stood and faced him. 'I am not experienced in these matters, but I do know that you have been unlike any man I've known, certainly unlike any man in my family, and I wanted more than anything else to be that close to you.'

'We cannot,' he said again.

'Why not, if I am willing?' she countered.

Because she was not experienced she would not know why not.

'Are you willing to give up your reputation?' he asked. 'We cannot keep this a secret. There are no secrets in a house like this. You would be giving up any chance to make a respectable marriage.'

'The chances of my marrying are slim, are they not? Besides, I wanted this with you.' She held on to the bedpost as if she had trouble standing.

He'd be making her his mistress. Because he was marrying Lady Agnes, there was no other choice. But he cared too much for her to make her his mistress. And there was nothing else she could be, not with him promised to another.

'Would it make a difference if I were not a governess?' she asked.

What an odd question.

'But you are a governess.' He searched for another argument. The obvious one. 'You would risk conceiving a baby. What would you do then?'

Rebecca lifted her chin. 'Raise the child. Love it.'

'How would you live?' He put on one shoe then

the other. 'No one would hire a governess with an out-of-wedlock child.'

She averted her gaze for a moment, then faced him again. 'You would support me and the child. You are that sort of gentleman.'

She knew with every fibre of her being that she could trust Lord Brookmore to take care of her and a baby. He did not abandon those who needed him. He was indeed that sort of gentleman.

He faced her and looked her directly in the eye. 'There is something else, Miss Tilson—'

She longed for him to call her Rebecca.

'Something I should have told you before.' His eyes held hers and it seemed an age before he spoke. 'I am betrothed. I am to marry the daughter of the Earl of Trowbridge. Lady Agnes. It is a good match.'

Rebecca felt as if all the blood drained from her body.

He was betrothed. He was to marry. An earl's daughter.

Like her.

'I cannot cry off,' he went on. 'It would be assumed that I found something objectionable in her. It would ruin her for other suitors.' He frowned. 'I cannot make love to you, Miss Tilson. It would dishonour you and her.'

Rebecca closed her eyes against the pain of her

foolishness. To weave this fantasy of sharing carnal love with him for one night. To convince herself it would have no consequences. To believe she could be content with one night.

All along he'd belonged to another woman, her social equal. It stung.

'I should return to London. To—her. Not remain here.' His brow furrowed. 'You will stay, will you not? You will stay with Pamela and Ellen?'

She crossed her arms over her chest. 'I will stay.'

Would he be honourable enough to give her a good reference if she wished to leave? What would he think if she told him who she really was?

She could not leave, though, or tell him the truth. Because she wanted to stay with Pamela and Ellen. Losing them would truly be like losing everything dear to her. Pamela and Ellen.

And him.

'I will stay.' She calmed herself. 'And so must you. You have been telling me for days how you must help your tenants and workers and give them a reason to work harder for the estate. You would be neglecting them if you left. How honourable would that be, my lord? I will not allow you to leave them because of me.'

His voice turned low. 'How can I remain with what passes between us?'

But even if he were not betrothed to Lady Agnes, there would still be a barrier between them. She'd given up her social status equal to Lady Agnes's and if she revealed herself to be Lady Rebecca, she'd lose Pamela and Ellen and they would lose her along with the other losses they'd endured.

'Then go,' she said, keeping her voice carefully even lest she reveal the confusion of emotions swirling inside her. 'Leave this house. Leave your nieces. Leave all these people who work for you and esteem you. Leave this room, too. I suddenly wish to be alone.'

He straightened, almost as if receiving a blow. With one long gaze at her, he turned and walked away.

Rebecca stood, grasping the bed post, watching him until the door closed behind him.

Chapter Eleven

Rebecca rose early the next morning, having slept little, fired by the emotions within her. About herself. About Lord Brookmore.

She'd been too impulsive once again, a fault her teachers told her would be the death of her. Perhaps Lady Rebecca, with all her illusions and fantasies, ought to pass away.

She needed to be Claire. A governess who knew her place. She'd made a choice to be Claire impulsively, but it could not be undone without hurting Pamela and Ellen and that she would never do.

If she had not pretended to be Claire, Lord Brookmore would have disappeared from her life, nevermore to be seen. She was glad to have made that impulsive choice, glad she'd had this time with him.

She was even glad to have been kissed by him. And refused to feel guilty for wanting to make love with him. After a day so harrowing, so filled with life and death, she'd needed him. That had been one impulsive choice she did not regret. She only regretted that he'd stopped. It had been her only chance to experience that sort of love and she'd only wanted that sort of love with him.

There was something between them, that elusive element for which she'd yearned, but had been absent in any other suitor. What she felt for Lord Brookmore bound her to him, even if he married another.

Still, he'd been right to stop. At that moment, she'd been wild with disappointment and still was, really, but he'd been right.

It was not right of him to leave his nieces and his estate because of her. That she could not allow.

One of the lower maids entered the room to tend the fireplace. She jumped when she noticed Rebecca seated in the chair by the window. 'Oh, miss!' the maid exclaimed. 'You startled me.'

'I am up early, I know.' Rebecca smiled at the young woman. 'Please tend to your task as if I were not awake.'

The maid swept the ashes into her bucket and placed new coals on the few that still glowed. She refilled the coal bin and wiped the hearth with a damp cloth.

She gathered up her things and started for the door. 'I'll be going, miss.'

Rebecca stopped her. 'May I beg a favour? You are Meg, are you not?'

'Yes, miss,' the maid said.

'Will you help me into my riding habit?'

The maid put down her things and wiped her hands. 'Yes, miss.'

A few minutes later Rebecca made her way down the back stairs, out of the house and across the park to the stables, determined to ride, as Lord Brookmore had once invited her.

She would ride until these emotions blew off her, like leaves off a tree, and hopefully she would be calm in time for breakfast with the girls.

And Lord Brookmore.

The stable door was open and she walked in.

'Is anyone here?' she called.

A stable worker emerged from one of the stalls. 'Miss?'

She lifted her chin. 'Lord Brookmore said I might ride. Is there a horse you could saddle for me?'

He wiped his hands on a cloth as if considering her request.

'I assure you, I am an experienced rider,' she added. 'The more spirited the horse, the better.'

'Yes, miss.' His voice was sceptical.

She walked through the stable until reaching the

tack room. She pointed to her saddle, one of two side saddles that hung there. 'That one is mine.'

He took the saddle and walked by two or three stalls, whose horses eagerly reached for him with their muzzles. He finally chose a lovely bay mare.

'This is Lily,' he told her.

While he saddled the horse, Rebecca introduced herself to the animal, stroking its neck and getting it used to the sound of her voice.

'You know horses, miss.' The stableman nodded approvingly.

'I love horses.' She pressed her cheek against the horse's neck.

The stable worker checked the saddle and led the horse to a mounting block. Rebecca was soon in the saddle and out in the crisp morning air.

The stable worker had chosen well. Lily was steady, but eager. When Rebecca accustomed herself to the feel of the horse, she lengthened the reins and gave Lily her head.

Galloping over the fields and jumping fences with the green mountains shrouded in fog gave Rebecca exactly what she'd craved. The pleasure of the ride. Freedom from thought and emotion.

Lily slowed and Rebecca turned back towards Brookmore House. They kept a sedate pace. Inhaling the clear morning air, Rebecca felt cleansed.

The day before, so filled with drama, was over and she could move past it, just as she'd moved past the shipwreck and entered Claire's life. Time would make everything better. She'd get used to being a governess. She'd get used to Lord Brookmore marrying an earl's daughter.

Rebecca would keep her distance from him, as she'd learned to do with her father whenever they were in the house together. Lord Brookmore would not have to leave because of her.

She patted Lily and drank in the beauty all around her.

As the house and stable came in to view, so did another lone rider making his way back, as well.

Lord Brookmore.

He saw her and stopped to wait for her to reach him.

'I heard you took a horse out,' he said when she came near.

He had invited her to ride, had he not? She felt her emotions bubbling to the surface. She pushed them down.

'I needed a good run.' She leaned forward to pat the horse. 'Lily is a wonderful horse.'

He rode beside her, not speaking, like that last day on the road, the day they'd arrived at Brookmore House.

Like that day she broke the silence. 'I suggest we leave yesterday in the past,' she began. 'I plan to devote myself to Pamela and Ellen, nothing more.'

She darted a glance towards him. Did he realise what she meant? No more kisses. No lovemaking.

He frowned. 'Very well, Miss Tilson.'

She bit her lip to keep from saying more and managed to accept his silence for the rest of the way to the stable.

They walked back to the house together, still not speaking. Rebecca still felt the same towards him, as if they were tethered together, but she could not indulge such a feeling.

They walked up the back stairs to the second floor and emerged into the hallway near the breakfast room. Would he eat with them this morning, Rebecca wanted to ask, but she held her tongue.

He started to walk away from her, towards his room, but he turned. 'I will see you and the children at breakfast.'

At least she had not spoiled that for Pamela and Ellen.

Garret expected great difficulty being in Miss Tilson's company, but over the next week she made it easy, never getting close, never turning the conversation to anything personal between them. How was she able to do that? he wondered. He still felt the physical yearning for her, but because she kept herself at an emotional distance, he managed to do the same. On the outside, anyway.

That he'd been busy helped, as well. He'd joined his tenants and workers in the fields, the stables, or wherever they toiled, and he'd asked them to tell him of their needs, their complaints, their ideas for improvement. He'd kept a log of everything they'd said and worked with Ben to begin with the most important repairs. He abandoned his plan to leave right away. He'd stay as long as he could.

He continued to eat dinner with Miss Tilson— he could not bear to give that up—but they limited their conversation to his work with the tenants and hers with the children, even though he longed to ask if she still had visions of the shipwreck, if her new dresses pleased her, if she were happy.

She rode almost every morning, as did he. Twice they'd ended their runs riding next to each other and all he could think of was of riding next to her on the trip from Moelfre, how his admiration of her grew on the trip, how he had kissed her.

Would another moment eventually come when he—or she—would weaken and they'd again be caught in a whirlpool of desire? He hoped for her sake he could resist.

This day was to be another busy one, busier than most, in fact. Today the sheep shearing was to begin. Garret was surprised how much he looked forward to this. It had been many years since he'd thought of the delights of the sheep shearing. He'd loved it when he'd been a boy.

That morning at breakfast he'd invited his nieces to watch the shearing, which meant, of course, that Miss Tilson would also come.

Garret walked with Ben to the pen set up for the shearing. Already they could hear the bleating of sheep.

'It sounds like the clipping has begun,' Garret said.

Ben responded, 'I am glad you are staying for the clipping. The sheep are everything to the workers and the sheep are everything to the farm.'

Garret nodded. 'I confess, I am itching to be down there with them.'

Ben grinned. 'Like when we were boys.' He turned serious. 'The workers like to see you out there with them, doing the work. That is something even your father did not do.'

Garret smiled. 'I remember my father standing with my brother, instructing him on the shearing. They never noticed me in the midst of the sheep.'

Garret had herded the sheep to the shearers or rolled the sheared wool into bales. In those days he'd do whatever the workers let him do, which was mostly the dirtiest jobs. Garret hadn't minded. The dirtier the better, he'd thought at the time.

The sheep had been brought down from the fells into a pen that funnelled them one by one to the shearers, several who were itinerant, making a living by going from farm to farm in July when the Herdwick sheep were typically shorn.

Miss Tilson and the girls were already at the wooden fence watching the operation. Pamela and Ellen had climbed on the slats of the fence so they could see over the top. Miss Tilson leaned on the top slat, her face alight with interest. Her eyes seemed involuntarily drawn to him for an instant, but she immediately turned her attention back to the sheep.

Garret greeted the men and joined the work, some of the older men joking with him that they'd give him the same dirty jobs they'd given him when a boy. The Herdwick wool did not bring in much money; it was too coarse for most clothing, but the sheep were valued for their meat and the shearing protected them from blowflies and bluebottles laying eggs in their wool.

Garret loved it all, loved the bleating of the sheep, the scraping of the shears and the voices of the workers as they toiled. He walked among them, helping when he could. There was no slacking off on this job as far as he could tell. Everyone worked with efficiency and skill. Ben said it was because Garret was among them.

Throughout the morning, though, Garret was aware of Miss Tilson. He felt her gaze as if it were an actual touch.

The afternoon wore on and eventually the numbers of sheep shorn exceeded those in the pen preparing for the clippers. Garret's skin softened with wool oil. His back was damp with sweat.

He was picking up stray bits of wool when Ben tapped him on the shoulder. 'A carriage is coming towards the house.'

Garret glanced to the road. A large black coach, an aristocrat's carriage drawn by four horses, approached, but was too far away for him to see the crest on the side.

'Who the devil could that be?' he said aloud.

He wiped his hands on a towel and made his way out of the sheep pen, striding towards the house.

'Where is Uncle Garret going?' Ellen asked, twisting around to watch him.

Rebecca, of course, had seen him leave the pen and cross the paddock. Her gaze had followed him wherever he'd been. Helping pull sheep into the shearing area. Holding sheep until the shearer had the animal well in his grasp. Rolling the wool and gathering the stray bits that scattered on the floor.

She turned to see. 'A coach is coming.'

'A coach!' Ellen cried. 'A big coach!' She jumped down from the fence. 'I am going to see who it is!'

'No, Ellen!' Pamela cried. 'Uncle won't like it.'

But Ellen paid her sister no heed.

'Ellen!' Rebecca called after her. 'Come back!'

Both she and Pamela left the fence and chased after Ellen.

'She should know better,' Pamela exclaimed to Rebecca. Pamela had become her ally in trying to rein in Ellen.

'Stay away from the coach's horses!' Rebecca cried after the little girl.

Lord Brookmore had already reached the front door. Two footmen emerged from the house as the carriage pulled up.

Rebecca and Pamela caught up to Ellen several feet away from the carriage. Rebecca caught the little girl by the nape of her jacket just in time to see a fashionably dressed young lady emerge from the carriage.

'Let us go see who it is!' Ellen tried to pull away.

'Not like little hoydens,' Rebecca said. 'We will walk like ladies and when I say stop, you must stop.

No running up to your uncle. He will tell you who it is if you are to know.'

'Yes, Ellen.' Pamela mimicked Rebecca's tone. 'Do not act like a little hoyden.'

Pamela took her sister's hand to guard against another impulsive run, Rebecca thought.

An older woman and a maid also disembarked from the coach.

Rebecca allowed the little girls to approach a little closer, close enough to hear, but not to be in the way.

'You weren't able to send a message?' Lord Brookmore asked the young lady.

'Brookmore, darling. I wanted to surprise you,' she replied.

Rebecca had a sinking feeling she knew who this was.

The young lady was petite enough to make Rebecca feel like an Amazon. Pale blonde hair peeked out from beneath her exquisite silk bonnet, the same deep blue as her perfectly tailored travelling dress. The hue complemented her blue eyes, their colour visible even from this distance.

Lord Brookmore wore the expression of someone punched in the stomach.

'Oh, are these sweet little girls your nieces?' the lady asked while her maid carried in a large piece of luggage.

Ellen skipped towards her and curtsied.

'Yes,' Brookmore said stiffly. 'May I present Miss Pamela and Miss Ellen.'

The young woman laughed, a musical sound. She smiled at the girls. 'Your uncle forgets to say who I am. I am Lady Agnes. His fiancée.'

Rebecca took in a gulp of air. As she'd guessed.

'What's a fiancée?' Ellen asked.

Pamela answered, 'It means that Uncle Garret is going to marry her.'

Both girls glanced back at Rebecca with unhappy expressions. Lord Brookmore's face remained stiff.

The fashionably dressed, beautiful, petite, blonde, blue-eyed fiancée then seemed to notice Rebecca. 'And you are the governess, I presume.'

Rebecca met the woman's gaze and executed an obligatory curtsy. 'Miss Tilson, my lady.'

'Not in the schoolroom, I see?' Lady Agnes said, ever so disapprovingly.

Rebecca smiled. 'On such a fine day? We were watching the sheep shearing.'

Lady Agnes wrinkled her nose. 'You do not say!'

'Lady Agnes,' Lord Brookmore finally spoke. 'Come in the house.'

Rebecca curtsied again and the girls mimicked her.

'May we go back to the sheep?' Pamela asked. The

once too-correct child had become enamoured of animals. The horses were still her favourites.

'I want to go inside with the lady,' Ellen insisted.

Rebecca scooted them away. 'We are not going inside to bother her. We will watch the sheep some more.'

Ellen was full of questions on the walk back to the shearing station. 'Where did she come from?'

'From London, I suppose,' Rebecca answered.

'Will she stay in the house?'

'I expect so,' Rebecca said.

'What room will she sleep in?'

Would Ellen's questions never stop? 'I do not know.'

'When will they be married?'

This question was the most painful. 'We will have to ask Uncle Garret.' Although Rebecca had no intention of asking that question.

They watched the sheep for another hour before returning to the house, but Rebecca could not tell what they had seen or what they'd spoken to each other. It had taken her a long time to even remember to breathe. She brought the girls into the house through the back entrance and up the back stairs to the children's wing where they washed their faces and hands and changed their clothes. Cook sent up a meal of soup and bread with blueberry tarts for dessert.

Afterwards the girls wrote in their journals and somehow Rebecca read to them from *The Shepherd Boy*, a book that seemed to suit the day—at least the sheep-shearing part of the day.

Mary helped the girls get ready for sleep and Rebecca kissed them both goodnight. So dear and sweet they were, she thought. Her efforts at being a governess might fall short, but she loved these little girls. She could not imagine having a stronger love, even for children of her own.

Not that she would ever have children of her own.

She left their bedchamber and sought refuge in her own room. On an ordinary night she would ready herself for dinner with Lord Brookmore, but this night she simply sat in the chair and stared out the window at the waning light. In mid-July it would be more than an hour before the sky turned dark.

She watched the setting sun paint the fells in shades of purple and wondered how to bear spending another day in this house. With *him*. With *her*. She imagined them together in the dining room, Lady Agnes dressed formally for dinner, seated in the chair near him. Rebecca's chair.

Lady Agnes was dazzling in a way Rebecca could never be, even if dressed in her finest gowns and jewellery, the ones lost at sea. Lady Agnes also had charm, although Rebecca detected a bite to it, hidden behind a smile. A governess was nothing in comparison.

She remembered what Claire had said—*'A governess is not important enough to notice.'*

Chapter Twelve

Garret felt like another person walked in his skin. From the moment Lady Agnes stepped from the carriage, he'd felt like an automaton, going through the motions. He'd walked Lady Agnes and her companion, an adoring aunt, into the house and called for Mrs Dodd to make rooms ready for them and serve them tea in the drawing room. All the while, his spirit was with Miss Tilson, wanting to explain that he hadn't known Lady Agnes was coming, that he would have warned her had he known.

Lady Agnes kept up enough chatter that he needed only to nod or speak one or two words.

Mrs Dodd readied Garret's sister-in-law's room. He trusted the housekeeper would remove Maryanne's personal items, items he must save for his nieces.

When the room was ready, he parted from Agnes and went to his room to change for dinner. He'd still had the mud from the shearing on his boots and bits of sheep's wool clung to his buckskin breeches. No doubt she'd been appalled.

As Brant dressed him, his mind whirled. Why had Lady Agnes come? The trip from London was a journey of at least five days in a private coach. She'd made it clear she disliked travel. He'd never expected she would make such a journey.

Garret hurried down the stairs and knocked at his sister-in-law's bedchamber door.

Lady Agnes's maid answered.

'Come in, Brookmore, dear,' Lady Agnes trilled. 'I am almost ready.'

She sat at the dressing table putting sapphire earrings in her ears. She wore a blue-silk gown and looked as if she'd be gracing a London dining room.

He remained standing.

'This room is charming,' she went on. 'All this oak wainscoting quite transports me to an earlier era.'

'Most of the house is panelled in oak,' he said.

'It is quaint, is it not?' She rose from her chair. 'Aunt Theodora will not be joining us. She is very fatigued.' She took his arm. 'So it is just you and me.'

His insides plummeted. What about Miss Tilson?

When he and Lady Agnes reached the dining room, Miss Tilson was not there and the table was set only for two. But for which two? For him and Lady Agnes? Or him and Miss Tilson?

Agnes surveyed the room. 'Now I do feel transported. Spanish leather wall covering!'

The wall covering had been on these walls since the sixteenth century.

Lady Agnes managed to keep conversation flowing throughout dinner, even though he could offer few words and his eyes kept wandering to the door wondering if Miss Tilson would appear, wondering why she had not.

She finally asked something about him. 'Tell me, Brookmore, what has been occupying you here?'

It took him a moment to focus his thoughts enough to answer. 'Estate business.'

She pressed for more. Why not answer her? If he were to share his life with her, why not tell her how he'd spent his time. At least some of his time.

'I've been meeting with the tenants and the workers, asking their needs, taking their complaints and planning to address them.'

'Goodness!' She blinked. 'That is what an estate manager is for. If you like I will write to Papa. He can certainly recommend someone who is up to the job.'

He took a long sip of wine. 'I have an estate manager.'

She laughed softly. 'I meant a good one.'

He averted his gaze. 'That is not necessary.' Miss Tilson had admired his efforts with the workers.

After dinner they retired to the drawing room. In the midst of her commentary, he gazed at her, perfect in every way a viscount's wife should be. It would be a good partnership, so why did his mood plummet to the depths?

What had changed inside him? Or, rather, who had changed him?

When he finally suggested they retire and she agreed, he escorted her back to her room.

On the way he said, 'I take breakfast with my nieces at eight-thirty in the morning.' *And Miss Tilson.* 'You are welcome to join us.' *But please don't.* 'Or you may have breakfast in the dining room, if you prefer.'

'How sweet.' She smiled. 'And a little absurd, too, is it not? The lord of the estate eating with children? I am certain I would be excessively entertained, but I believe I will sleep in and ask for breakfast in my room.'

'As you wish.' They reached her door.

She put a hand behind his neck and urged him to

lean over. She kissed him on the lips, a lingering kiss, but one as cool as the evening air.

'Goodnight, Brookmore,' she murmured before slipping into the room.

Garret strode away and climbed the stairs to his room, putting his hand on the door handle, but he did not open the door. Instead he walked down the hallway to the children's wing.

And knocked on Miss Tilson's door.

Rebecca answered the door in her nightgown, expecting Mary coming to offer her food one more time.

'Lord Brookmore.' Her heart leapt at the sight of him, but she quickly steeled herself.

He stared at her with his intense blue eyes and she remembered that, once again, he'd encountered her in her nightgown.

Finally he spoke. 'You did not come to dinner.'

'Surely you did not expect me?' She almost laughed.

'I did not know whether to expect you or not.'

She lowered her gaze. 'I would not intrude.'

His brows knitted and again he paused before speaking. 'Did you eat?'

He should not trouble himself of whether or not she ate. 'I ate,' she lied. She started to close the door.

He stopped her with a hand on the door. 'May I speak with you?'

She should say no. She should close the door and turn the key in the lock.

But she opened it the rest of the way and stepped aside so he could enter. The last time he'd entered her room was after a passionate kiss that sent them both to her bed—something he regretted, but even now she could not regret.

She waited for him to speak, her arms folded across her chest.

He walked over to the window and looked out into the night, as she had done before his knock.

Finally he turned. 'I did not know Lady Agnes would come.'

'I see.' Claire would not have expected to be informed of invited or uninvited guests. Rebecca must not either.

He pressed his lips together. 'I would not have invited her.'

Why did he believe it mattered? Merely because the governess developed romantic notions about him?

'But had I known of her visit, I would have told you,' he added.

She lifted a shoulder. 'It is of no consequence.'

He took a step towards her. 'I want to explain.

When I inherited the title, I took my duty very seriously, including the duty to make a good marriage and ensure the line of succession. I was not prepared—'

She stopped him. 'You do not have to tell me this.'

He shook his head. 'I do need to tell you. I need you to understand.'

He was making it difficult for her to build a cage around her emotions. 'I do understand,' she murmured. 'You are trying very hard to do all that is required of a viscount.'

'It is not what I wanted,' he shot back. 'And I have not done well. I've made mistakes. Big mistakes.' He sounded pained. 'I tried to do as my brother would have done, but then I discover he was a terrible model.'

She looked directly into his eyes. 'You are nothing like your brother.'

'How could you know that?' he snapped.

'For one thing, you care about other people, even your tenants and workers.' She added, 'You care about his little girls, which certainly he did not.'

He turned his face away. 'You give me too much credit.'

It struck Rebecca like a bolt from the heavens that she, too, had often thought only of herself and not others. Perhaps she ought to have considered her father's grief over losing her mother with more sympathy, rather than be hurt at being ostracised by him. Perhaps she could have seen that her brother had been the most unloved of them all. After marrying her mother, her father had not cared a fig about his son. Perhaps she even should have understood Lord Stonecroft's desire for an heir.

This was new territory for her. Lord Brookmore had been the cause of it. She'd watched him being kind to her, being loving to his nieces and concerned about his workers. She'd opened her heart to Pamela and Ellen, because she'd seen them through his compassionate eyes.

She could not tell this to him, though. They could no longer share confidences. He could never be her lover, nor could he be her friend. She must remain in her place as governess.

Rebecca lowered her arms and softened her voice. 'I will tend to Pamela and Ellen,' she told him. 'But I'll have no expectations of dining with you or otherwise placing myself in your way. You can rest easy on that score.' She paused. 'But I would like to continue to ride in the mornings.' Without that release she feared she'd go mad, because, although she was acting strong and noble, inside she felt as if every organ was shredded.

She knew how to keep her distance; she'd perfected the skill with her father.

'Of course you may ride. You must go on as you were,' he insisted.

'No.' Sadness filled her voice. 'That is what I must not do. I will act the governess from now on.' She forced herself to smile. 'And a governess must not entertain the Viscount in her bedchamber.' She walked to the door, which he'd kept open. 'I bid you goodnight, sir.'

He crossed the room, but slowed as he passed her. His hand rose and she thought he might touch her, but he dropped it again. 'Goodnight, Miss Tilson.'

The next morning Lady Agnes did not sleep as late as she'd told Brookmore she would. She rose early, sent her maid down to the kitchen to get her a pot of chocolate and something sweet to eat.

Her Aunt Theodora sat in the ancient upholstered chair that must have been a century old, while Lady Agnes stood at the window overlooking the park and the outbuildings, one of which showed signs of activity. More sheep shearing, no doubt.

'It is very rural here, is it not?' Agnes remarked, her lip curling.

'Indeed,' her aunt agreed. 'Quite rural.'

She gazed at the far hill, dotted with grazing sheep.

Lord Brookmore had smelled of the vile creatures the day before. She hardly could stand it until he washed and changed for dinner. This was not something she would tolerate.

But she knew that was a battle to be engaged in at a later time. No husband of hers would smell like a farm labourer.

He was less elegant than she would have liked, possibly from all those years in the army, but she intended to give him polish and working with farm animals, alongside unwashed underlings, would not do it. The previous day he'd seemed preoccupied with these farm people. Well, after their marriage he'd discover she had no intention of spending her days on a farm.

But first she had to get him to the altar.

His delay at returning to London and accompanying her to Brighton had worried her. Something was afoot and she'd come all the way to this… wilderness…to discover what it was.

She moved the curtain—how old was that piece of cloth? she wondered.

Two riders approached the outbuildings and it took only a moment's observation to recognise Brookmore and that governess. They were not riding side by side, but they were both riding early in the morning and returning to the stables at the same time.

Agnes felt her neck tense the way it always did when she sensed trouble.

She'd noticed the way he'd looked at the governess the day before. And this nonsense about breakfasting with the children every morning. Undoubtedly the governess was present. Now both he and the governess were riding?

The night before, he'd avoided any discussion of a wedding date. Or of a time he would be ready to leave this rustic area. Was it because of this governess?

Her maid entered the room with a tray bearing the pot of chocolate, two mugs and a plate of sweet breads filled with currants.

Agnes turned to her maid. 'Holly, put the tray on the table and go find Mrs Dodd, the housekeeper. Ask if she might come speak with me.'

Holly curtsied. 'Yes, m'lady.'

'And bring another chocolate cup when you return,' Agnes added.

Aunt Theodora sat at the table, but waited for Agnes before eating or pouring the chocolate.

Agnes joined her.

A few minutes later Holly brought the chocolate cup. 'M'lady, Mrs Dodd said she would call on you directly.'

'Excellent!' Agnes turned to her companion. 'Aunt,

would you mind taking your breakfast in your room? I should like to speak with the housekeeper privately.'

Aunt Theodora immediately stood. 'Of course, dear.'

Agnes signalled to Holly. 'Help her.'

When Mrs Dodd knocked on the door, Agnes was quite alone.

'You wished to see me, Lady Agnes?'

The housekeeper appeared cordial enough and well she ought. Lord Brookmore had introduced Agnes as his fiancée. Mrs Dodd would eventually answer to Agnes when she became Lady Brookmore. Assuming Agnes would ever set foot in this antiquated house again.

'Thank you so much for interrupting your busy day to speak with me.' Agnes smiled her sweet smile. 'Please do come in.'

Mrs Dodd entered and Agnes gestured for her to sit. 'Please have a cup of chocolate with me.' These upper servants sometimes liked such niceties.

'Thank you, my lady.' Mrs Dodd sat.

Agnes started the conversation with polite enquiries as to Mrs Dodd's health and her satisfaction with her position and her staff, complimenting her lavishly as she went on. She finally reached the point of her request to see the housekeeper.

She poured Mrs Dodd more chocolate. 'And what of this governess? I understand she is new.'

Mrs Dodd pursed her lips before answering. 'She is an odd one. I will say that for her.'

Agnes's brows rose. 'Odd one? How so.'

The housekeeper leaned forward. 'When she arrived with Lord Brookmore, she rode on horseback with him. Most unseemly!'

'Oh, I agree. Most unseemly. Can you imagine?' Agnes readily agreed.

The housekeeper went on. 'She had only a very small bag with her. Almost no clothing. No personal items at all. The children's maid said she'd been in a shipwreck, which would explain it, but...' She trailed off, clearly sceptical.

'Do go on,' Agnes encouraged.

Mrs Dodd took a sip of chocolate. 'She takes the children outdoors most of the day. They hardly ever are inside the schoolroom. Not like the dear governess who came before.'

'What can they be doing out of doors all day?' Agnes asked.

'Well.' She took another sip. 'One day she almost got Miss Ellen drowned. His lordship had to rescue Miss Ellen and Miss Tilson.'

'You do not say!' Agnes put on a shocked expression. 'How did such a person become a governess?'

The housekeeper seemed eager to impart information. 'She came with an excellent reference from the lady of the house whose children she cared for. And she was registered with a reputable agency, but there is something havey-cavey about her.'

Agnes suspected as much!

'I cannot abide this!' Agnes said. 'Those poor dear children.' She put a hand to her chest. 'I must make certain that dear Brookmore was not deceived. Perhaps I could write to the agency. Or to her previous employer. Only I would like to do this without Brookmore knowing.' She smiled conspiratorially. 'I do not wish to worry him, of course.'

'I have the letters from the agency and the reference,' Mrs Dodd said. 'I will show them to you so you have the proper address.'

Agnes stood. 'Thank you. You may spare these children from irreparable harm.'

Mrs Dodd also rose. 'I will bring the letters to you right away.'

After the housekeeper left, Agnes paced the room. Her instincts were never wrong. She was certain there was something to discover about this governess that would sour Lord Brookmore on the young woman.

Yes. Mrs Dodd confirmed Agnes's suspicions. The governess was the problem and Agnes excelled at eliminating problems.

Chapter Thirteen

Garret managed to endure the day in a tolerable fashion. Breakfast with the children and Miss Tilson that morning had been difficult, but he and Miss Tilson had already become practised in remaining remote while still engaging the children. Afterwards he invited Lady Agnes and her aunt on a tour of the house and garden, which served only to remind him of when he'd done the same for Miss Tilson and the children. He'd next seen Lady Agnes and her aunt at dinner. By then he'd endeavoured to be more civil than the previous night. Lady Agnes's aunt excused herself after dinner and Garret spent the rest of the evening alone with his fiancée.

He'd had one piece of happy news that day. In an effort to please the children, as well as Miss Tilson, he'd asked his stable master to scour the countryside for suitable ponies to purchase for Pamela and Ellen. The man found two perfect fell ponies just the right size and temperament for the girls. They'd arrived that afternoon and Garret planned to surprise the girls the next day.

In an attempt to be convivial, he'd spoken of it to Lady Agnes.

'Ponies?' Her brows rose. 'Are not they a bit young for riding?'

'I was younger than Pamela when I started,' he said. 'And she is pining to learn.'

'But you are a man,' she exclaimed. 'Riding is a necessity for a man.'

Necessity or not, no one could have kept him off a horse in those days. Pamela had that same passion for horses—as did Miss Tilson.

'These are gentle animals,' he said. 'The girls will be safe.'

'I was not thinking of safety, although that is important, of course,' she countered. 'There is a risk of indulging a child's every whim, especially little girls. One does not wish them to grow up horse-mad, does one? They will have to make a good match some day and that means embracing feminine pursuits.'

Garret frowned. 'I intend to indulge whatever whims give my nieces pleasure. They have lost their mother and father and the governess they'd known since birth. They deserve to be indulged. I will do what makes them happy.'

Her expression turned sympathetic. 'Of course you are right, my dearest. The poor darlings. How are they getting along?'

He nodded. 'They are doing well now.' Because of Miss Tilson.

The next morning at breakfast Garret told Pamela and Ellen—and Miss Tilson—that he had a surprise for them in the stables. He told them to meet him at the stables at ten o'clock. He was rushing to get there before them when he encountered Lady Agnes on the stairs.

'Brookmore!' She smiled. 'How are you this morning? How was your little breakfast with the children?'

'Pleasant, as always,' he responded. Not counting the ache he felt whenever he was with Miss Tilson.

She gave an amused look. 'I was about to take a turn in the garden. Will you join me?'

He shook his head. 'I cannot. I am on my way to the stables. The children are to meet me there soon, but I want to make it there before them. I am surprising them with the ponies.'

'The ponies.' Her face fell, although she quickly smiled. 'How very sweet of you to make it a surprise.'

He hesitated, sensing her disappointment and feeling guilty for having an excuse to avoid her company. 'You may come, too, if you wish.'

'To the stables?' She wrinkled her nose, but again put on a smile. 'I would love to, but I must change my shoes, I fear.'

She lifted her skirts to show she wore dainty slippers that would be ruined in any bit of mud or muck. The glimpse of her ankle should have been alluring, but Garret was unmoved.

'I must hurry there now,' he said. 'Come as soon as you are ready. Any footman can show you the way.'

Her smile lit her beautiful features. 'I will hurry, as well.'

His guilt rose again for feeling his surprise gift to the children would be a bit spoiled if she came.

Rebecca and the girls hurried down the back stairs, the fastest way to leave the house and reach the stables.

'What is the surprise, Miss Tilson?' Ellen asked for the hundredth time.

'I still do not know, Ellen,' Rebecca replied, laughing.

Pamela piped up, 'Stop asking!' But her eyes, too, were filled with excitement.

Rebecca thought she knew the surprise, though,

and she, too, could hardly wait to see if she was correct.

When they reached the door, Lady Agnes was there, about to leave with a footman.

'Good morning, children,' she chirped.

'Good morning, Lady Agnes,' they responded, both their voices dampened.

'May I walk with you?' she asked. 'I believe you are off to the stables for the big surprise.'

She knew of it?

'Are you going, too?' Ellen's enthusiasm quieted somewhat.

'Yes,' Lady Agnes replied. 'But I do not know the way to the stables.'

Rebecca's insides clenched. 'You may walk with us.'

What right would she have had to refuse, even though the lady had not acknowledged her, only the children?

Lady Agnes turned to the footman. 'Thank you so much, Mason, but I will not need you now.'

The footman looked pleased that she'd addressed him. 'M'lady.' He bowed and held the door for them.

Pamela and Ellen ran ahead, leaving Lady Agnes to walk with Rebecca.

Lady Agnes wrapped her shawl around her. 'It is cold for a summer day, is it not, Miss Tilson?'

'Yes, my lady.' Rebecca kept repeating to herself that her status was now lower than this earl's daughter.

'The children are quite excited, are they not? Running like that.'

There it was again, Rebecca noticed. That sweet tone that held a bite.

'Indeed,' she responded.

'Well they might be,' Lady Agnes said with a little laugh.

'You know the surprise?' Rebecca could not help feeling hurt that Lord Brookmore had apparently confided in her.

'Yes, of course.' Lady Agnes looked pleased. 'But I will not spoil it for you.'

Rebecca felt a pang of jealousy, but what right had she to feel such an emotion? They were not rivals. He would share confidences with this lady that he would never do with her.

Lord Brookmore stood outside the stables and Rebecca's heart lurched when he scooped up Ellen into one arm and put the other around Pamela's shoulder.

'We must wait for Miss Tilson,' she heard him say.

He glanced her way and his smile faltered for a moment when he saw her walking with Lady Agnes.

When they came closer, he acknowledged his fiancée. 'Lady Agnes.'

Her smile turned more dazzling. 'See? I did not need an escort after all.'

'I do see.' His gaze slipped to Rebecca for an instant, before he turned again to the children. 'Well, shall we see the surprise?'

'Yes! Yes!' cried Ellen.

He carried Ellen, but held Pamela's hand as he entered the stables. Lady Agnes followed. Rebecca waited to be last.

The stables were dark compared to the sunny day outside and it took a moment for her eyes to adjust. There, held by two of the grooms, were two ponies, one light, one dark, one larger than the other, but the perfect sizes for Pamela and Ellen.

'Oh!' exclaimed Pamela, her tone awed. 'Oh.'

Lord Brookmore put Ellen down. 'The larger one is yours, Pamela. Go say hello.'

Rebecca could tell Pamela wished to run to the pony, but she forced herself to approach slowly.

She turned back to Lord Brookmore. 'Mine, Uncle Garret?'

'Yours,' he repeated, his voice soft.

Pamela stroked the pony the way Rebecca and Lord Brookmore had taught her. The little horse nuzzled her and Pamela threw her arms around its neck.

'What is her name?' she asked.

'Biscuit,' the groom told her.

The pony was a dappled grey, a pretty creature any little girl would fall in love with. Already the horse was delighting in Pamela's affection.

'Biscuit is a perfect name!' Pamela placed her cheek against the horse's neck.

Tears stung Rebecca's eyes. She exchanged a glance with Lord Brookmore and saw he understood. Pamela was truly happy.

Ellen, still a bit wary of horses, held back. 'The other one is mine?'

'Yes, yours,' Lord Brookmore assured her. 'Her name is Pixie.'

Pixie was a bay mare, a rich reddish brown with a black mane.

'Will she bite?' Ellen asked.

He squatted down to her level. 'She won't bite. She likes little girls. She'll like to be petted the way Miss Tilson and I showed you.' He gave her a gentle push. 'Go to her.'

Ellen crept forward. 'Hello, Pixie,' she said in a slightly anxious voice.

The pony did not wait, but stepped towards her, already nudging her with her muzzle. Ellen drew back, but soon laughed and patted the pony's neck.

Lord Brookmore again shared a glance with Rebecca. His tenderness to the girls nearly undid her.

She gulped to keep from becoming a complete watering pot.

'May I ride, Uncle Garret?' Pamela asked. Rebecca thought she would leap on the pony at any moment.

'You will have your first lesson right now, if you like,' he responded.

'Yes!' cried Pamela.

A few moments later both girls were on the ponies' backs, being led around the paddock. Lord Brookmore walked beside Ellen, reassuring her all the way. Pamela spent the time either talking to her Biscuit or exclaiming that she could not wait to ride on her own.

Rebecca watched the scene with her heart full of happiness for the girls.

Lady Agnes sidled up to her. 'They look so sweet, do they not?'

'Yes, indeed,' Rebecca responded, not inclined to do anything to further the conversation.

'I must confess,' Lady Agnes went on. 'I told Brookmore I was concerned about Pamela and Ellen riding at such an early age.'

Early? Pamela and Ellen were latecomers. 'Where I come from children begin riding as soon as they can walk.'

'And where is that, Miss Tilson?' Lady Agnes asked sweetly.

Rebecca had said too much, but she'd cause more suspicion if she did not answer. 'Ireland.'

Lady Agnes smiled as if amused. 'Oh. Ireland.'

Rebecca caught the implied aspersion.

'I do worry about Pamela.' Lady Agnes sighed.

'Why?' Rebecca asked.

'I suspect she is the driving force behind acquiring these ponies.' Lady Agnes shook her head in disapproval. 'I believe it is dangerous to let children dictate what they must have and what they must do.'

Rebecca was appalled. It was such a profound misunderstanding of how reticent Pamela had been to ask for anything.

'I do not believe it is dangerous for young girls to tell us what they need,' Rebecca said, trying to keep her voice calm. 'I believe girls need to learn to think for themselves and speak their minds. They should feel free to pursue what interests them, to do what makes them happy.'

She'd hate to think of Pamela or Ellen forced into thinking they must please others and do what others say. Or marry whomever they were told to marry.

'Oh, dear,' said Lady Agnes in a humorous tone. 'Have you been reading Wollstonecraft?'

Rebecca had, indeed, read *A Vindication of the Rights of Woman* when she'd attended her very progressive school, but she declined to respond to Lady Agnes.

She watched Lord Brookmore walk around the paddock with Ellen and wished that his fiancée was someone she could like. Lady Agnes definitely was not.

The next three weeks gave Garret no pleasure at all, at least not in the company of Lady Agnes. If only she would see how wrong their marriage would be and cry off, there would be no harm to her reputation. Surely her time at Brookmore House showed her how ill-suited they were.

She detested common labour, but he was happiest when fully immersed in the farm and the quarry. He loved to be in the thick of things, with the people he counted upon and who counted upon him. It was close to riding into battle, but without the risk. She disliked horses, but he, like Miss Tilson, felt the need to ride every day. He needed the release of a fine gallop across the fields.

Garret still enjoyed sharing breakfast with his nieces, who seemed happier and more relaxed as his days became unhappier and more tense. Breakfast gave him his only opportunity to see how Miss Tilson was faring. She'd been resolute in keeping her distance from him. He thought she looked more strained.

Like him.

Garret spent part of his day teaching his nieces to ride, a task in which Miss Tilson enthusiastically participated and about which Lady Agnes complained.

Her complaints were couched in words of concern, of course. Might the children be harmed by being out so much in the sun? Would they be falling behind on their lessons? Would it be prudent to engage a piano teacher or a dancing master as well for some balance?

He realised Lady Agnes must be going mad from boredom. There was very little for her to do but write letters, do needlework, play the pianoforte and read ladies' magazines he brought her from Grasmere, since she disliked the books in his library.

How many letters could she write, though? How much needlework could she finish? How did her poor aunt stand it, as well? The older lady seemed to nap most of the day, probably from lack of anything more interesting to do.

In this past week, Lady Agnes had begun to press him to make her acquainted with other good families in the area, meaning other land owners with titles, if possible. Garret had neglected to call upon his neighbours. He'd always meant to, but he wanted to see to the estate's needs first.

At Lady Agnes's request he sent a servant to Ambleside every day for the mail. She received more letters than everyone else in the household combined and he franked all the letters she sent in return. He did not care enough to notice to whom they were addressed.

This afternoon he carried some ledgers into the house, planning to go over some figures he and Ben had discussed. Agnes encountered him in the drawing room.

'Brookmore! How lovely to see you,' she chirped. 'I was about to take a turn in the garden. Would you join me?'

To deny such a little request seemed churlish. 'Certainly.' He put the ledgers in a desk drawer. 'Which gardens?'

Brookmore House had, of course, more than one garden. He'd toured them all with her when she first arrived. As he had toured with Miss Tilson and the children.

Lady Agnes took his arm. 'The topiary. It is so quaint.'

Quaint was a common word she used when talking about the house and its gardens.

Garret walked with her out the front entrance and

through the gate to the topiary. This day she did not remark at all about the whimsical shrubbery. She talked of the unseasonably cool weather and lamented that Garret had been working too hard which could not possibly be good for him.

Suddenly a screech came from behind the shrubbery and two laughing little girls ran straight for them.

Lady Agnes cried out in surprise.

'Uncle Garret! Uncle Garret!' Ellen ran up to him. 'We are pretending we are afraid of a snake, but we aren't really, because the snake is a garden snake and only does good by eating bad things.' She paused. 'At least that is what Phibbs tells us.'

'You gave me such a fright!' Lady Agnes fanned herself.

Pamela eyed Lady Agnes and spoke mechanically. 'Sorry, Lady Agnes.'

Lady Agnes took a step backwards. 'Is there truly a snake?'

'A very long one,' Pamela said.

'A garden snake is harmless,' Garret told her.

'But we were pretending it was a viper,' Ellen explained. 'Phibbs said there are vipers in the gardens, too.'

Lady Agnes trembled. 'Do not say so!'

Garret reassured her, 'Vipers prefer to hide. You

have nothing to fear. Even the gardens in London have them.'

'We saw a big garden snake, though,' Ellen said. 'Want to see it?'

Lady Agnes smiled stiffly at the little girl. 'Are you two unsupervised?'

'No, Lady Agnes.' Miss Tilson appeared from behind the shrubbery. 'I am here.'

Miss Tilson looked lovely in the wide-brimmed hat she wore for excursions like this one, her colour heightened by the summer air. The little girls looked like miniatures of her, in similar hats and a healthy glow to their faces.

'Goodness!' Lady Agnes laughed. 'Do you stay out of doors all day? Riding all the morning and now playing in the garden? When do the girls do their lessons?'

Miss Tilson lifted her chin. 'Their lesson is about the flora and fauna found here. Phibbs has shown the girls plants of all varieties and insects and this lovely snake.'

'Phibbs?' Lady Agnes looked quizzically towards Garret.

'The gardener,' he responded.

Lady Agnes's lip curled. 'The gardener!'

'He is a fine man,' Garret said.

'I am certain he is,' laughed Lady Agnes. 'And apparently a suitable playmate, as well.'

'Not a playmate,' Miss Tilson broke in. 'I could think of no one more knowledgeable about plants and insects and the like.'

When he'd been a boy, Garret learned much from Phibbs, but he'd escaped his governess to do so. He had to admit he sometimes wondered if his nieces received any lessons in the schoolroom. Miss Tilson certainly did not teach as he had been taught, but the little girls had blossomed under her care and that was enough for him.

'If you will pardon us,' Miss Tilson went on, 'we will return to our lesson. Come, girls.'

Garret watched her walk away, holding the hand of each of the girls who skipped at her side. It was a sight he wanted to embed in his memory.

'Such an interesting person.' Lady Agnes took his arm again. 'Do you not agree?'

He did agree. And that was what made life so difficult at the moment.

Chapter Fourteen

Lady Agnes seemed to dismiss Miss Tilson more easily than Garret could. She took his arm again and turned down a path away from where Miss Tilson and the children had disappeared.

She spoke. 'I have a surprise for you, Brookmore, dear.'

'A surprise?' Garret suspected he would not like a surprise from Lady Agnes.

Her expression was that of a mischievous child. 'You know how often I have mentioned to you that it would be a courtesy to call upon your neighbours?'

He nodded.

'I decided you have been much too busy, so I took matters into my own hands so to speak.'

'What did you do?' His voice turned cold.

She grinned. 'I have planned a dinner party.'

'A dinner party?' She planned a dinner party without his knowledge?

'Do not concern yourself,' she said quickly. 'I consulted with Mrs Dodd and Glover regarding the guest list. I will show it to you when we are in the house, but I know you will approve it.'

'I am not certain this is a wise idea,' he said carefully.

'Of course it is a wise idea!' She laughed.

'You should have consulted me, not Mrs Dodd and Glover.' *You are not my wife and hostess yet,* he wanted to say.

'It has been a lovely diversion for me, Brookmore,' she went on. 'Surely you can see how much pleasure it gives me to do this for you.'

Not for him. For her. Because she wanted it.

'Please, Brookmore?' She blinked up at him. 'Please let me show you how skilled I am at giving a party like this?'

Having her so publicly act as his hostess felt like another link in the chain of a marriage he no longer desired.

A marriage that was inevitable, though.

'Show me the guest list.' He had no intention of approving this dinner party without knowing who would be invited. 'Then I will decide.'

'I am very happy to show you the guest list,' she retorted. 'But it is too late for you to decide.'

His anger kindled. 'What do you mean too late?'

She smiled her sweet smile. 'The invitations have already been sent.'

'You sent out the invitations?' His voice rose.

She faced him, nonplussed. 'You know you've neglected your duty to your neighbours. This dinner party will remedy that. You have a standing in this area. You must assert your importance.'

He did not mind dining with neighbours and hearing of local matters. What he did not like was Lady Agnes manoeuvring to get what she wanted in an underhanded way.

'You have made it impossible for me to refuse, have you not?' he snapped.

She laughed and put her arm through his again. 'Of course I have! But know I have done it all for you, my dearest one.'

That did nothing to appease him. 'When is this dinner to be?'

She squeezed his arm. 'In a week's time.'

'A week's time?' How long had she been working on this in secret?

'You will love it, I promise you,' she insisted. 'It will be the loveliest dinner party!'

He'd get through it, he was certain. He'd got through many a dinner party, ball and other entertainments in London.

He must accept some of the blame for this, as

well. He'd not troubled himself to know how she occupied her days. He'd left her too much to her own devices.

'Next time, no secrets, Lady Agnes.' He much preferred plain speaking. Like Miss Tilson engaged in.

'I shall never hide anything from you, Brookmore.' She sounded sincere for a woman who'd kept this secret for some length of time.

She pulled him towards the garden gate. 'Come inside with me! I will show you the guest list and the menu. I am sure you will be more than satisfied.'

He let her lead him back inside the house. As soon as they entered through the front door, the butler approached him.

'What is it, Glover?' he asked.

'A caller,' Glover replied. 'A gentleman who wishes to see Miss Tilson.'

Lady Agnes dropped his arm.

'Miss Tilson?' he asked. Who would call upon Miss Tilson? Who would she know? 'Did the gentleman give his name?'

'Sir Orin Foley, m'lord,' the butler replied. 'He is seated in the hall.'

Lady Agnes started for the door of the hall. 'Let us see what the gentleman wants.'

Garret followed her.

A man who looked to be in his thirties stood at their entrance. He was not as tall as Garret and was fair, with red hair that was starting to recede from his forehead.

He stepped forward with an ingratiating smile. 'Lord Brookmore, I presume? I am Sir Orin Foley.' He bowed.

Garret looked at him suspiciously. Where had this fellow come from? 'And you are here to see Miss Tilson?'

'If she will receive me.' Foley smiled again.

'Is she acquainted with you?' Garret asked.

He laughed softly. 'Indeed. I am her former employer.'

'And your business with Miss Tilson?' Garret pressed.

Lady Agnes broke in. 'Brookmore, maybe the business is private.'

Garret did not care.

'I have no secrets, I assure you,' Foley said. 'I am her former employer and, to be frank with you, I am here to ask her to return with me.'

Take her back to Ireland?

Lady Agnes spoke again. 'You must let her speak to the man, Brookmore. It is her affair, certainly.'

He supposed he must, although every piece of him

wanted to toss the man out before Miss Tilson knew he was here.

'Very well,' he said. 'I will send someone to find her.'

Lady Agnes watched Brookmore stride out of the hall. She approached Sir Orin.

'I am Lady Agnes, sir. I wrote to your wife to enquire about Miss Tilson, but I would prefer you not tell Lord Brookmore that. He likes to believe he must do everything.'

Sir Orin's expression turned mournful. 'I regret to say my dear wife passed away shortly after Miss Tilson left us. I am here to entice her back. We need her desperately.'

Lady Agnes touched his arm. 'My condolences, sir. How very sad for you and the children.'

'Yes.' He sighed. 'The children need Miss Tilson to return to them.'

'I do understand,' she assured him. 'You found her services satisfactory?'

He smiled again. 'She was an angel!'

That would not be Agnes's description of her. Obviously the men who hired her saw her much differently. In Sir Orin's case, though, this might be the answer she'd been hoping for.

'Until your letter, I did not know where Miss Tilson had gone,' he said. 'I am very indebted to you.'

'I confess, I wished to know more about her,' Agnes told him. 'For the children's sake. I was not involved in hiring her—' She broke off. 'But I should tell you I am betrothed to Lord Brookmore, so soon it will be my duty to take care of such matters.'

Agnes asked him more questions, keeping an eye on the doorway for Brookmore's return.

'I am so sympathetic to your plight, sir,' she said. 'To have no one. At least Brookmore's nieces have me. I will do what I can for you, but you must let no one know that I sent that letter.'

He gave her a shrewd look. 'It is a bargain, Lady Agnes.'

Rebecca and the children knelt by a bed of sweet alyssum, watching a bumblebee dart from one tiny white flower to another. She looked up at the sound of footsteps.

A footman hurried up to them. 'Miss Tilson, you have a caller.'

'A caller! For Miss Tilson!' Ellen parroted excitedly. She jumped to her feet. 'Let us go see who it is!'

Rebecca rose as well, her heart pounding. Who would call upon her? She knew no one here.

'The caller is for Miss Tilson, not you,' Pamela chided her little sister.

'I want to see who it is!' Ellen cried.

Rebecca brushed off her skirt. 'I had better go alone. You children stay in the garden. I'll be back in a few minutes.'

She could not imagine this taking long. It must be a mistake.

She followed the footman back to the house. When she entered the front door, Lord Brookmore waited there for her.

'Who is it calling upon me?' she asked him.

He did not look happy about this visitor. 'Your former employer.'

'My employer?' Claire's employer, he meant. A man? A woman? She did not know who to expect. What to expect. Would her masquerade be exposed?

'He is in the hall,' Lord Brookmore told her.

He. A man. That answered one question. But she did not even know his name.

She pulled off her hat and walked into the hall, legs trembling.

A red-haired man, talking with Lady Agnes, glanced over at her and broke into a smile. 'Claire!' he cried.

Lady Agnes gave Rebecca a knowing look. 'I will

leave you two.' She nodded to the man. 'A pleasure to speak with you, Sir Orin.'

Sir Orin. Sir Orin was his name.

Rebecca remained where she was as Lady Agnes swept by her. Sir Orin strode over to her.

'Claire, it is so good to see you.' He reached out to touch her, but she stepped back.

She came directly to the point. 'Why do you call upon me?'

'You must know why.' His eyes scanned her from head to toe in a manner that made her skin crawl.

'I do not. I wish you to tell me,' she demanded.

Goodness. She was not acting like Claire, was she? Claire would not have demanded anything. Rebecca needed to be direct, though. The less time he was with her, the better the chance of him not seeing she was not Claire.

'When I just discovered your whereabouts, I came right away.' He moved closer to her.

She stepped back again.

'My wife is dead, Claire,' he told her excitedly. 'You must come home with me now.'

A *frisson* of alarm crawled up her spine. He sounded almost happy about his wife dying.

Oh, why had she not asked Claire about her employment in Ireland? She'd certainly filled Claire's ear about her situation. She'd never thought to ask Claire anything about hers.

Rebecca tried to remain calm. 'I am employed here now, Sir Orin. I am content here.'

His eyes flashed with anger, but he quickly altered his demeanour and lowered his voice. 'The children need you. *I* need you. You must come.'

Rebecca looked him in the eye. 'I choose to stay here. You must find another governess for the children.' She had no idea how many children he had. Boys? Girls? Their names? She knew nothing.

'Let me persuade you.' He looked at her entreatingly.

'No.' She stepped back again. 'I am very sorry you travelled all this way, but you should not have come. I am not going back to Ireland.'

'It does not have to be Ireland, my dear,' he purred. 'I can move the children to England. Anywhere you desire.'

My dear? This intimate tone unnerved her. So did his use of Claire's Christian name. *Claire, what happened to you there? With this man?* she asked silently.

'I have given you my answer.'

'How may I change that answer, my dear?' he murmured. 'I must change your mind.'

This man looked harmless enough, but his words and manner made the hairs on Rebecca's neck rise.

She raised her voice. 'My position is here now. I do not wish to discuss this further.'

'Claire, you must let me persuade you!' he pleaded, extending his hand.

She turned away. 'Please leave now.'

'But—' he began.

A voice from the doorway broke in. 'She has asked you to leave, sir.'

Lord Brookmore must have been standing there. Rebecca's shoulders relaxed in relief.

Sir Orin did not move, however.

Lord Brookmore repeated, 'You must leave. Now.'

Lady Agnes stepped into the hall, walking up to Sir Orin. 'Come. I will walk you out.' She took his arm and he left with her.

Lord Brookmore turned and watched them leave before speaking to Rebecca. 'I could not hear your conversation, if you are wondering. Something about him… I did not think you should see him alone.'

She was grateful to him. Excessively. 'It was nothing. He came for nothing.'

'He upset you,' Brookmore said.

She wanted so badly to ask for his comfort. She wanted him to hold her and tell her Sir Orin would never bother her again and she would never have to worry about her deception being exposed.

But she could not ask him for comfort. Lady Agnes was here now.

Rebecca waved a hand. 'He wants me to be his children's governess again.'

'And what do you want?' he asked.

She met his gaze. 'I wish to remain here.'

Lady Agnes walked Sir Orin all the way out the front door where no one could hear them.

'Best you not press her now,' she told the dejected man.

'I am determined to have her back.' He put on his hat and pulled his gloves over his fingers.

'Then you must try another day.' Agnes certainly was not ready to give up. 'Where are you staying, sir?'

'Ambleside. The Unicorn Inn,' he said.

She nodded. 'Enjoy your stay there. I will contact you soon, I promise. Do not lose hope.'

He smiled charmingly. 'I am so very grateful to you, Lady Agnes. I am obviously in need of an ally.'

'As am I.' She returned his smile. 'I should tell you she rides early every morning, but do not make use of that information tomorrow. Give her a day or so.'

'She rides?' He looked puzzled. 'I had no inkling she was a horsewoman.'

'She is quite enamoured of the out of doors, actually.' Anything to do with the farm.

'Is she?' His brows rose. 'That is a change. I can see there is more to discover about Claire Tilson.'

'She did not spend her time out of doors with your children?' Agnes asked.

'Not at all,' he responded. 'Oh, she took the occasional walk, but most days she closeted herself in the schoolroom with the children.'

This was curious indeed, Agnes thought. Of course, she could favour the out of doors because that was where Brookmore was likely to be, working on the farm like a common labourer.

Sir Orin brightened. 'Perhaps I can entice her back with some prime horseflesh!'

'An excellent idea.' Extravagant gifts never hurt.

'I will work on that.' He tipped his hat to her. 'You have been very helpful, Lady Agnes. I will remember all you have told me.'

He headed down the lane leading to the gate. How gauche to have walked from Ambleside.

She went back into the house and joined Brookmore and Miss Tilson in the hall. 'I've sent him on his way,' she told them.

Miss Tilson actually looked grateful. 'Thank you,

Lady Agnes.' She released a breath. 'I am much relieved.' She slid a glance to Brookmore before turning back to Agnes. 'I really should get back to the children. Will you both excuse me?'

'Of course,' Agnes said in her sweetest voice. 'The children.'

Miss Tilson curtsied and left the room.

'Well, that was certainly dramatic,' Agnes remarked to Brookmore.

'The whole matter is odd, if you ask me.' Brookmore's words were more spontaneous than usual when he spoke to her. 'Why did he show up in the first place?'

'I attempted to discover his reasons while you sent someone to find Miss Tilson.' She might as well have him think she was trying to be helpful to him. 'He told me his wife died and he needed Miss Tilson to return to care for his children. They are all alone now, you see.'

'They are alone, so he travels all the way here?' Brookmore huffed. 'He might have stayed with his children and written a letter.'

It was pathetic, really, these two gentlemen fawning over that plain spinster of a governess. She was too tall. Too…robust. And lacking in refinement.

She shook her head. 'A letter would not do, you

see. A personal contact like this is much more convincing.'

He darted a fiery glance at her. 'You sound as if you are taking up his cause.'

'Do I?' She laughed. 'I do not mean to sound that way. I do have some sympathy for Sir Orin, losing his wife. And his little children, losing their mother. If Miss Tilson returned to him, his children would regain some stability.'

'I want stability for my nieces,' Brookmore stated. 'They lost both their parents.'

She slid her arm through his, brushing her breast against him. 'Don't get in high dudgeon, Brookmore, dear. I am excessively proud of the way you have taken care of your nieces. Those dear little girls. But, I must say, Miss Tilson is not like any governess I ever knew.'

'Nor I,' he said absently.

She seized on this. 'She seems to take them outside all day. Is she ever in the classroom? Do you know if they are learning French? Italian? Or doing needlework? Or learning the social graces?'

'I have not discussed the details of Miss Tilson's lessons with her,' he admitted.

What did he discuss with her, then?

They walked into the drawing room. He went over to a cabinet and took out a decanter.

'Some claret?' he offered.

'Please.' She smiled.

While he poured, she draped herself gracefully on one of the sofas. He handed her a glass.

She took a ladylike sip. 'Would you like me to involve myself with the nursery? I could visit the schoolroom and see what exactly Miss Tilson is teaching your sweet nieces.'

'No,' he shot back. 'Leave it. Ellen and Pamela are starting to be happy again.'

She took another sip. 'As you wish.'

Chapter Fifteen

It took Rebecca three days to calm down from Sir Orin Foley's visit. The day of his visit, she'd gone into Lord Brookmore's library and looked up Sir Orin in *Debrett's*. She'd had to comb through all the listings, which were by title and not given name, but she'd found it finally. Orin Foley of Newpark, Second Baronet. As of 1814, that issue's publication date, Sir Orin had been married to Anne Walsh, daughter of the Earl of Branard and had issue, one son, Charles, and three daughters, Mary, Margaret and Bridget.

She wished she could discover what had happened to Lady Foley and what had happened to Claire to make her leave her position.

But the days settled into their usual order and her thoughts about Claire and Sir Orin became more fleeting. Her feelings regarding Lord Brookmore settled into a quiet ache and she sometimes could see him without feeling like the wound had been re-opened to bleed all over again. Lady Agnes more and more took over the house as if it were hers, which, of course, it was destined to be.

Rebecca's teaching had settled into a routine, as well, if one could call her haphazard lessons a routine. Sometimes she remembered to teach them sums and French, but mostly she read to them from Lord Brookmore's extensive library or they went outside and looked at everything. How the plants grew, how the animals behaved, both those on the farm and in the wild, how the weather changed, although it didn't change much. It remained unseasonably cold.

Every morning the girls had riding lessons on their ponies. Pamela was taking to riding as though she was born on a horse, but Ellen, the typically intrepid one, was slow to giving up her fear. Her pony was the sweetest creature, though, and was steadily winning her over.

She encouraged them to talk to her about their thoughts and feelings or to write them down in their journals. If nothing else, she was determined they know their own minds.

This morning, as the sun merely peeked over the mountains, Rebecca mounted Lily, the horse that was hers in her heart, although she'd never again own a horse. Galloping on the fields, she and Lily seemed to have one mind. She loved her morning rides. For a few minutes every day, Rebecca could feel free as the wind whipping through the fells.

On her way back, in the distance a man on horseback appeared on the next hill. Rebecca's heart thrilled, as it always did when she saw Brookmore unexpectedly, but a second later she realised it was not Brookmore. She rarely saw anyone else on her early morning runs, except workers beginning their day's toil.

The figure rode down the hill out of her sight and she put him out of her mind. The ride back was when she talked herself into being grateful for what she had. Life, for one. So many others on the ship lost theirs. She again thanked Claire for the chance to live Claire's life, even though nothing turned out like she thought.

She made herself think of Pamela and Ellen, of how they were blossoming under her care. Inept as she was as a governess, something she was doing made these little girls happier. She and Lord Brookmore, of course. He daily showed he cared about them.

Lily climbed the far hill where Rebecca had seen the man. She started to plan her lessons for the day. They always seemed so organised in her mind. In practice, though, it never worked out so neatly.

She rode over the hill and was startled to see the rider waiting there.

Sir Orin.

'What a surprise to see you riding, Claire!' He spoke to her as if continuing an ongoing conversation. 'I did not know you rode.'

'There is much you do not know about me.' Like the fact that she was not Claire.

He started riding beside her. 'Yes, indeed. You are so changed. I find it exciting.'

Anxiety crept up her spine. 'Why are you still here, Sir Orin? I told you that I am happy in my position here. I'm not returning to your employ.'

'Can I not tour the Lake District? It is becoming fashionable to do so, I understand.' He smiled at her.

'You should go home to your children,' she admonished.

'Not without you,' he said.

'You must not speak to me that way.' Can Lily gallop home? she wondered. She didn't wish to try for fear of overworking the horse.

'Why did you leave, Claire?' He acted as if she'd not spoken. 'I told you I would find a way for everything to work out.'

Had he romanced Claire? It certainly seemed as if he had, but he wasn't precisely stating so. She did not want to say the wrong thing.

'I am quite content here, sir. There is nothing more to discuss. I am riding back to Brookmore House and I do not want you to follow me there.' She signalled Lily to canter and she did not look back, but she could hear no hoofbeats behind her.

Later that day Lady Agnes asked to be taken to Ambleside for shopping. Her aunt did not accompany her. Ordinarily Agnes preferred riding in her carriage, but, since the ride to Ambleside was only three miles, she allowed herself to be taken in the gig. One horse instead of four. Her coachman drove instead of one of Brookmore's stablemen.

'Take me to the Unicorn Inn,' Agnes said as they neared the village. 'I have an errand there before shopping.'

'Yes, m'lady.' Her coachman would spend the time in the inn's tavern, she guessed. And he lacked any curiosity as to her business.

Agnes entered the inn.

A man, obviously the innkeeper, attended the hall.

'Good day to you, my fine lady,' he said in the jovial manner so common to these sorts.

She gave him one of her charming smiles. 'Good day to you, sir. I am looking for a gentleman of my acquaintance. Sir Orin. I wish to speak with him. Is he here, do you know?'

'Sir Orin.' He nodded. 'I believe he is in the parlour reading the newspaper. Shall I get him for you?'

Silly question. 'Either that or show me to the parlour.'

He extended his arm. 'This way, madam.'

She was not a madam yet, not until she got Brookmore to the altar. This plan of hers would get the deed done, though, she was certain of it.

Sir Orin fortunately sat alone in the parlour.

'A lady to see you, sir,' the innkeeper announced.

Sir Orin looked up and smiled. He stood and walked over to her. 'Lady Agnes. How good to see you.'

When the innkeeper closed the door, Agnes spoke. 'I told you I would come.'

He gestured for her to sit.

She brushed off the upholstery of a chair and lowered herself on to it.

'I hope you are well,' he said as he chose a chair facing hers. He leaned forward as if eager to hear what she had to say.

'I am glad you have not given up,' she said.

His expression turned serious. 'I shall never give up. Do you come to offer me some hope?'

She turned serious, as well. 'I wish you to be very honest with me.'

A slight smile lit his lips. 'I am the soul of honesty, my lady.'

Then he was a fool. Everyone needed to tell a falsehood now and then.

She refrained from rolling her eyes. 'Tell me truthfully. Do you wish Miss Tilson back as your children's governess or is there another reason?'

He clamped his mouth shut as if considering whether to answer her question or not. Or to lie or not.

Finally he spoke. 'I am determined to make Miss Tilson my wife. I wish this above all things.'

She leaned back. 'I suspected as much.' How convenient that his wife had died. 'And does she return your regard?'

He glanced away. 'How could she have done? She was too honourable. And she was loyal to my wife.'

Who now was conveniently out of the way.

Agnes straightened her spine. 'Well, I have contrived another opportunity for you.'

'Excellent,' he said. 'I rode this morning and intercepted her, to no avail. I did not recall her being so stubborn.'

'I think there are other factors at play here.' She was not going to divulge them to him, though. He was a man, after all, and men could so easily ruin things. 'In any event, you are invited to my dinner party this Saturday next. Five other couples, all I could find who would be suitable. I will insist she be a member of the party, as well, and that you have an opportunity to speak with her privately.'

'A dinner party?' He did not look convinced.

'Let her see you with other good people.' Or at least the best she could find in this remote area of England. 'Put on the charm.'

He gave her an earnest look. 'Do you believe I have seemed too eager?'

'Absolutely.' She believed he'd played this all wrong. 'Be a gentleman. Make the others like you. Let her see you through their eyes.'

He sat back and grinned. 'I dare say I can do that.'

'I am certain you can.' She stood. 'Come at eight o'clock. Come by carriage. Do you have proper attire?'

He rose, as well. 'I do indeed.'

He extended his hand. She put her gloved hand in his and accepted the handshake.

'Until Saturday, then, Sir Orin,' she said.

When Agnes returned to Brookmore House she changed out of her walking dress and went in search of Miss Tilson. She climbed the stairs to the second floor and passed what she supposed was Brookmore's bedchamber. At least, it was the room his valet exited as she walked by.

'Good day, m'lady,' the old man said.

'Good day,' she said brightly.

The valet shuffled off and Agnes wondered why Brookmore did not pension off such an ancient servant. Surely the man had no sense of men's fashions today. It could not be pleasant to have such a wrinkled creature touch him or his clothes.

But, never mind. That was a task for another day.

She continued down the hallway until coming to what she supposed was the children's wing. She heard a voice and listened through the door.

The voice was Miss Tilson's, sounding as if she was reading from a book:

'"*The elk is twice as big as a hart and bigger than a horse in Norway and Sweden. It is tamed and put into a coach, chariot or sledge to draw men through great snows and upon the ice. It is said to be more swift and to run more miles in one day than a horse...*"'

Agnes opened the door without knocking.

'Lady Agnes!' Miss Tilson closed the book.

The little girls were seated at the table, their backs to the door. They whirled around to the doorway.

'Stand and curtsy to Lady Agnes, girls,' Miss Tilson said.

They scrambled off their chairs and did as she said.

'How darling!' Agnes let her gaze encompass the three of them. 'What were you reading?'

Pamela answered. '*A Description of Three Hundred Animals.*'

'*Beasts, Birds, Fishes, Serpents and Insects,*' Ellen added.

'Animals,' Agnes repeated. 'How delightful.' She turned to the governess. 'May I speak to you alone for a moment, Miss Tilson?'

As Miss Tilson made her way to the doorway, she handed the book to Pamela. 'Read some of this to Ellen while I speak with Lady Agnes.'

Agnes stepped back out to the hallway. Miss Tilson joined her and closed the door behind her. She did not speak, but merely gazed at Agnes.

Agnes smiled. 'Do not fear, Miss Tilson. I bring you very pleasant news.'

The governess looked sceptical, but still did not speak.

Agnes took a breath. 'I am inviting you to our dinner party on Saturday night. I have invited some of the area's important people and it would be so kind of you to join us.'

It took Miss Tilson several seconds to finally speak. 'I must respectfully decline, my lady. I do not have suitable clothes to wear.'

Agnes waved a dismissive hand. 'Simply wear your best dress. It will do, I am sure.'

'I do not think so,' Miss Tilson said.

Agnes gave her a steely smile. 'I must insist. I need you at the table, otherwise the numbers will not be even. Come to the drawing room at seven-thirty.' She nodded a dismissal, turned on her heel and left.

Rebecca watched Lady Agnes walk away. The tension from the encounter came in a rush and she tried to quiet her breathing.

Refusing to attend this dinner would likely cause more drama than enduring it. She'd have to attend.

She wished she were a man so she could curse!

Her fists clenched and unclenched.

Finally when she felt like she could act with some semblance of normalcy, she opened the classroom door.

Pamela and Ellen both jumped back with guilty looks on their faces.

'Were you two listening at the door?' Rebecca asked, although she knew very well they were.

'Yes, Miss Tilson,' Pamela admitted.

Ellen's eyes grew big. 'Are you really going to a dinner party?'

'I don't know, Ellen.' Rebecca sat in her chair and the two girls came to her side.

Ellen's brow furrowed. 'What is a dinner party?'

Pamela looked exasperated. 'It is when you invite people to eat dinner with you and they come dressed in pretty clothes. Do you not remember Mama and Papa having dinner parties?'

Ellen shook her head.

Pamela turned to Rebecca. 'You do not have pretty clothes, though, do you, Miss Tilson? Your pretty dresses are all at the bottom of the sea.'

'I am afraid so.' Rebecca looked down at herself. 'I'll have to wear this.'

'You cannot wear that,' Pamela insisted. 'The other ladies will be in silks and laces and such.'

Ellen jumped up and down. 'I have an idea!' She pulled Pamela some distance away and whispered in her ear.

Pamela's face brightened and she whispered something back. Ellen jumped up and down again. This time Pamela pulled her back to Rebecca.

Pamela took Rebecca's hand. 'Come with us, Miss Tilson.'

Ellen grabbed her other hand and they pulled her out of her seat.

'We'll need a lamp,' Pamela said.

Rebecca picked up one from the schoolroom and followed them into the hallway. They led her to another staircase, one she had not seen before.

'This is the attic,' Pamela said.

They climbed the stairs up to a third floor and opened the door to a cavernous area dotted with trunks, wooden boxes, furniture covered with cloth. The girls walked over to a trunk stashed near the entrance. It was made of the same carved oak wood that panelled most of the rooms in the house.

It took the two girls to lift the lid.

'Come see, Miss Tilson!' Ellen cried.

She carried the lamp closer and placed it on the lid of a nearby wooden box. She peered inside the trunk. There appeared to be women's clothes carefully folded.

'What are these?' Rebecca asked.

'Mama's dresses,' Ellen said. 'You could wear one to the dinner party.'

Rebecca stepped back. 'Oh, no. Not your mother's clothes.'

The girls could not possibly know how it would feel to see their mother's clothes on someone else.

'It is all right, Miss Tilson,' Pamela said. 'Mama never wore these. They were delivered after…after the accident. Nobody has ever worn these.'

'But I could not…'

Pamela put her hands on her hips. 'Did not Uncle say that our mother's things belong to Ellen and me now?'

He'd told them that at breakfast many times.

'Then we can say who wears these dresses,' Pamela added.

'Miss Ellen! Miss Pamela!' Mary's voice reached them.

Ellen ran to the doorway. 'Up here, Mary!'

Mary's footsteps sounded on the stairs. 'You girls know you are not supposed to play up here.' She reached the top. 'Oh, Miss Tilson.'

Ellen looked up at her. 'Miss Tilson is going to the dinner party and she doesn't have a pretty dress and Pamela and I want her to wear one of Mama's—the ones Mama never wore.'

'You've been invited to the dinner party?' Mary looked surprised.

'I am afraid so,' admitted Rebecca. 'Lady Agnes has demanded I attend.'

Mary rolled her eyes. 'The dinner party. She has everyone below stairs at sixes and sevens over it. Except Mrs Dodd. Mrs Dodd is over the moon that there will be a party.'

'The children want me to wear one of these dresses.' Rebecca gestured to the trunk.

'Oh, the dresses that came after.' Mary knew instantly which dresses she meant. 'We did not know what to do with them so we simply put them in this trunk in the attic.'

'Otherwise she'll have to wear an ugly dress,' Ellen explained.

The children's maid laughed. 'We cannot have that. Not if Miss Tilson is invited to the *dinner party*.' She put an exaggerated emphasis on *dinner party*. 'Let's have a look.' Mary knelt next to the trunk and lifted one dress out. 'It is too dark here. Let's look at the dresses in Miss Tilson's bedchamber.'

Mary pulled out three dresses and draped them over Rebecca's arms. Mary carried three more. 'Miss Pamela, you carry the lamp.'

'What can I do?' Ellen whined.

'You must close the door,' the maid said.

They made their way to Rebecca's room and spread the dresses over the bed. There was one dress Rebecca could not help but love. A deep green patterned silk with a flounce at the hem and a gold ribbon tied under her breasts. It was plain, but elegant. She knew instantly that it would complement her colouring and make her eyes turn green.

It was just the sort of dress Rebecca would have worn in her real life.

'Which one?' she asked, thinking the girls would like to choose for her, since it had been their idea.

'The green one,' Mary, Pamela and Ellen said together.

Rebecca laughed. 'That is the one I like the best.'

Ellen came over and hugged her. 'We will dress you up and you will be as pretty as Mama.'

That night at dinner Lady Agnes seemed especially cheerful. No doubt it was due to the impending dinner party. She hardly talked of anything else.

Garret wished it would never take place, but not because guests were invited. He'd known these people most of his life. He objected because Lady Agnes manipulated the whole event and he disliked being manipulated. More reason to dread marrying her.

'How was your day?' he asked Lady Agnes out of politeness.

'It was lovely!' Her colour was heightened, which made her even more beautiful. 'I went to Ambleside to do some shopping and you will never guess who I encountered there.'

He detested guessing. 'Who?'

'Sir Orin.' She took a sip of her wine.

'Sir Orin, yes.' Her aunt who sat across from her nodded approvingly. 'You told me about him. A baronet, you said.'

Sir Orin? Garret remembered him. Miss Tilson's former employer. 'He is still here?'

'He is indeed,' Agnes responded. 'I invited him to the dinner party.'

'How very nice, dear,' her aunt said.

Garret put down his fork. 'You did what?'

'I invited Sir Orin to the dinner party,' she repeated.

This was too much. 'Un-invite him, then. He is nothing to me.'

She spoke calmly. 'Now, Brookmore, another couple is needed to balance out the table. And he is a baronet. This area is quite thin of aristocracy. A baronet will improve the company.'

Sir Orin Foley had pressed Miss Tilson to return to his employ. He'd used her Christian name. 'This dinner was supposed to fulfil a social obligation to my neighbours. Sir Orin is not a neighbour. I do not want him here.'

Her eyes twinkled. 'There is another reason,' she said, but did not immediately elaborate.

'What other reason?' he asked finally. Why the devil did she not simply tell everything instead of feeding it to him piecemeal?

'He confided in me.' She leaned towards Garret. 'He is sweet on Miss Tilson.' She laughed as if that idea was amusing. 'He wishes to convince her to marry him. That is why he has remained in the area.'

'Marry him?' Garret felt his skin turn cold.

'How nice,' her aunt broke in.

It was not nice. It was decidedly not nice. 'How

can you think she will welcome his suit? She sent him away when he called here.'

'Yes, but that was when she thought Sir Orin merely wanted her as governess.' Lady Agnes speared a piece of roast fowl with her fork. 'It is quite another matter to be a baronet's wife.'

Garret's appetite fled. 'I fail to see how inviting him to the dinner party furthers his aim to marry Miss Tilson.'

Lady Agnes swallowed and took another sip of wine. 'Oh, I invited her, too, of course. She evens out the numbers.'

Garret frowned into his plate. Miss Tilson would not desire this. 'I dislike these machinations, Lady Agnes.'

Her aunt wiped her mouth with her napkin. 'Agnes, dear, I am feeling a bit ill. I believe I will retire.' She turned nervously to Garret. 'With your permission, sir?'

He nodded.

Lady Agnes avoided looking at him until her aunt left the room. Then she turned to him with a wounded expression. 'These are not machinations, Brookmore dear. I did need one more couple for the dinner party. And more elevated company. And I can only see this as a favour for Miss Tilson. You must admit, her life would more vastly be improved by marriage. She would have a household of her own to manage. She would have wealth and security.'

Everyone knew the life of a governess was a dismal one. Long hours. Little chance of meeting a respectable suitor. A victim of those on whose employment she was dependent. Was he right in wanting nothing to take her away from here? From his nieces, he meant.

'Am I not correct?' Lady Agnes pressed.

He faced her. 'Does she know all this?'

Lady Agnes glanced away and back. 'Well, she does not know he seeks her hand in marriage. To tell her seemed like too much interference.'

It all seemed like too much interference to Garret.

'And she is willing to attend the dinner?' he asked.

'Certainly she is,' Agnes said brightly.

He didn't believe her. He hoped he could contrive an opportunity to ask Miss Tilson if she wished to attend this cursed dinner party.

They finished the meal with little conversation.

Lady Agnes took his arm to be escorted from the room. 'Do not fear, Brookmore, dear. This dinner party will be a success, I assure you. I know precisely what I am doing.'

Chapter Sixteen

The night of the dinner party came quickly. Mary and the little girls were so excited for Rebecca she couldn't help feeling a bit of their enthusiasm herself. The only detail she knew about the party was that she was expected to show up in the drawing room at seven-thirty. Mary and the girls insisted they devote the whole afternoon to preparing for it.

Rebecca had successfully avoided being alone with Lord Brookmore the last three days. He'd spoken of the dinner party at breakfast, letting her know she was free to decline.

But she wasn't really free. To decline only brought more attention on her. She would attend and be precisely what Lady Agnes wished—a person in a chair so the party had symmetry.

After the girls ate their midday meal, they would join Rebecca in her bedchamber. Lady Agnes did not know—no one knew—that Rebecca knew exactly how to prepare for a party, although she did not have any tools to do so. She would do the best she could with what she possessed.

'Look what we found,' Ellen cried from the hallway.

Rebecca stepped out of the room.

Pamela and Ellen carried a big wooden box, so large it took the two of them to manage it.

What had they got into now? Rebecca took it off their hands before they dropped it and did themselves an injury.

'What is it?' she asked.

Ellen jumped up and down in excitement. 'Bring it to your room! You will see.'

She carried it into the bedchamber, the two girls following at her heels. She placed it on a table. Ellen immediately pulled up a chair and knelt on it. Pamela was tall enough to open the box.

'Oh, my!' Rebecca picked through the contents. 'This is everything I need. Where did you find it?' There were curling papers, pomade, rouge, ribbons and hair pins.

'It is Mama's things,' Pamela said solemnly.

The girls somehow discovered the box in which their mother's dressing table had been packed away.

Rebecca closed the box again. 'Oh, no. I cannot

use your mother's things.' The items were too personal, too intimate.

'You must,' Pamela pleaded. 'We used to watch Mama make herself ready for parties. We want to see you do it, too.'

'She looked very pretty.' Ellen's bottom lip trembled.

'We want you to look pretty, too,' Pamela said.

'Prettier than Lady Agnes!' Ellen added.

Rebecca opened the box again. Was she to live this part of Lady Brookmore's life, as well as living Claire's? Perhaps she could use Lady Brookmore's things so her little girls could once more watch her dress up.

She could make it a lesson, as well. Some day the girls would be dressing up for some social event. They needed to learn.

'Shall we start with my hair?' Since she'd become Claire, she'd not arranged her hair in any way more decorative than Claire's plain hairstyle.

Rebecca took out the curling papers, triangle-shaped tissue paper. She searched through the box and found what else she needed at the bottom.

'Here it is!' Rebecca pulled out an iron instrument similar to a small coal tongs, but with disc shapes on the ends.

'What is that?' Ellen asked, reaching for it.

Rebecca let her hold it. 'It is a *papillote*. We will use it to curl my hair.'

There was a quick knock on the door and Mary entered, carrying the green-silk dress. 'I've cleared away the girls' meal and have everything else done, so I am at liberty to assist you.' She saw the box. 'Lady Brookmore's things. I packed them up from her dressing table when Lady Agnes arrived.'

'The girls brought them in,' Rebecca explained.

'Miss Tilson is going to curl her hair.' Ellen held up the *papillote*.

Mary put one hot coal from the fireplace into the coal scuttle and brought it over to Rebecca's dressing table. She placed the *papillote* in it. 'Now you girls must not touch it. It will become quite hot.'

Rebecca took the pins from her hair and brushed out the tangles. She separated her hair into sections. 'Now I will show you how to make *papillote* curls, Pamela, Ellen. Watch carefully.'

Explaining each step as she performed it, Rebecca placed a tiny amount of pomade on to a strand of hair and wound it around her finger, so that it was the size of a coin. She wrapped it in the curling paper and Mary carefully pressed the curl with the heated *papillote*. She continued until every strand on her head was wrapped in paper.

'Now I let it cool and you will see what comes next,' she told the girls.

'I remember!' Pamela cried abruptly. 'Mama's head was all full of curls.'

'That's right,' Rebecca told her.

The girls' eyes had been large as saucers as they watched her wrap her curls. They were eager and happy observers. At least this measure of fun, sharing her preparations with the girls, would make this event worth it.

'Would you girls like curls, too?' she asked impulsively.

'Yes! Yes!' they both cried.

She and Mary carefully curled the girls' hair, then the girls insisted Mary have some curls, too, and the four of them laughed at how silly they looked with paper stuck all through their hair.

Mary had Rebecca try on the dress which needed more minor alterations. Mary had lengthened it by letting out the hem and sewing the flounce at the very bottom. With another tuck or two, the gown would fit Rebecca perfectly.

While waiting for the dress to be finished, Rebecca went through every item in the box of Lady Brookmore's things, making the girls guess at items they should know and giving the names and purpose of items they did not.

They all stopped for tea as the afternoon headed into evening and soon it was time for her to complete her *toilette*. Rebecca enhanced the colour and shape of her eyebrows with burnt cloves. She dabbed her cheeks and lips with a faint tint of rouge and she dusted her face with a tiny bit of powder.

'Is it too much?' she asked Mary.

'No!' the girls replied.

Mary surveyed her carefully. 'It looks very natural to me.'

She took a deep breath and looked into the mirror. 'Time for the hair.'

She pulled out the curling papers and her head was a mass of curls. She pulled her hair on top of her head, secured it with ribbons and pins and let the curls cascade wherever they wished. The shorter hair curled around her face in a nice frame.

She turned to see what her audience thought.

Ellen threw her arms around her. 'You look so pretty!'

After fixing the girls' hair in a similar style and Mary's into some curls that would not cause her trouble with Mrs Dodd, it was already seven-thirty and she would be late.

As if she cared to be on time.

Mary helped her into the dress and she donned a pair of slippers and gloves they'd found in the attic.

Mary gasped. 'You need to see yourself! Come with me.'

Mary picked up a lamp and took Rebecca's hand. She led Rebecca and the girls to one of the bedchambers on the hallway near Lord Brookmore's room. She stood Rebecca in front of a full-length mirror.

Rebecca took in a quick breath. Her legs trembled.

The reflection in the mirror looked nothing like Claire Tilson, the governess. In the mirror stood Lady Rebecca Pierce.

She'd almost forgotten about her.

This evening would be a social engagement much like those Lady Rebecca would have attended. The company would be like the company with whom she would have conversed. Lady Rebecca was the social equal of Lady Agnes. She might even have precedence over her.

Lady Rebecca was also the social equal of Lord Brookmore.

Tonight, just this one night, she would be Lady Rebecca again, she decided.

She turned to Mary and the girls with a grin. 'Will I do?'

The girls ran to her and she hugged them close, not even thinking about how her dress might get a wrinkle. When she released them, she kissed them goodnight and promised to tell them all about the party the next day.

They walked her back to the hallway where she hugged the girls again and hugged Mary. 'Thank you, Mary. Thank you, Pamela and Ellen.' She swept her arms from her head to her toe. 'This is all due to you.'

Rebecca hurried to the stairway, turning to wave at the girls one more time. When she descended to the first floor and entered the hall, she straightened her spine and lifted her head and again became Lady Rebecca.

All the guests had arrived and had been served glasses of claret, but Garret kept glancing towards the door.

Had Miss Tilson decided not to come?

Lady Agnes approached him when others were not close by. 'I do hope your governess has the courtesy to show up. I shall be excessively peeved if she ruins the numbers in my dinner party.'

He said nothing, knowing he'd given Miss Tilson permission to stay away. He refilled Lady Agnes's wineglass and poured another to hand to Mr Henson, Reverend Elliman's curate.

Sir Orin walked up to him and handed him an

empty glass. 'It was kind of you to include me in your party, sir. I have been missing good company.'

Garret filled his glass. 'You must thank Lady Agnes. She tendered the invitations.'

Sir Orin smiled charmingly. 'I do thank her, then.' He lifted his glass to Garret and glanced at the door.

He's waiting for her, too, Garret thought. He looked at the clock. Ten minutes to eight. Lady Agnes had been clear that Glover should announce dinner precisely at eight.

Glover stepped inside the drawing room. 'Miss Tilson,' he announced.

All eyes went to the door. Garret worried on her behalf. She would not expect this attention.

She appeared and Garret felt the air leave his lungs.

Here stood a different person, tall and regal, wearing a fine green dress that perfectly complemented her colouring and her statuesque figure. Her features, always striking, could only be described as beautiful.

'Who is she?' gasped the curate.

'My nieces' governess.' Garret stifled an urge to laugh in appreciation of her triumph. She outshone every woman in the room. Especially Lady Agnes.

Sir Orin took a step towards her and Lady Agnes put a stilling hand on his arm, showing more consideration than Garret gave her credit for.

Miss Tilson directed her gaze to Garret and started to walk towards him, but Lady Agnes intercepted her.

'Everyone,' Lady Agnes said, 'this is the girls' governess. She has kindly offered to even our numbers at dinner.' She took Miss Tilson's arm and guided her to the guests, starting with Sir Orin.

Miss Tilson turned white at the sight of him.

'Sir Orin you already know,' Lady Agnes chirped.

He bowed. 'Claire.'

Her eyes flashed. 'Sir,' she said curtly, turning her head away.

Agnes, following precedence, introduced her to Mr and Mrs Howard of Levens Hall, Squire Lloyd, Mrs Lloyd, Reverend Elliman and his wife, the curate, and Mr and Mrs Wordsworth.

Her eyes brightened. 'Mr Wordsworth! This is a pleasure! *"I wandered lonely as a cloud, That floats on high o'er vales and hills, When all at once I saw a crowd, A host, of golden daffodils."'*

He beamed with pleasure. 'You read poetry, Miss Tilson?'

She smiled at him. 'I read your poetry, Mr Wordsworth.'

Agnes guided her away.

Garret spoke up. 'Would you care for a glass of claret, Miss Tilson?'

Her gaze turned to him again. 'Thank you. I would.'

She stepped away from Lady Agnes and walked up to him, her back to the rest of the room.

He handed her the glass. 'You did not know Sir Orin was invited, did you?'

'No,' she snapped. 'You might have warned me.'

'I was told you knew.'

She turned away from him and walked over to Mrs Howard and Mrs Wordsworth.

Glover entered the drawing room again. 'Dinner is served.'

Garret clasped Lady Agnes's arm and spoke through gritted teeth. 'You told me she knew of Sir Orin's invitation.'

Lady Agnes gave him an innocent look. 'I am sure I never did say that.' She glanced towards Miss Tilson. 'Where did she find that gown? Did it conveniently survive the shipwreck?'

'Ask her,' he shot back. '*She* will tell the truth.'

Lady Agnes had been cruel to not tell Miss Tilson that Sir Orin would be among the guests. Worse, she'd lied about it.

Cruelty and lies. Two things Garret could not abide. He'd seen enough cruelty and was told enough lies while in the army. And now Lady Agnes seemed to have a strong capacity for both.

* * *

Garret's anger persisted throughout dinner. At least Lady Agnes was at the other end of the table, too far for him to converse with her. He talked politics and the army with Mr Howard, who was a Member of Parliament and had been a lieutenant colonel in the Irish 9th Garrison. He'd lost an eye in the Helder Expedition. He also spoke with Reverend and Mrs Elliman. Elliman had been the vicar when Garret was a boy and the man cared passionately for his parishioners. He and Squire Lloyd knew all the news and gossip in the local area.

In the middle of the table Sir Orin was busy entertaining the ladies, making conquests of Mrs Wordsworth, Mrs Lloyd, Mrs Elliman, even Lady Agnes's aunt Theodora. Mrs Howard looked at him with some scepticism.

Squire Lloyd leaned over to Garret. 'Who is this Sir Orin?'

He frowned. 'Someone Lady Agnes wished to invite.'

Garret watched Miss Tilson, who seemed to converse comfortably with Mr Wordsworth and the curate, who was clearly smitten. She held herself regally and confidently.

She was full of surprises and that intrigued and

captivated him. He wished he could get her aside and tell her how beautiful she looked.

But he could not speak to her that way.

If it were not for Sir Orin and Lady Agnes, Rebecca might have enjoyed herself. She was beyond thrilled to actually meet the poet Wordsworth and his dear wife who so clearly worshipped him. Mrs Howard was another interesting person. Shrewd, but kind, the sort of lady who would make a formidable friend.

Rebecca was very aware of Sir Orin's eyes upon her and aware of a seething animosity underneath Lady Agnes's sugary exterior. It was painful to think of Lord Brookmore being fooled by her sweet facade. Rebecca was certain Lady Agnes's aim had been to hurt her. She'd succeeded, but Rebecca had no intention of letting her know.

'Miss Tilson,' Lady Agnes asked in her sweet tone. 'Wherever did you get that dress? It is so lovely.'

Rebecca smiled at her. 'Did you ever read "Cinderella"?' It was one of the tales in the book by the Brothers Grimm that she found in the schoolroom.

'Is that a novel?' Lady Agnes smirked. 'I am not overly fond of novels. I prefer reading something more edifying.'

'Very true,' agreed her companion, her aunt Theodora.

'Not a novel,' Rebecca retorted. 'A tale for children. Edifying, in that it instructs how kindness is eventually rewarded. Cinderella received her gown for a ball from some helpful doves.'

'Your dress came from doves?' Lady Agnes laughed derisively.

'Two little doves,' Rebecca responded, daring a quick glance towards Lord Brookmore.

'A tale for children,' Lady Agnes repeated. 'Was that one of your lessons?'

'A lesson about kindness, yes,' Rebecca retorted.

Lady Agnes addressed the dinner guests, 'Miss Tilson has a unique way of teaching. One wonders if she ever attended school.' She turned to Rebecca. 'Where did you attend school, Miss Tilson?'

Such a question risked exposure. She knew very little about Claire's schooling. 'A boarding school in Bristol.'

'Its name?' Lady Agnes pushed.

'You would not have heard of it,' Rebecca said. 'It was a school for gentry and merchants' daughters and the like.'

Lady Agnes glanced at the other ladies. 'Her lessons are conducted mostly out of doors.'

Rebecca cringed inside, but she refused to let Lady Agnes see her discomfort.

'Rousseau,' Mrs Howard piped up. 'She is following Rousseau. Are you not, Miss Tilson?'

Rebecca remembered learning about Rousseau at school, but all she could recall was that he was a French philosopher who had something to do with the French Revolution.

'It is odd,' Sir Orin broke in. 'When Miss Tilson was in my employ, she kept my children in the schoolroom most of the day.'

'Miss Tilson worked for you?' Mrs Elliman asked, giving Sir Orin an opportunity to wax poetic over her excellence as a governess.

Lord Brookmore looked grim during this discourse.

Rebecca wanted the attention off her. She turned to the curate, who was perhaps as young as she, and asked him questions. Where he was from. Where he attended university. When he became ordained. She asked him if he read poetry in university and whether he had read any of Mr Wordsworth's poems. This led to a discussion with Wordsworth about the inspiration of his poems, which started him talking about his love for the Lake District, a topic that was joined by the rest of the table, barring Sir Orin, Lady Agnes and Aunt Theodora.

* * *

Soon the dinner was over and the ladies retired to the drawing room again. Lady Agnes gathered all the women around her and poured tea for them. Rebecca remained on the periphery, by Lady Agnes's design, she supposed, although Mrs Howard and Mrs Wordsworth sent friendly smiles her way.

After a time, Lady Agnes shivered. 'It is chilly in here, is it not?'

The other ladies professed to be comfortable.

Lady Agnes persisted, though. 'Aunt, are you chilly? Do you need your shawl?'

Her aunt looked uncertain at first at how to respond. 'I am a bit chilly,' she finally said.

Lady Agnes turned to Rebecca. 'Miss Tilson, be a dear and fetch Aunt Theodora's shawl from her room, would you please?'

Rebecca's cheeks burned. This certainly was a pointed insult, no matter the sugary language in which it was made. There was a footman in the room—a servant—whose job it was to see to such tasks.

But she was not going to nip at Lady Agnes's bait. 'Certainly, my lady.' She stood and walked out of the room, passing the footman who gave her a surprised look.

There was another footman attending the hall. She

could have asked him to do the task, but it seemed easier merely to do as Lady Agnes asked. She'd already brought more attention towards herself than she'd desired by her Cinderella story. Lady Agnes had not been pleased.

Rebecca entered the corridor to the first-floor bedchambers and a man's hand seized her arm. Sir Orin.

'Claire,' he murmured, close to her ear.

She pulled away. 'Unhand me, sir.'

He moved closer to her, his eyes sweeping her body. 'You look so different, Claire. Even more beautiful than before. I am quite enamoured.'

She raised a hand to fend him off. 'Do not speak to me.'

He made a quick move and pinned her against the wall, holding her shoulders. 'Do you not see, Claire, my darling. Do you not see what I want? What I yearned for? What I can finally possess?'

Claire, I know now what you fled, Rebecca said silently.

She glared at him. 'Take your hands off me.'

He dropped his hands, but her back was still against the wall. She could not move away from him. 'If you think this is the way to hire a governess, you are very mistaken, sir.'

'A governess?' His eyes grew dark as he perused

her again. 'I do not want you back as a governess. I want you for my wife.'

'No!' It was unthinkable. 'How can you ask? Your wife is hardly cold in her grave.'

His eyes flickered with a cold emotion. 'She was the one thing in our way.'

At that moment he looked dangerous enough to have caused his wife's death.

She took a careful breath. 'I will never marry you, sir. Now, allow me to continue on my errand for Lady Agnes. She will be wondering where I am.'

'Lady Agnes will understand,' he said with a knowing smile.

She understood why Lady Agnes had sent her on an errand. Lady Agnes had arranged this meeting.

'Release me now!' Rebecca demanded.

He put his hands on her again.

The door opened and he backed away from her.

Lord Brookmore stepped into the hall. 'Miss Tilson? Lady Agnes's aunt needs her shawl.'

Lord Brookmore rescued her. 'Yes, my lord.'

Sir Orin moved out of her way. She hurried to the elderly woman's room, trusting in the fact that Lord Brookmore would make certain Sir Orin would not accost her again.

Chapter Seventeen

Sir Orin gave Garret an angry look. 'That was a private conversation, Lord Brookmore. You interrupted it.'

Garret returned a steely gaze. 'When Miss Tilson returns I will ask her if she wishes a private conversation with you. If she does, I will summon you. Until then return to the drawing room or take your leave.'

Sir Orin huffed, but he turned on his heel and walked through the doorway to the hall. Garret waited and a few minutes later Miss Tilson appeared carrying the shawl Lady Agnes's aunt did not need.

'Thank you,' she said when she reached him. 'I could not get away from him.'

'I take it you did not desire that encounter?' Lady Agnes had insisted she would welcome it.

'Indeed not!' she exclaimed. 'He asked me to

marry him. His wife could not be dead more than a few weeks and he asked me to marry him.'

'His suit is unwelcome?' Garret asked.

'How can you ask me that, Lord Brookmore?' she said crisply. 'Of course his suit is unwelcome. I do not want anything to do with him.'

Garret felt relieved. He wanted her to stay. For his nieces.

'I am sorry. I fear Lady Agnes arranged that encounter.'

Their gazed locked. He felt that pull of attraction he always felt when near her. He had nothing but admiration for her this night. From her appearance to her deft handling of the dinner-table conversation to her quiet dignity in the face of Agnes's mistreatment. Agnes had tried to cow her, but Miss Tilson had kept her head high.

She glanced away and lifted the shawl in her arms. 'I should bring this to Lady Agnes's aunt.'

He smiled wryly. 'I should return, as well. I am supposed to be the host of this party.'

They walked side by side to the door.

Garret put his hand on the door handle. 'I suppose the two doves who brought you the dress were named Pamela and Ellen.'

She grinned. 'They just happen to be.' Her expression sobered. 'They were very sweet to me.'

He softened his voice. 'You look lovely, Miss Tilson.'

Two spots of pink tinged her cheeks. 'Thank you,' she murmured.

He began to open the door, but turned to ask her one more question. 'I do not suppose those two doves arranged your hair, as well?'

She lowered her gaze, but smiled. 'No, that was my doing. With Mary's help, of course.'

He nodded. 'You did well. It is very becoming.'

As he opened the door, she shot him a glance. 'I believe you will see plenty of curls tomorrow morning at breakfast, my lord.'

He stepped aside and held the door for her. She walked briskly to the drawing room. He followed more slowly.

He reached the door to the drawing room as she handed the shawl to Lady Agnes's aunt.

'I am sorry I took so long,' she told the elderly woman. 'I was detained.'

The poised, well-spoken woman she had become returned as she conversed with Mr and Mrs Howard.

Garret walked over to Lady Agnes who was momentarily alone. 'That was not well done of you, Lady Agnes.' He turned away from her to converse with the Ellimans and the Wordsworths. Sir Orin stood in a corner of the room, consuming a brandy and alternately glaring at Garret and watching Miss Tilson.

After what seemed like an interminable period of time, the guests began to say goodnight. The Howards were the first to leave, having a carriage ride of at least two hours before they reached Levens Hall. Miss Tilson slipped away when they were saying their goodbyes, as did Lady Agnes's aunt.

Garret had made his carriages available for the other guests—except for Sir Orin, that was. He did not care how the devil the man made it back to Ambleside.

When they were finally all in their carriages and riding away, the lamps on the carriages danced down the lane to the gate.

Garret turned to Lady Agnes, who gave him a bright smile. 'That was a success, do you not think?'

'In spite of your machinations, do you mean?' He spoke severely.

Her eyes widened in all innocence. 'I do not know what you mean.'

'Manipulating that meeting between Sir Orin and Miss Tilson.'

She looked wounded. 'I told you, I merely was trying to help them. Sir Orin managed to tell me it did not go well. I do hope that was not because of you interrupting them.'

'Stop any assistance to Sir Orin. Miss Tilson does not welcome his suit. I expect you to respect that.'

'She doesn't?' Lady Agnes sounded surprised, but at this point Garret did not believe anything she said. 'I am astonished. It is a better match than a governess could expect. She is a fool not to secure him while she can.'

'You are to respect her decision and stop your interference. I mean that.' He added, 'And I will not have you belittle those who are lower status than you. Not in this house.'

Her mouth dropped. 'When did I ever do that?'

He looked her in the eye. 'You called attention to Miss Tilson's position, not once but twice in a manner that was belittling.'

She blinked. 'I would never do that. Never. If she took it that way, I am very sorry.' She stepped closer to him and threaded her arm through his, clasping his arm so that her body touched his. 'I will apologise to her tomorrow. I promise.'

'No,' he said. 'Leave it. Leave her to her duties.'

'Are you sure?' She batted her eyelashes at him. 'I am desolated that she believes I belittled her.'

'She has not said so. I say so.' He stared into her fluttering eyelashes. 'Leave her alone.'

She squeezed his arm. 'Whatever you wish, Brookmore, dear.'

Agnes knew Brookmore did not want to walk her to her bedchamber, but by taking his arm, she ensured he would. At the door, though, she was forced to let go of him.

He stepped away quickly, saying only a curt, 'Goodnight.'

She entered the room, kicked off her shoes and threw them against the wall with a cry of frustration.

Her maid appeared from the dressing room. 'Shall I help you prepare for bed, m'lady?' the maid asked.

'Yes. Be quick about it,' she snapped. 'I am very tired.'

When she was finally ready for bed, though, she could not settle down. She threw things around the room. Nothing that would break. Her clothing mostly. Things her maid would have to tidy up in the morning. She let herself have a proper tantrum until she flung herself on the bed.

Everything had gone wrong. Lord Brookmore was angry with her and if she did not do something to fix it, he might cry off. Think of the shame of that!

She sat up. It would never happen. She would cry

off first and tell some horrible tale of how wicked he was. Or worse, how very provincial.

She pounded the pillow. No! She would not give up so easily. He needed her. She was the perfect wife for him. Everyone said so.

That governess was the problem. Agnes knew it from the moment Miss Tilson entered the drawing room and Brookmore could not stop looking at her.

If Agnes had thought Miss Tilson could dress like she had vouchers for Almack's, she might never have included her in the dinner party. She'd hoped only that the dinner would give Sir Orin an opportunity to propose to the governess. How could Agnes know that Miss Tilson would refuse?

She was a fool. Sir Orin was a baronet. She was a nobody.

Unless she was holding out for a viscount. Which, of course, she was.

Brookmore would not be so foolish to consider marriage to a governess with no name and no position in society. A dalliance with her, perhaps, but not marriage.

At this point, though, if he fancied himself besotted with the creature, he might very well call off the wedding.

Agnes certainly would not stand for that.

* * *

The next morning when Garret entered the Tower Room to share breakfast with Miss Tilson and his nieces, he was greeted with two smiling faces framed with bouncing curls. Even Miss Tilson's curls remained.

When the children's maid walked in for a moment, Garret laughed out loud. She also sported some curls.

'All four of you?' He grinned. 'I've never seen so many pretty curls in all my life.'

Pamela and Ellen giggled.

'Miss Tilson says there is another way to make curls without using the *papillote*.' Ellen frowned. 'I didn't like the *papillote*.'

'So we might come to breakfast with curls every morning,' Pamela added.

He pulled on one of Pamela's curls and watched it bounce back into a spiral. 'You are very pretty with or without them.'

He loved these little girls and was as proud of them as if he'd sired them. They'd emerged from a cloud of grief and found their way back to the sun.

Thanks to Miss Tilson.

They all sat down to bowls of porridge and cups of tea. It was a breakfast Garret relished, only realising during this time how it evoked those more carefree days of childhood. In a way he'd thrived on his father's neglect. He'd been free to explore every part of the estate, learning of the work by doing it and learning of the people by working beside them.

'Was your dinner party enjoyable, Uncle?' Pamela asked, sounding like a young lady making conversation.

He glanced towards Miss Tilson who had raised her teacup to her lips.

'There were many fine moments,' he said. 'Although I am certain your mother and father had parties that were much more successful.'

'Mama loved parties.' Pamela sighed.

'Did you like the party, Miss Tilson?' Ellen asked.

'Much of it,' she said, brushing her hand through Ellen's curls. 'I was asked about my dress and I told them it was like Cinderella—do you remember us reading "Cinderella" in the fairy tale book?'

Ellen nodded.

'I told them two doves brought me the dress!' She grinned at the girls.

Pamela's eyes grew wide. 'Did they believe you?'

She darted a glance towards Ellen and winked at Pamela. 'I dare say they did. And did you know there was a famous poet who came to the party? William Wordsworth. He lives near Ambleside in a fine house called Rydal Mount.'

Pamela appeared very impressed. 'May we read the poems he wrote?'

Garret spoke. 'I believe there are some volumes of his poems in the library. You are welcome to them.' He looked directly at Miss Tilson. 'You are welcome to use the library as freely as you wish. I hope you knew that.'

She glanced at both the girls. 'Thank your uncle.'

'Thank you, Uncle Garret,' they said in unison.

Ellen wiggled in her seat. 'Tell us more about the party.'

Miss Tilson told the girls about the other ladies' dresses and how they wore their hair. She told them what food was served and described the cakes and tarts and fruit that were eaten at dessert. She made no mention of how mistreated she'd been by Lady Agnes, how trapped she'd been by Sir Orin, but, of course, she wouldn't mention such things to the children.

Garret saw so clearly how his nieces adored her and how caring she was of them, making them a part of the dinner party, fussing over them by curling their hair, making an exciting story out of a rather dismal gathering. She seemed more like a loving mother than a governess, cuddling them and making them feel important and special. He was glad of it.

When they finished eating Mary came in to stack

up the dishes and place them on a tray for one of the kitchen maids to collect. She left again.

'What now, Miss Tilson?' Ellen asked.

'May we go see the ponies?' Pamela asked. 'May we ride?' Pamela was riding on her own, but only in the paddock.

Before Miss Tilson could answer, Garret said, 'Wait in the schoolroom for Miss Tilson. I wish to speak with her a moment.'

The girls ran out of the room and their footsteps clattered down the hallway to the schoolroom.

Now that he was alone with Miss Tilson, Garret did not know what to say.

She waited, a wary look on her face.

He finally asked her, 'How do you fare?'

She paused for a moment before answering. 'I am well enough.'

'I mean after last night,' he clarified.

She answered in a careful tone. 'I was unharmed.'

She stood in a ray of sunlight streaming through the Tower Room windows, making the curls in her hair gleam and her hazel eyes sparkle. He did not dare take a step closer to her for fear he'd not be able to keep from wrapping his arms around her.

'I apologise for it.' He added, 'For Lady Agnes. She disappointed me greatly last night.'

Miss Tilson lowered her eyes. 'Please do not discuss Lady Agnes with me.'

Garret went on, though. 'I fear I have made a grave error.'

She lifted a hand. 'Say no more, Lord Brookmore.'

But he wanted to explain. To her, of all people. 'I was convinced she was the sort of woman my brother would have chosen and in many ways she was the perfect wife for a viscount.'

She looked into his eyes, then. 'From what the children say to me, their mother was nothing at all like Lady Agnes and you are twice the Viscount your brother could be.' She glanced down quickly. 'I really should see to the children.'

She turned and left.

Garret made his way down the stairs. His morning ride had not settled the restlessness inside him, but he could think of nothing at the farm to engage him this day. Perhaps he should go to the quarry and see how the workers fared there. Or he could walk to the workers' cottages and see how the repairs were coming along. Check on the crops.

He entered the hall.

From a corner, Lady Agnes rose from a sofa. 'Brookmore! There you are. I waited in hopes of seeing you.'

He nodded curtly. 'Lady Agnes. You are up early.' The last person he wished to see this morning.

'I could not sleep a wink.' She walked towards him. 'I was desolated that you felt I had been… demeaning last night. I want to make it up to you and especially to Miss Tilson. What can I do? Shall I ask her to share dinner with us? Some governesses do eat with the family, you know.'

And further expose Miss Tilson to her sugary venom? Never.

'Leave it. Do nothing. I told you this last night.' He walked towards the door. The footman attending the hall brought his hat, gloves and topcoat. 'Was there anything else? I have much to do.' He just was not certain what it was.

She lowered her head. 'You are still angry with me and I cannot blame you. This is not the time to ask you…' Her voice trailed off.

The footman helped him on with his topcoat. 'Ask me what?'

'If we should announce the banns here.' She quickly added, 'I would not mention this, but Mr Elliman did ask me last night.' She smiled wanly. 'It is a lovely idea, is it not? Announcing the banns in the church of your childhood.'

Not a lovely idea at all. Announcing the banns

felt like hammering another nail in his coffin. 'No banns,' he said before walking out the door.

Lady Agnes fumed as she watched Brookmore stride out of the house. All her careful plans were fraying into useless strings. She spun on her heel and crossed the hall to the stairs.

Aunt Theodora was in her room eating her breakfast. 'Do eat, Agnes,' the elderly lady said. 'You need your nourishment.'

Agnes slumped into a chair. 'He will barely speak to me.'

'Now, dear, is it that bad?' Her aunt patted her hand.

Agnes pulled her hand away and threw the napkin on to the floor. 'It is that bad. I need a plan, something to turn his affections back to me.' She crossed her arms over her chest. 'I need to be rid of that governess.'

'Yes, dear,' her aunt said meekly.

Chapter Eighteen

Three days went by and Brookmore House seemed to settle into its former routine. Garret no longer attempted to speak about Lady Agnes to Miss Tilson, and, since she was only in his company at breakfast and rarely otherwise, he hardly spoke to her at all.

He'd spent much of his time trying to consider what to do about Lady Agnes. She'd reverted to the sweet, charming woman he'd known in London, never setting a foot out of place, correct and considerate.

He no longer believed any of it.

One evening he'd stared at her while she played the pianoforte, wondering what it would be like to have children with her. Good God, he feared they would turn out as manoeuvring and manipulating and cruel as she was.

She carefully avoided any mention of banns or marriage, which was good, although he'd soon have to have a frank talk with her. Each day more convinced him he could never marry her.

This morning Garret rode as usual, hoping, as usual, that he would encounter Miss Tilson. He knew she was riding because her favourite horse, Lily, was not in the stable. He scanned the countryside, hoping to catch sight of her.

To his right, he saw movement and stopped to see if it was her. It was a horse, but a riderless one. He rode towards the animal and, when close enough, saw it was Lily, Miss Tilson's horse. He managed to grab the horse's reins and calm the animal.

'Where is she, Lily? Lead me to her?' Garret feared she'd been thrown from the horse and lay injured.

He'd scour every inch of this land to find her, if necessary.

Lily turned and retraced her tracks. When they reached the crest of a hill, he spotted another riderless horse, a striking white steed, and quickened his pace. Both his horse Skiddaw and hers nickered anxiously. Lily pawed the ground.

Garret scanned the area and found her. Sir Orin pinned her against a tree.

'Damned man,' he said beneath his breath.

He galloped towards them, slowing enough to jump off and seize Sir Orin by his collar and pull him off her. Sir Orin cried out and swung around to strike him, but Garret blocked his fist and threw him to the ground. Sir Orin leapt up at Garret and both men fell, rolling on the ground. Sir Orin fought like a man possessed, but Garret had battled far worse. He rose to his feet, backed off and waited for Sir Orin's next attack.

Sir Orin stood and readied himself to rush at Garret again, but suddenly Miss Tilson appeared from behind him. She swung a large stick at Sir Orin and struck him across the back. He staggered and Garret seized the opportunity to grab him in a choke hold, immobilising him.

'Shall I finish you?' Garret could easily snap his neck. 'I've killed before.'

'No!' rasped Sir Orin. 'No.'

'Wait!' Miss Tilson cried.

Garret did not heed her.

'Go away,' he growled to Sir Orin, in his most ferocious soldier voice. 'Go back to Ireland. Never show your face here again. Or else.' He squeezed harder. 'Do I make myself clear?'

Sir Orin made choking sounds.

'Lord Brookmore, do not kill him,' Miss Tilson said in an even tone.

But Garret knew what he was about.

'Do I make myself clear?' Garret raised his voice and tightened his grip.

Sir Orin's legs buckled under him.

Garret loosened his hold.

'Yes. Yes,' Sir Orin managed to gasp. 'Give my word.'

Garret released him and the man fell down on his knees, taking in loud gulps of air. Garret pulled him to his feet and shoved him towards the white horse he assumed Sir Orin had ridden.

Garret turned to Miss Tilson, wanting to touch her. 'Did he hurt you?' Garret thought he might kill Sir Orin if he had.

'No.' She rubbed her upper arms. 'At least nothing to signify.'

Her horse came up and nuzzled her.

'Lily!' She pressed her forehead against the horse's neck.

Garret walked towards Sir Orin, who was trying to mount his horse. The horse edged away from him.

Garret held the horse's head. 'I meant what I said, Sir Orin. Leave this area and never contact Miss Tilson again. Or I'll finish what I started.'

Sir Orin finally reached the saddle. 'You do not understand.' His voice rasped. 'She was not like this in Ireland.'

'No matter. She has told you to go away. That is all you need to know.' Garret turned the horse in the opposite direction of his farm and tapped its rump.

The horse bounded away, Sir Orin hanging on.

Garret returned to Miss Tilson. 'Are you feeling ready to ride back? We can wait, if you are not.'

'I need a minute.' Her whole body trembled.

Garret enfolded her in his arms. 'You are safe now. He will not bother you again.'

He was in no hurry to release her. To hold her again filled an emptiness he'd possessed since the night he'd told her about his betrothal, the night he'd almost made love to her.

'He was waiting for me,' she said, her voice shaking. 'The horse was supposed to be a gift. He wanted me to ride to Holyhead with him.' She took a breath. 'When I refused, he pulled me off Lily and—and pinned me against that tree. I—I was afraid he would—'

She couldn't finish, but Garret knew what she would have said. Had he known this, he might have indeed killed the man.

'He won't hurt you now, I promise,' Garret murmured.

He'd warn the estate workers and servants about Sir Orin and make certain he never again came near her. He'd check in the village and ensure Sir Orin left.

Garret felt her relax. She took in a deep breath and he released her.

He walked her over to Lily and boosted her into the saddle. Touching her had heightened his senses. If only he could hold on to her for ever...

Garret whistled for Skiddaw, who trotted over immediately. He mounted and he and Miss Tilson started towards the farm.

Garret gestured towards her horse. 'Lily led me to you, you know.'

'She did?' She leaned forward and gave the horse an affectionate pat. She turned back to Garret. 'I wondered how you found me. You have rescued me over and over, Lord Brookmore. How can I ever thank you?'

Those words again. Did she remember those were the words she spoke before they kissed that first time? And nearly the same words before he'd almost ravished her? And all he wanted now was to keep her safe and never allow any harm to come to her.

Had Lady Agnes sensed his attraction to Miss Tilson? He'd certainly tried very hard not to act upon his feelings, nor show them to anyone else. But had Lady Agnes somehow seen through these efforts? It would explain why she'd gone out of her way to assist Sir Orin in his pursuit of Miss Tilson. But nothing excused Lady Agnes's belittling Miss Tilson in front of guests.

Lady Agnes had certainly hidden her true character when he'd met her. In a way he was fortunate to have discovered this mean spiritedness before marrying her.

Rebecca was grateful that Lord Brookmore said little on their ride back to the stables. She needed the time to sort out this experience and to shed it from her once and for all. Brookmore's strength and violence had alarmed and thrilled her. He was the only man of her acquaintance who would have been willing to fight to protect her, to even kill to protect her.

The thing was, he would have been equally as willing to protect, to kill, for any person on his estate, for any person in jeopardy from one more powerful.

She glanced at him, so tall and comfortable in the saddle. She tried to imagine him in his red coat and shako, charging into a battle, slashing with his sabre, firing his pistol, fighting with fists like he'd done with Sir Orin. Her insides fluttered at the thought.

A flash of memory intruded, a memory of Sir Orin pressing his hand against her breast, of him jutting his leg between hers and rubbing it against her most private place. She shuddered. Sir Orin had been about to take what Rebecca so freely wished to give to Lord Brookmore. Rebecca was so very grateful to Lord Brookmore for arriving when he did.

Her heart filled with love for him.

And filled with pain.

He could not be hers. The most she could hope for was that he would not be Lady Agnes's.

As they neared the stables, they passed some of his workers ready to start a day of toil. Each worker doffed his hat and greeted Lord Brookmore with a cheerful voice. Even the stablemen, to whom Lord Brookmore and Rebecca handed over their horses, looked pleased to see him and eager to tend to his horse.

They walked out of the stable together.

'G'morning, m'lord.' Another worker tipped his hat. 'Miss.'

She wondered how his list of repairs and improvements was faring. What a caring thing it was to ask what his workers and his tenants needed from him. When had she ever heard of a gentleman so mindful?

Another reason to love him.

They neared the house.

'Please tell no one what happened today,' she asked him. She could not bear to speak of it to anyone or even to endure their sympathetic looks.

'Lady Agnes needs to know.' He glanced at her. 'She needs to know what sort of man she foisted on you. I would like to tell her.'

'Very well,' Rebecca conceded. 'But only Lady Agnes.' She frowned. 'You might tell her that Sir

Orin may be even more dangerous than he showed today. His wife died so conveniently I cannot help but be suspicious.'

He paused, still holding her gaze. 'When did she die?'

It must have been after Claire left Ireland. Sir Orin gave it as new information that Claire did not know.

'I do not know precisely, but very recently or so Sir Orin says,' she responded. 'The timing of it seems very convenient for him and he is not at all sad about her death.'

'A dangerous man indeed.'

They walked across the lawn behind the house.

A wave of fear washed over her. 'Will he leave here like you asked?'

His expression turned dark and fierce. 'I will make certain he leaves.'

Her fear receded as quickly as it had come. Lord Brookmore would protect her.

'What a stupid man Sir Orin is.' She shook her head.

'In what way?' he asked.

She'd meant it rhetorically, but she tried to piece together her thoughts. 'He could not have behaved more abominably. How did he think that would appeal?' Why had Sir Orin not believed her when she spurned him the night of the dinner party? Why had he thought assaulting her would further his cause?

They reached the garden gate that led to the back entrance to the house.

'Indeed,' Lord Brookmore responded. 'Surely he knew that was not the way to gain your affections.'

That feeling of connection with him returned, but Rebecca steeled herself against such feelings. She'd become accustomed to staying distant from him, just as she'd done with her father, but since he'd acted as her protector that night of the dinner party, her resolve had broken and she yearned for that closeness they'd briefly shared.

He went on. 'For Sir Orin to come all the way from Ireland claiming a wish to marry you, then behaving like this… It makes little sense.'

It made no sense to Rebecca.

Lord Brookmore opened the gate. 'What happened in Ireland before you left?'

She went cold. 'What do you mean?'

'I mean, there must have been something that happened between you and Sir Orin, something that led to this. His behaviour must have risen from something.' He touched her arm, stopping her from proceeding through the gate. 'Did he assault you there?'

She glanced up into his concerned eyes. Her heart pounded. How was she to answer such a direct question? Should she make up a story? Lie to him directly, lie to this man who had just rescued her once again?'

She could not do it.

'Did he assault you when you were in his employ?' he asked again, his voice more insistent.

She held her gaze steady. 'I do not know.'

He released her arm and stepped back. 'What do you mean you do not know?'

She passed through the gate, but turned to face him again. 'I mean, I do not know what happened in Ireland.'

His expression turned sceptical. 'Miss Tilson, you must know what happened. You were there.'

Rebecca released a pent-up breath. 'Come with me.'

She led him to a secluded spot near the willow labyrinth. There was a bench there, but she had no wish to be seated.

'Well?' He crossed his arms over his chest, waiting for her explanation.

She averted her gaze. 'It is a long story. One, I suspect, you will not like hearing.' She drew in a deep breath. 'I was never there.'

'Never where?' He looked confused.

'I was never in Sir Orin's house. I never cared for his children. I never knew his wife.' She breathed again and made herself look him in the eye. 'I am an imposter, Lord Brookmore. I am not Claire Tilson.'

'Not Claire Tilson?' His confusion turned to a flinty anticipation. 'You had better explain.'

'I met Claire on the packet boat. We looked exactly alike—' She swallowed. 'Like twins, but we have no family in common—'

'Say no more.' He held up a hand. 'You expect me to believe you happened to meet a woman, unrelated to you, who looked exactly like you?'

'Yes. That is it,' she responded. 'Claire Tilson looked exactly like me. So much so even the maid sent with me could not tell us apart.'

Nolan! Rebecca had not thought of the maid for weeks. Now she again saw the woman rolling over in her bed, refusing to leave the ship with her.

'Miss Tilson was lost in the shipwreck?' His voice brought her back to the present.

Rebecca's throat became raw as the events of the shipwreck rushed back to her. 'When the storm came, she was washed into the sea. She—she died, but I survived. But everyone thought it was me who died and that I was Claire—' She swallowed. 'Then you came and thought I was Claire. So I decided to be her.'

'You decided to deceive me, you mean.' Colour rose in his face. 'Who are you, then?'

Her hands trembled. 'I am Lady Rebecca Pierce. My brother is the Earl of Keneagle.'

He looked sceptical. 'Are you? Why would the sister of an earl change places with a governess?'

'I was headed for London and an unwanted marriage.' She again felt Lord Stonecroft's appraising eye and his wet, dough-like lips. 'My brother made it impossible for me to refuse this marriage. I decided being a governess would be preferable.'

'Being a governess was preferable to marrying?' He scoffed. 'Who was the man? Some kind of monster?'

'Lord Stonecroft,' she said.

'Stonecroft?' he cried. 'I have met Stonecroft. Being a governess was preferable to marriage with him?'

She averted her gaze. 'It was. It still is. And you can probably guess that I know nothing of being a governess.'

His voice turned cold. 'Did you not consider that two children would be victims of that ignorance?'

She felt a shaft of pain pierce her heart. 'No, I did not consider it. When I chose to be Claire, I thought only of myself. But I did not know Pamela and Ellen then. How dear they would become—' She paused to fight back tears. 'I have tried my best for Pamela and Ellen. I would never do anything to deliberately hurt them.'

But he would not believe that.

'Depriving them of a real governess was not hurting them?'

She felt the shaft stab deeper. 'I admit they have not had proper lessons—'

He waved a hand. 'Never mind that. You are playing us all for fools, pretending to be what you are not. Making yourself into someone you are not. Using a dead woman's life because it was convenient for you.' He paced in front of her.

She lifted her chin. 'I did not perceive it as using Claire, but as living life for her.'

He stopped and leaned into her face. 'Do not try to vindicate yourself by pretending you did this for her. You did this for you.'

He might as well have slapped her, but she swallowed the pain—and her shame—and boldly met his eye. 'At the beginning, yes, I did it for me. But I did not celebrate Claire's death. She deserved to live so much more than I did.'

He kept on. 'Why? Did she have integrity? Would she have refused to masquerade as someone she was not?'

'Certainly.' Could he not see? Rebecca meant no one any harm, even if her decisions were self-serving. It wounded her that this man she so ad-mired—loved—would think the worst of her. 'While we are speaking of pretending to be someone one is not, what about you, Lord Brookmore?'

He blew out a breath. 'I am not pretending to be someone I am not.'

'Are you not?' she shot back. 'You've tried to be your brother or your father. You thought you had to be them to be a viscount. Where has that idea taken you, Lord Brookmore?' She did not give him a chance to respond. 'I will tell you where it has taken you. To a betrothal with Lady Agnes.'

His eyes flashed. 'See here, Miss T—!' He shook his head. 'What am I to call you? I do not even know.'

She held her head regally. 'Call me Lady Rebecca.'

'Lady Rebecca,' he spat out.

Her anger rose higher. 'At least I have always acted like myself. I have used Claire's name, but I have acted like Lady Rebecca. You must have acted like a shell of who you are when you pretended to be your brother, the Viscount. When you are you, you are a better viscount than your brother ever could have been.'

He glared at her. 'You did not know my brother.'

She glared back at him. 'I have learned of him from your nieces and have overheard your workers talking about him. They admire you, not him. Because you listened to them and acted on their behalf.'

He held up a hand again. 'Stop. Do not turn this discussion on to me. This is about your lies, your deception.'

She shot back. 'Yes. I have deceived you, but I have not lied to you.' What did it matter now? This time she told the truth and look what happened.

His eyes looked wounded. 'I am sick of people who are not what they seem. I thought you were different.'

She lowered her gaze. He was about to send her packing. Her pain returned. 'You will wish me to leave, I know, but may I beg for a little time? The children are just now coming out of their grief. It would be another loss for them, would it not?'

'You use them as an excuse,' he accused.

Was she? Perhaps he was right, but she felt shattered at the idea of losing Pamela and Ellen, as well as him.

His voice remained hard. 'You will stay. I'll not have my nieces suffer another loss so soon. You will stay until I say it is time to find them another governess.'

Her spirits lifted, but only slightly.

'I will leave,' he said. 'I'll go back to London. Or go to Brighton. I dare say Lady Agnes will be happy to leave here.'

'No, don't leave!' she cried, then bit her lip. He belonged to this place. He did not belong with Lady Agnes.

'No more discussion,' he said. 'I am going to the house. You do what you wish.'

What she wished? When had she ever received what she wished?

Chapter Nineteen

Garret strode away, a kaleidoscope of emotions spinning inside him.

Was no one honest? Did no one reveal their true character or was everyone hiding who they were?

He was furious at being deceived by her, by being played for a fool. He'd been attracted to a fiction, not a real person. She was no better than Lady Agnes. Or even Sir Orin.

Or even himself.

It angered him, what she'd said about him.

Because it was true.

He had tried to be a viscount like his father and brother, until he discovered that his brother had been a terrible viscount and a worse father. Then he'd tried to make it up to everyone. To his workers, his servants, his nieces. He couldn't leave. Not with everything half-done.

Pamela and Ellen were what mattered most and,

after them, the estate and its people. Not his wounded feelings. Not even Miss Tilson's—Lady Rebecca's—deception. Both he and Lady Rebecca must stay and he must endure it.

He entered the house and climbed the back stairs. As he reached the first-floor landing, Lady Agnes appeared. He stopped on the stairs, two steps below her.

'Brookmore!' she said brightly. 'I had hoped to catch you.'

'Lady Agnes.' He had no wish to speak to her. 'You are awake early.'

'With purpose, sir!' She smiled. 'I rose early so I might join you at breakfast with your nieces. I wish for them to know me, you see, and I simply can never catch them at another time of day. They are always outside, it seems. Who knows where?' She laughed.

She just could not resist a dig at…the governess… could she? Angry as Garret was at *Lady Rebecca*, he would not be so cruel as to inflict Lady Agnes on her. Not after what happened this morning. With Sir Orin. With him.

'Not today, Lady Agnes.' He put a foot on the step to rise past her.

She moved in front of him, her face nearly level with his. 'Is something amiss, Brookmore? You look so preoccupied. I do worry about you.'

He kept his foot on the step. 'This day has already been…disturbing. Now if you will pardon me…'

She did not move. 'I was watching for you from the window, so I would know when you were back in the house. I saw you enter the garden with Miss Tilson. Is she the source of your disturbance? Perhaps I can help.'

He'd already seen what her efforts to help could do. She'd brought Sir Orin back into his house. She'd encouraged his pursuit of… Lady Rebecca.

'I will tell you what happened, Lady Agnes.' He faced her on the landing, elbows akimbo. 'Your friend, Sir Orin, forced himself on Miss… Tilson while she was riding. Fortunately I was able to stop the assault before he did worse to her.'

'No.' She looked genuinely shocked. 'Sir Orin? But he was so besotted! Believe me, Brookmore, I had no idea he was such a man. He fooled me completely!'

She did not ask about Lady Rebecca's well-being, Garret noted.

'I have sent the man packing. I expect him gone, but if he shows up here, he is not to be admitted to the house and he is not to come near Miss Tilson.'

'Oh, my goodness, of course not,' she agreed.

He rose to the landing and she did not stop him this time.

He started to pass her, then turned. 'Do not speak

of the assault to anyone. Miss Tilson does not wish it to be known.' He looked her directly in the eye. 'Do you understand? Speak of it to no one. I mean this, Lady Agnes.'

'Why, Brookmore, I would never pass on such gossip.' She blinked in all innocence.

Not unless it suited her, he thought.

Garret continued up the stairs.

Garret's valet had the good sense to remain quiet as he helped him change into other clothes. He would be only a few minutes late for breakfast with his nieces.

He thought about skipping breakfast, not wishing to see the lady imposter so soon.

Lady Rebecca.

The name suited her, did it not? She was more of a lady than a governess, more outspoken, more independent, more...regal. She was never a governess employing the ideas of Rousseau, as Mrs Howard had suggested; she was the daughter of an earl playing at being a governess.

He left his room, determined to stop thinking of her. To wipe his mind of all that had happened and behave as his nieces would have been accustomed. As unsettled as he was, he did not wish for anything to disturb Pamela and Ellen.

Lady Rebecca had better feel the same.

He walked down the hallway and entered the Tower Room.

'You are late!' Ellen cried.

The two girls were seated at the table, but were alone in the room. The bowls of porridge were at each place at the table and the tea, milk and some other fare were set in the middle.

Would Lady Rebecca not show?

'Pamela showed me on the clock,' Ellen went on. 'You are late and so is Miss Tilson.'

He walked over to each of them and kissed them on their heads. 'Some mornings are like that.' He took his usual seat. 'Shall we begin eating before the porridge gets cold?'

Pamela shook her head. 'We should be polite and wait for Miss Tilson.'

But she might not come.

'You are right.' He pointed to the clock. 'We will wait five more minutes, but then we must start eating.'

Ellen got out of her chair and pulled it over to the mantel, climbing atop it so she could see the clock. 'When is five minutes?'

Pamela answered her. 'When the big hand is on the nine.'

Ellen climbed down and pulled her chair back to the table.

The door opened and Lady Rebecca entered. Her face looked strained, but her bearing was tall. Unbowed.

'Miss Tilson!' Ellen cried happily. She bounded over to her governess and was enfolded in a hug.

Pamela was included in the embrace.

'Good morning, my little ladies,' Lady Rebecca said, although Garret could tell her cheerful tone was forced. 'I am so happy to see you this morning. And I am sorry I am late.'

Garret stood.

Lady Rebecca released the girls and shooed them towards their chairs. The girls sat adjacent to each other, which meant that Lady Rebecca was adjacent to Garret. At least they were not forced to face each other.

As Lady Rebecca took her chair, she glanced at Garret. 'Good morning, Lord Brookmore,' she said formally.

He inclined his head.

'What made you late?' Ellen asked her.

Lady Rebecca paused, probably to invent an excuse. She looked from one girl to the other. 'Remember how I go riding most mornings?'

They both nodded.

'I was detained, so I came back a little late.'

That was the truth, although with no details.

'Uncle Garret was late, too,' Ellen said.

He made himself smile at the child. 'I was detained, too.'

Pamela regarded them. 'You were detained together.'

He exchanged a glance with Lady Rebecca. 'That would make us both late, wouldn't it?'

She averted her gaze and poured the tea and spoke of the food while the children ate their porridge. Garret noticed that she ate only a few bites of hers. When the children were not looking her way, her smile faded.

He refused to feel compassion for her. She'd created this situation for herself. It was none of his doing. She'd deceived him and the girls. That was despicable, was it not?

He watched her hide the tension in the room— the tension between him and her—from Pamela and Ellen, by focusing on their thoughts, their wishes, their desired plans for the day. Her behaviour towards the children was completely kind and unchanged.

He remembered their first days eating breakfast together and those first evenings when he'd shared dinner with her. He remembered how they'd managed an ease between them, even after that emotional night when he'd nearly seduced her. By God, he was only a little more contemptible than Sir Orin, was he not?

He wished those early days could have lasted. He wished they would have been real.

'What would you like to do today?' she asked the girls.

Now he knew why she did not do the things he expected a governess to do. She was never one in the first place. What governess would ask the children what to do?

'May we ride our ponies?' Pamela asked.

Ellen looked less excited about this prospect, but she nodded her agreement.

'Very well,' Lady Rebecca said.

Her love of horses. That was genuine, Garret supposed. One could not disguise such skill and enthusiasm.

Ellen turned to him. 'Uncle Garret, will you come, too?'

He'd enjoyed the time he'd spent helping them learn to ride, but he could not be with her, not even with the children there. This breakfast was difficult enough.

'Not today, Ellen,' he said. 'I have estate business.'

She jumped out of her chair to come and hug him. 'We will miss you, Uncle Garret.'

He would miss this, too, even though some of it was not real.

Later that morning when Lady Agnes was certain Brookmore was otherwise occupied, she had her coachman drive her to Ambleside, to the Unicorn Inn.

She marched into the hall and demanded of the innkeeper, 'Find Sir Orin. I wish to speak with him privately in the drawing room.'

The innkeeper pulled on his forelock and bustled off to do her bidding. Lady Agnes swept into the drawing room, which was empty. A good thing because she would have sent anyone there packing. She was too agitated to sit. She paced the room.

Finally Sir Orin appeared, with a cut on his cheek, a large bruise forming under his eye and pouting lips.

'Lady Agnes,' he said unenthusiastically.

She walked right up to him, glaring. 'What an idiot you are, Sir Orin. You forced yourself on Miss Tilson? How could you be so stupid?'

'I was tired of her spurning me.' He rubbed his jaw. 'I purchased a beautiful horse for her. She would not even look at it. I tell you, she is so changed.' He glanced away. 'Had to sell the horse, too. Lost a bundle on him.'

She faced him. 'I only speak to you because I want to be rid of her and you are still my best chance. Do you still want her or not?'

'I want her,' he responded earnestly. 'But she will have nothing to do with me. I do not have the luxury of time to change her mind. Your fiancé made it clear I was to leave the area. I only await the mail coach which is expected in a couple of hours.'

She waved her fingers. 'We can work around Brookmore's edict.' She stared into his face. 'Are you willing to force her to leave with you? How far are you willing to go to achieve this desire of yours.'

'There is nothing I would not do.' The look in his eyes turned malevolent. 'I have already gone quite far.'

She liked a man who went after what he wanted, even if this one was not smart enough to achieve it on his own. 'We need a plan. We need some way to force her to come to you.'

He gestured for her to sit down. Her restlessness had abated now that she could focus on her desire— to have Miss Tilson gone. She lowered herself into one of the chairs and he sat across from her.

'What of Brookmore?' He touched the cut on his face. 'I suspect he will check to see I've gone.'

This part was easy. 'Ride the coach as far as Outgate, then disembark there. Then find a secluded cottage to rent. Somewhere apart from other people. Send me word of where you are.' She could not receive mail from him at Brookmore House. 'Send word here. I will arrange for my coachman to pick it up.'

'How am I to entice Claire there?' he asked. 'She will not want to come.'

Lady Agnes's mouth stretched into a smile. 'We must provide her with incentive.'

Lady Agnes's plan came to her quickly, but it was foolproof. Miss Tilson would come running to Sir Orin and Lady Agnes would be rid of her at last.

Then, she was convinced, Brookmore would turn to her once again and the marriage could take place very quickly.

The next few days brought disruption to the routine which had so recently made Rebecca restless. She rarely saw Lord Brookmore. He'd stopped sharing breakfast with her and the children, but not because of Rebecca. She'd heard through Mary that the crops were suffering from the unusual cold and that Lord Brookmore spent most of his time with the tenant farmers and his estate manager trying to figure out how to keep the people and livestock fed throughout the winter. They'd decided to purchase stores now in anticipation of hardship later. He and the manager would be gone for a couple of days to accomplish this task.

It was the first time he would be away from Rebecca since she woke to see him standing over her in Moelfre, after the shipwreck. He'd made a point to inform her that Sir Orin had left Ambleside in a mail coach bound for Liverpool, but still she felt rudderless without him.

When he'd spoken to her about Sir Orin's departure, he had been cold. She could not blame him. She'd deceived him and now she could see the real harm that came from that decision.

At least she could relax in her role as governess. It did not matter if she performed like a real governess or not. He knew she was not. She and the girls simply did whatever came into their minds. They learned writing and spelling by keeping their journals. They read the books in the schoolroom and Rebecca read to them books she found in Lord Brookmore's library. On a rainy day they explored the attic, finding many of the children's mother's things and some of their governess's things, prompting the girls to talk about both of them. Rebecca even started them on needlework, a skill at which she was only passable, but she knew enough to teach a nine- and seven-year-old.

And they rode the ponies.

Pamela and Ellen finally did ride enough to venture out of the paddock. Rebecca led them on Lily and the girls followed. One of the stablemen rode along for a little more security. Though it was unusually cold, it felt delightful to ride amongst the fells and waters, the mountains and lakes.

This day Rebecca and the girls were in the schoolroom practising their needlework. To Rebecca's surprise Lady Agnes came to the door.

'May I join you?' Lady Agnes asked, walking in before her question could be answered. She looked at what the girls were doing. 'Oh, needlework! I adore needlework.'

'Say good day to Lady Agnes, girls,' Rebecca told them. 'As I taught you.'

Pamela and Ellen got out of their chairs, faced Lady Agnes and curtsied. 'Good day, Lady Agnes,' they parroted.

'How charming!' Lady Agnes clapped her hands. 'Now show me your needlework. Are you making samplers?'

'We are merely practising stitches,' Rebecca said. 'Pamela is practising ten basic stitches and Ellen is practising the running stitch and the backstitch.'

Ellen lifted her embroidery hoop so that Lady Agnes could see her efforts.

Lady Agnes sat next to the little girl. 'Shall I show you how to do it?'

Ellen politely allowed Lady Agnes to criticise her childish efforts, making her start over again. Rebecca watched this performance and tried to guess why the woman had come to the schoolroom, when she'd never shown an interest in doing so.

When Ellen had her hoop and needle in hand again, Rebecca asked, 'Is there some purpose to your visit with us, Lady Agnes?'

Lady Agnes sighed. 'I am afraid I am missing dear Brookmore. My aunt naps and I am feeling quite lonely. I decided to see if I can make myself useful and become more acquainted with Brookmore's nieces.' She smiled at Rebecca. 'You do not mind?'

To be in her company, especially after all she'd said and done at the dinner party? 'Of course we do not mind,' Rebecca said.

Pamela, who sat so only Rebecca could see, rolled her eyes. Rebecca winked back.

What she could not figure was Lady Agnes's true reason for this visit.

Lady Agnes came back to the schoolroom the next day and the next and she invited Rebecca to join her and her aunt for dinner. Rebecca might have seen this behaviour as an attempt at friendliness, perhaps even some empathy for the assault Rebecca endured from Sir Orin, but often enough Lady Agnes said something unkind to or about someone, revealing her true nature. Her words were always spoken in the most amiable tone and her barbs were subtle, but Rebecca heard them. Lord Brookmore had not yet returned and perhaps Lady Agnes's cordiality was simply so she could tell him how good she'd been while he was away.

In any event, Rebecca suspected it would cease when Lord Brookmore returned.

This morning, Lady Agnes stopped Rebecca in the hallway outside the schoolroom where the girls were waiting after they all finished breakfast.

Lady Agnes pressed her fingers to her temple. 'May I ask a favour of you, Miss Tilson?'

'Very well.' Rebecca held her breath.

Lady Agnes attempted a pained smile. 'Would you ride into Ambleside and purchase a headache remedy from the apothecary? My head is pounding so I cannot go myself.'

'I have to attend to the children,' Rebecca responded.

'I will stay with them,' Lady Agnes said. 'If I sit my headache is not so bad.'

'Could your maid not go?' Errands for guests of the household were not the responsibility of the governess. What was Lady Agnes's true motive?

'She's attending to my aunt, who is feeling unwell today.' Agnes looked at her with slitted eyes. 'Please, Miss Tilson? I do so need your help. There is no one else I can ask. My coachman will drive you.'

'Then send your coachman on the errand!' Rebecca said.

Lady Agnes produced tears. 'I cannot ask him! The man is illiterate. I need someone who can discuss things with the apothecary. How do I know he will have the right powders? If he doesn't, I need someone with judgement to make a decision what to buy! Please, Miss Tilson!'

Rebecca was either being manipulated by an excellent actress or Lady Agnes truly had a terrible headache. In any event, the argument over whether she should go or not was likely to take longer than the errand itself. She could be back in an hour or so.

'Ambleside is not far. I can walk it faster than the horses could be hitched to a coach.'

'Then you will do it?' Lady Agnes's smile turned grateful. 'He could take you in the gig.'

Rebecca was still uncertain about this. 'I will walk. What do I ask for from the apothecary?'

Lady Agnes handed her a folded piece of paper and a purse full of coin. 'I have written it down.'

'Very well. Let me tell the children and I will go.' Rebecca entered the schoolroom and Lady Agnes followed.

'I have an errand in Ambleside,' she told the girls. 'Lady Agnes will sit with you.' She turned to Lady Agnes. 'Really, teach them anything you like.'

Lady Agnes nodded. 'I will.'

Rebecca returned to her room to collect her bonnet, gloves and the shawl Lord Brookmore had given to her that first day on the road. She told the footman attending the hall where she was going and stepped out into the morning air, which was a bit warmer than when she rode Lily earlier. A brisk walk would warm her.

She might even enjoy the exercise and the solitude.

Chapter Twenty

Lady Agnes made the girls practise their needle-work and while they did so, she leafed through the latest issue of *La Belle Assemblée*.

After a half-hour, she glanced at the clock and stood.

She clapped her hands. 'Pamela! Ellen! I have the most fabulous idea.'

The girls looked up at her.

'Do you know how Miss Tilson had to do an errand for me in Ambleside?'

They nodded.

She went on. 'Well, she said she would walk there.' How lucky Lady Agnes was that Miss Tilson decided to walk. It made matters so much easier. 'Would it not be the loveliest surprise if I asked my coachman to drive the two of you to Ambleside to meet her so she will not have to walk home? Would that not be the very best surprise?' She could see she'd kindled their interest. She intended to make it impossible for them to refuse. 'I will give you coins so you may purchase some gingerbread. Would you like that?'

'I would,' cried Ellen, bursting with excitement. She turned to her sister. 'Pamela, you would, too, would you not?'

'I suppose.' Pamela was obviously a little wary.

No matter. Agnes was not about to allow a nine-year-old child to stop her.

'Wait here a moment.' She hurried to the door. 'I will see to my coachman.'

Agnes descended the back stairs and left the house through the back entrance, careful that no one saw her. She walked through the garden and across the park until she could see a village cart waiting on the road, obscured from view by a group of trees. She waved to Sir Orin and he waved back.

When she returned for the girls, she made herself animated again. 'We are so lucky! I caught him already driving a village cart. Would you like to ride on a village cart?'

'Yes!' cried Ellen.

'Then you shall. I have another idea!' Agnes went on. 'Let's tell nobody what we are doing. Let us leave them a note.' She took a piece of paper and opened an inkwell. She wrote on the paper and folded it, leaving it on the table.

In no time they were walking through the garden and out the back gate.

'He will meet us on the road.'

It did not matter that the children could tell Brookmore or anyone else that Agnes arranged their little wagon ride. She would just say they were making it up. Who would believe children?

'Hello there!' The driver of the cart jumped down and helped the girls over the stone fence.

After he put both girls on the seat and climbed up next to them, Pamela cried, 'Wait, Lady Agnes. Are you not accompanying us?'

She laughed. 'Of course not! There is not enough room. As it is, one of you will have to ride on Miss Tilson's lap coming home.' She reached in her pocket and handed Pamela several coins. 'This is for your gingerbread. Do not lose it.'

Pamela closed her small hand around the money and glanced up at the sky. 'It is all grey today. Maybe it will rain.'

'It will not rain,' Agnes assured her. And if it did, a little rain would not hurt them.

'I do not think we should do this,' Pamela said as Sir Orin pulled away. 'It might rain and we might become ill with a fever.'

'Nonsense,' Agnes said, waving them off.

Agnes heard Sir Orin say in a jovial voice, 'Do not worry, little lady. It will be an adventure.'

Agnes grinned to herself as she watched the cart drive away. It was a masterful plan she'd created. She'd wait a half-hour before sounding the alarm that the children were missing. Sir Orin would be well on the road by then. He would take the girls to a rented cottage on Lake Windermere, where he would entertain them until Miss Tilson arrived to secure their release. She would be handed a letter while she was in Ambleside saying that the children had been abducted and her acceptance of Sir Orin's suit was the ransom she must pay.

Of course, the abduction was merely a ruse. The children would be returned later with a dramatic tale to tell, but Agnes had already invented a much more plausible explanation that surely would be believed. The best part was Miss Tilson would have already left with Sir Orin.

'When wanting someone to do your bidding, find their weakness,' she said aloud.

The children were Miss Tilson's weakness.

Agnes turned towards the house and started walking back.

Rebecca left the apothecary with a vial containing the headache remedy Lady Agnes had requested.

She no sooner stepped out into the street when a boy approached her.

'Are you Miss Tilson, miss?' he asked.

'I am.' She was puzzled he would ask.

He handed her a folded piece of paper that bore a plain seal, bowed and left.

She broke the seal and read.

Dearest Claire,
I cannot live without you. I must have you. I am desperate. I have abducted Lord Brookmore's nieces. If you value their lives, you will come to me.

Go to the Unicorn Inn. There is a carriage waiting for you that will take you to Far Sawrey. From there you will walk two miles along the coast of Lake Windermere. I will find you and bring you to the children.

Tell no one. Leave immediately. If you do not follow my instructions to the letter, I cannot vouch for the well-being of the children.
Yours, etc.
You know who I am.

She folded the paper, her heart pounding.

She should tell Lord Brookmore! But he would not return until tomorrow. She could not wait. The children's lives depended on her. There was no choice but to do what Sir Orin said.

How could he have known she would be here?

Rebecca felt the blood drain from her face. Lady Agnes.

This was why Lady Agnes befriended her. This was why she sent her on this errand. Surely she was not so depraved she would risk the lives of the children?

Sir Orin was that depraved, however.

She stopped a man on the street. 'Please direct me to the Unicorn Inn.'

It was almost two hours before she alighted at Far Sawrey and began walking. The coastline of the lake was heavily wooded and the breeze through the trees chilled her to the bone. She could not think of her comfort now. She thought only of the children.

She half-expected Sir Orin to jump out from behind a tree, accost her like he'd done on her morning rides. She half-hoped there would be other people on the road, someone who might help her, but she was very much alone.

She walked on. Surely she'd walked two miles already? Finally she spied a cottage, far from the road at the edge of the lake. Her senses heightened. Was this where he would be? She slowed her pace, carefully surveying her surroundings. There was the cottage and one outbuilding, both difficult to see from the road.

Sir Orin stepped from a path that she assumed led to the cottage. He smiled.

'Claire, you are finally here.' He approached with arms outstretched. 'I knew you would come.'

She stepped back. 'Where are the children?'

His smile faltered, but remained on his face. 'They are in the cottage.' He gestured for her to follow. 'Follow me.'

The path was bordered with scrubby brush and jagged rocks.

Sir Orin swept his arm over them. 'One way in to this cottage.' In an open area, a village cart stood. He pointed to it. 'Our transportation.'

'Are the children unharmed?' she demanded.

He turned back to her. 'I have no wish to harm them.' He grinned. 'That is, unless you do not cooperate with me.'

A chill went up her spine.

The path led to the outbuilding, which was a stable. Rebecca could see the horse inside. Fat raindrops started to fall, kicking up the dirt of the path.

Sir Orin stopped and looked up at the sky. 'Rain. I had not anticipated rain.'

The raindrops fell faster.

They finally reached the door of the cottage. Sir Orin took a key from his pocket and unlocked it.

When he opened the door, Rebecca rushed through. 'Pamela! Ellen! Are you here!'

Footsteps sounded from a back room. The children appeared, running towards her. She knelt down and scooped them into a hug. They looked unharmed. They felt unharmed.

She examined them more closely.

'See! I told Pamela you would meet us here,' Ellen cried. 'Just like John Coachman said.'

'John Coachman?' Was there another man here?

'That is what he told us to call him.' Ellen pointed to Sir Orin. 'He said all coachmen are called John Coachman.'

'I am here now and all will be well,' she said, hugging them again. 'Have you had something to eat?'

'Sweetmeats and tea,' Ellen said. 'And we've played games. But Pamela was worried you would not come.'

Pamela nodded. 'It is a diversion to Ellen.' She spoke this in a way that showed she thought it anything but a diversion.

Pamela looked sad. 'I hope we will be home soon.'

Rain pattered the roof of the cottage, louder and louder, until it sounded like one constant din.

Sir Orin went to the window and looked out. 'It

appears we are here until tomorrow unless this rain lets up.' He shooed the girls towards the back room. 'Leave us now. I need to talk to Miss Tilson.'

The girls looked reluctant to leave her.

'Go,' she told them. 'I will be with you in a moment.'

Pamela took Ellen's hand and pulled her into the room.

Sir Orin closed the door and turned the key in the lock. 'Do not worry. They have cards to play with. And spillikins.'

'You do not need them now. I am here. Take them back to Brookmore House.' She needed them to be safe.

He gestured to the window. 'In the rain?'

In rain, snow, anything as long as they were away from him. He was more dangerous than being caught in the rain.

He came closer. She backed away.

'Do not fear, Claire, dear, I am not going to force myself on you. Not like before. I do apologise.'

'What do you want from me, then?' she asked.

He became serious. 'I still want you to marry me. Marry me and come back to Ireland with me.'

'Or?'

His eyes turned cold. 'Or you will be very unhappy.'

'You cannot want me,' she insisted. 'You know I despise you.'

His forehead creased. 'You do say the most frightful things to me now. In Ireland you protested only that I was married and that you had no wish to betray my wife. Now you simply refuse me.'

'Never mind about me. Please let the children go. Take them to Far Sawrey, at least. It is only two miles.' She could think of nothing else.

He walked to the window, turned and smiled. 'I would not wish them to get wet. That was not in the plan.'

'The plan.' Of course, this abduction was planned. 'You planned this with Lady Agnes, did you not?'

'She has proved to be a valuable ally,' he responded.

'What was supposed to happen, if not for the rain?' she asked.

He laughed. 'According to Lady Agnes, the children were to be returned once I secured your…*affections*, shall we call it, then you and I were to be in a carriage on our way to Gretna Green before the sky turned dark.'

What did he mean *according to Lady Agnes*? 'And according to you?'

He lowered himself into a chair and looked up at her. 'I was thinking, what would make you stay if the children were returned safely? Lady Agnes did not consider that, did she? So they will come with us to Gretna Green, after which I will not need them any more, because you will finally be mine.'

Rebecca trembled inside. Did he mean he would return the children safely or not? A man who most likely killed his wife would be equally as capable of doing away with children. Rebecca could not take the chance. They must escape him.

He continued. 'You have left a note, asking for money in exchange for the children, with elaborate instructions for its delivery. That is all a humbug, you see. Some poor fool will find the money and be thought to be your accomplice. No one will suspect me, of course, because I left Ambleside the day after Lord Brookmore threatened me.'

Sir Orin and Lady Agnes had no idea exactly how plausible this scheme would be to Lord Brookmore. It was the sort of thing an imposter with no money might do rather than risk being kicked out without a reference or pay.

If that imposter had no love for the children and their uncle, that was.

Her heart raced wildly, but she needed to remain calm.

She sat in a chair near him. 'It seems you and Lady Agnes have thought of everything.'

He turned pensive. 'I did need her, at least before this. I've no doubt that I might have devised a workable plan on my own, but—' He gave her a meaningful look. 'I was in the throes of passion. My head is clear now, though. I will not make any future mistakes.'

If he did not make another mistake, the children were doomed. No matter what, she must not make any mistakes either. No more defiance. She must make herself as much like Claire as she could be until a way to escape offered itself.

He gestured to a kettle on the fire in the fireplace. 'Make me some tea, Claire. Have some yourself, if you like.'

At one end of the room there was a scullery with dirty cups, saucers and plates piled in it and a pantry where she found a tea caddy, some sugar, a large jug of milk and a tin of biscuits.

'Is this all there is to eat?' she asked.

He shrugged. 'That is all I bought. That and some sweetmeats for the children, which they have eaten already.' He waved an arm. 'Bring me some biscuits, as well.'

She put some tea in the pot and poured water from the kettle into it. 'May I offer some tea to the children?' she asked.

'The children.' He laughed. 'I quite forgot about

them. You may serve them after you serve me. I prefer they stay in that room.'

She did as he bid as deferentially as she could manage, although she had considered throwing boiling water on him and making a run for it. She didn't think she could release the girls from their prison fast enough, though.

When she'd finished serving him, she picked up the tea tray. 'May I spend some time with the children? I fear if I do not, they may become alarmed and hysterical.'

'Excellent point, Claire.' He rose and unlocked the door. He even opened it for her so that she could carry the tea to the children.

He left the door open.

Pamela and Ellen rose from their seats and came to her.

'I brought us some tea.' She set the tray on the table and set out the tea cups as if they were in the Tower Room at Brookmore House.

'When will we go home?' Pamela asked.

Ellen stood next to her chair and leaned against her. 'I want to go home, too.'

She did not want to alarm them. 'Our adventure is going to last a bit longer than expected.'

She glanced out the window. The cottage overlooked Lake Windermere. Wind whipped the trees that grew at the lake's edge and the water's waves washed over a stone jetty. Tied to a post by the jetty was a rowing boat bobbing in the water like a bucking horse.

Rebecca's stomach roiled and she felt as if she were in another rowing boat being tossed by waves. She closed her eyes and turned back to the girls.

'Do not worry,' she told them. 'I will not leave you.'

Chapter Twenty-One

The rain fell in sheets, but Garret and his estate manager decided to push through the bad weather and make it back to Brookmore House before dark rather than stay in one more uncomfortable inn.

Being away had been good for Garret. He'd at least solved one of his problems, securing enough stores to get them through a bad harvest. His more domestic problems remained unresolved, but the distance from them had done him some good. That and spending his days on Skiddaw's back like in the army. Garret felt more himself than he'd felt since his brother died. He was not certain what that meant ultimately, but it felt much better to be in his own skin again.

He'd missed Pamela and Ellen. He'd even missed Lady Rebecca.

The roads had turned muddy and the horses made slower progress, but eventually Garret saw the

Brookmore gates and knew they'd soon be warm and in dry clothes.

As they approached, a woman emerged from the house and ran towards them, hatless and coatless and unheeding the pouring rain.

'Lord Brookmore! Lord Brookmore!' It was Mary Beale, the girls' maid.

'Mary?' He halted his horse.

She grabbed on to a stirrup. 'Sir! The children are missing! They are missing! And Miss Tilson.'

His calmness fled. 'What? When?'

'We found them gone late this morning. They haven't returned!' she cried.

'Have you searched for them?' Ben asked.

'Yes!' She took a breath. 'Mr Glover sent several men out, all over the countryside. No one found any sign of them.'

Visions of Ellen and Lady Rebecca in the lake assaulted him. They wouldn't be so foolish a second time, would they?

'Here.' He extended his hand to her and pulled her up on to his horse.

They hurried to the house. When they reached the door, Garret helped Mary down and dismounted himself.

'I'll take the horses,' Ben said. 'When they're settled I'll come back. See how I can help.'

Garret rushed inside.

Glover, Mrs Dodd and several of the other servants were in the hall. A footman came over and helped peel off his wet clothes.

He wasted no time. 'Tell me what happened.'

Mary, shivering from dashing out into the rain, spoke. 'I was coming to the schoolroom to see if Miss Pamela and Miss Ellen wanted nuncheon when Lady Agnes ran out, saying the girls and Miss Tilson were gone.'

'Lady Agnes?' Garret's suspicions rose.

'She'd been spending time in the schoolroom the last couple of days,' Mary explained.

'In the schoolroom?'

Mary nodded. 'We sent up an alarm in the house, but no one had seen them and no one had heard them go out, but we knew they did, because their hats, gloves and jackets were gone.'

'I saw Miss Tilson,' one of the footmen said. 'She left to do an errand in the village, but she never came back.'

Glover spoke up. 'We sent men to search the estate and the countryside, but we didn't find them. A villager saw a cart and driver with what might have been two little girls, but he was not certain.'

Brant made his arthritic way down the stairs. 'I found this!' He waved a letter in his hand, but halted when he saw Garret. 'My lord! You are back. Thank God.'

Garret bounded up the stairs to his valet, who handed him the letter. Still on the stairs he broke the seal and saw it was written in a careful hand.

He read it.

Dear Lord Brookmore,
I have taken your nieces to a place where you will not find them. Follow these instructions carefully or you will never see them again.
I want five hundred pounds for their safe return...

There followed instructions on when and where to leave the ransom.

Garret skipped to the end of the letter.

Yours,
C. Tilson

Claire Tilson.

He crushed the paper in his hand. 'Where is Lady Agnes? I wish to see her immediately.'

'The poor dear is in her room with her aunt,' Mrs Dodd responded. 'She is quite shaken by this, as well we all are.'

Garret continued up the stairs to Lady Agnes's

room. He opened the door, not bothering to knock. 'Lady Agnes.'

She sat on the sofa, leaning against her aunt, patting her hand. At his abrupt entrance both ladies jumped.

Lady Agnes emitted a cry. 'Brookmore! You are here.'

Was that shock on her face? He was not expected until tomorrow.

He looked pointedly at her aunt. 'Leave us.'

He must have appeared fearsome, because the aunt's eyes widened in fright.

'I should st-stay,' she stammered. 'Not proper.'

'Leave,' he said again.

Lady Agnes wiped her eyes with a lace-edged handkerchief. 'Oh, leave us, Aunt Theodora. These are special times. Brookmore needs me now, I am certain.'

Her aunt needed no more encouragement.

When she'd gone, Lady Agnes flung herself against the sofa. 'You've heard! They are gone. I am certain something terrible has happened to them.'

He walked through the room, stopping by the writing desk, opening its drawers.

'Are you looking for something, Brookmore, dear?' she asked sweetly.

He was looking for something with her handwriting on it.

'Tell me what you know.' His clothing was still wet and dripped on the carpet.

She acted as if she were stifling a sob. 'I do not know much. I spent some time with Miss Tilson and the dear children—I thought I must do something to make up for the night of the dinner party—I had been with them earlier. When I came back, they were gone and no one knew where they were.' She wiped her eyes again. 'That is all I know.'

'What of this?' He shoved the letter in her face.

She took it from his hand and smoothed out the paper.

'Oh, my goodness!' she cried as she read the letter. 'I do not believe it.'

'I do not believe it either.'

She shook her head. 'I had no idea Miss Tilson was capable of such treachery! I mean, she was odd, not like a governess at all, but...this?'

'You spent time with her,' he said.

She sighed. 'I treasured the time I spent—not with her, but with Pamela and Ellen. Those little girls are so sweet.' She looked him in the eye. 'I could not have guessed Miss Tilson would ever threaten to harm them.'

He seized her by the shoulders and pulled her to a

standing position. 'Tell me what you did.' The letter fluttered to the floor.

She wriggled beneath his grasp. 'Stop being brutish!' Her despairing tone fled. 'You are cold and wet.'

He released her. 'You wrote this.' He picked up the letter.

'Me?' She made a nervous laugh. 'Do not be absurd!'

'Who else wanted her gone?' He glared at her. 'Now tell me where she and the children are.'

'How would I know that?' She twisted her face into a wounded expression. 'I am desolated that you would think such a thing of me.' She took a shuddering breath. 'You simply do not wish to believe she wrote that.' She blinked as if fighting back tears. 'She must have written it. I know it is painful to think of her doing it. After all, you trusted her with your nieces. But it makes no sense for anyone else to write it.'

She was trying too hard to convince him.

'I know she did not write it.' He shoved the paper at her again.

She perused it once more, as if examining it carefully. 'I am so sorry, Brookmore.' Her voice turned a sugary sympathetic. 'But how well did you know her, really? Did you know her writing?'

He did. She'd written a note to him. He could not remember her handwriting specifically, but this was not hers. He knew it.

He pointed to the letter. 'I know this is not her writing.'

She put a hand on his arm as if in consolation. 'Dear Brookmore. You waste time. You must do as the letter says, for the children's sake. She is missing and the children are missing and she left you a letter explaining it all. You cannot know this is from anyone but her.'

He removed her hand. 'I do know.' He knew because she would not have signed her name Claire Tilson. He was not about to divulge her secret to Lady Agnes.

He took Lady Agnes by the arm and sat her back on the sofa. 'Let me tell you what I think you have done. You have colluded with Sir Orin who has kidnapped the three of them. Tell me where I am to find them before it is too late.'

She brushed off where he'd touched her. 'Did not Sir Orin leave here after you brutalised him?'

He leaned over her. 'Did he tell you I brutalised him?' She'd just confirmed his suspicion that she was involved.

She flushed. 'I do not know what you mean.'

'If I send someone to Ambleside, will they find

an innkeeper who remembers a meeting or two between Sir Orin and a lady?'

'It is too rainy to go to Ambleside.' She glanced away and back. 'Besides, perhaps the lady could be Miss Tilson.'

He turned her head back. 'Blonde hair. Blue eyes. Fine clothing?'

She jerked away.

He turned her back again. 'Now tell me everything. Tell me where they are.'

'You are making a fuss over nothing!' she protested. 'The children will be home tomorrow and your precious governess will be gone. All will be well.'

'You are a fool, Lady Agnes. A man like Sir Orin is not going to release the children.' He was likely a murderer already. What would be one or two more?

'Tell me.'

She sighed. 'Oh, very well. But I assure you no one would come to harm. Your nieces will have had a lark and that woman would have another chance to accept a marriage proposal.'

She explained the plan.

When she was finished, Garret stepped back, his hands flexing into fists. 'You remain here. If they are unharmed, you will leave. You will tell everyone you broke our engagement. You will tell them you simply changed your mind. If you say otherwise, this story will be told with you as the villain.'

She glared at him.

'If they are harmed in any way, I will call in the magistrate and you will pay for your petty treachery.'

He turned on his heel and left the room.

Sir Orin allowed Rebecca to stay in the room with the children for over an hour. She played simple card games with them and spillikins, but all the time she was aware he watched them from the other room.

The sky turned dark but the sounds of the wind, rain and waves reached Rebecca's ears, pricking at her memory of another storm, another time of danger. She needed to stay in the present, even though the past tugged her backwards.

'Claire, my love,' Sir Orin called to her. 'Come sit with me now.'

'One moment, Sir Orin.' Rebecca hugged both girls. 'I'll just be in the other room.' There was a sofa in that room, right beneath the window. 'Lie down on the sofa and try to sleep.'

The girls climbed on the sofa and she covered them both with her shawl. She kissed them on their heads, blew out the lamp and walked out of the room, closing the door behind her.

'I am here,' she told Sir Orin.

He patted a chair next to his. She obediently sat next to him.

He turned his chair a little so that he looked directly at her. 'You are so good with children, Claire. That is one of the first things I loved about you.'

Her entire experience with children had taken place in these last few weeks.

'You have not asked about the children. Do you not wonder how they fare?'

She did not know them. 'How could they fare? Their mother died and their father left them.'

He scowled. 'I must curb that biting tongue of yours.'

Better she curb it. She had no wish to agitate him.

She glanced around the room. There was just the one door and windows facing the front.

'The children were inconsolable when you left, you know,' he said.

'Were they?' She could see how they might be. She'd become instantly fond of Claire. 'But do you not think they miss their mother more acutely?'

He shrugged. 'I suppose. She did dote on them.' He waved a hand as if wiping that thought away. 'I thought you would have more to say about the children. You must have cared for them deeply. They said you cried when you said goodbye.' He wagged a finger at her. 'You sneaked away without me knowing. I would not have let you go, you know.'

Had Claire realised what this man was capable of? Was that why she left? She'd run away, obviously.

He smiled. 'Guess which one of the girls cried the most after you left?'

Rebecca felt panicked inside. She struggled to remember the names she'd read in *Debrett's*. 'Margaret?' she guessed.

He frowned. 'Margaret, you say?'

She struggled to remember the others. 'Was it Mary? Not Bridget, certainly.'

He peered at her. 'Why do you call them Margaret and Bridget?'

She remembered correctly, she was certain. 'Those are their names.'

'We have always called them Meg and Biddy. You should know that.' His eyes turned suspicious.

Her muscles tensed.

He leaned a bit closer. 'Tell me the name of my estate.'

Had it been in *Debrett's*? She could not remember.

His voice rose. 'Tell me the name of the village. The county.'

She was discovered.

Rebecca straightened. 'I cannot tell you those things.'

His expression turned dark. 'Why not?'

She lifted her chin. 'Because I am not Claire Tilson.'

He made a sound like the low growl of a wild dog.

She taunted him. 'I look like her. A lot like her, but not exactly. I wonder that a man so besotted with Claire would not see the difference.'

'You are deliberately toying with me,' he said, his voice low.

She went on. 'You said so yourself. That I was not like myself. Of course I was not. I was never Claire.'

'How can this be?' His voice turned smaller.

'By chance. We met on the packet boat. We instantly saw the resemblance and we formed a friendship over it. We even fooled my maid into thinking Claire was me.'

He shook his head. 'Who are you, then?'

She gave him a regal look. 'I am Lady Rebecca Pierce. I am of the aristocracy and I am well connected with men of power.' Of course, all her connections were gone. Lady Rebecca was thought to be dead.

'Why are you pretending to be Claire?' he asked.

She was not about to confide in him. 'My reasons were private ones. You need not know them.'

He swung away from her. 'No. No. You are playing with me. You are Claire.'

'I am not. I do not know where you live. I do not know your pet names for people. I know nothing of your life. I can only imagine what a nightmare it was to be married to you. Not so horrid to lose one's life over.' She should stop herself, but her words came out like a tidal wave.

He stood and paced in front of her. 'Where is Claire, then? Where is she? I demand to know.'

She did not know how he would take this news. 'Sir Orin, Claire is dead. Our packet boat was caught in a terrible storm. She drowned.'

'No.' He groaned. 'No.'

He paced away from her and twisted back. 'This changes everything, you know.'

She hoped so. 'You do not really want me. I'm not Claire. There is no reason why you cannot simply walk away from us.' She spoke soothingly, as she might to a spooked horse. 'You could leave now. You would get wet, of course, but you would be long gone before anyone would know.'

'No.' He spoke more to himself than to Rebecca. 'No. You'd tell. You'd tell.'

Her hands shook. 'I won't tell. I—I do not want attention called to myself. All I wish is for you to be gone and for the children to return home safely. I must disappear, too, you know.'

'No,' he said again.

There was a loud crack and a crash that put Rebecca back on the packet boat, when the mast had broken above their heads. The room grew dark and images of the angry sea overwhelmed her.

'Blast.' He walked to the window and peered out. 'A tree. It looks like it hit the stable. He walked to a hook on the wall where his topcoat hung. He put it on and grabbed a lantern.

He opened the door and turned to her. 'Do not try to escape. I will see you. There is only this one door and one path to the road and one road. Do not do anything foolish.' He walked out the door.

She immediately ran to the room where the children were. When she opened the door, they jumped back.

'We were listening,' Ellen said. 'Are you really not Miss Tilson?'

'Never mind that. We have to get out of here.' She ran to the window.

She pushed on the window and it finally opened wide enough for them to climb through. The distance to the ground was one storey high.

She had to think fast. 'Put your jackets on.' She helped them. 'I am going to climb out the window and hang over the side. Pamela, you climb down on me and drop to the ground. Then wait to help Ellen down.'

Rebecca climbed out into the rain. The window sill was slippery, but she hung on.

'Pamela! Come out now.'

Pamela scrambled out and climbed down Rebecca, holding on to Rebecca's dress as she lowered herself, finally letting go. Rebecca heard her hit the ground.

'I'm ready for Ellen,' she said in a loud whisper.

Rebecca's arms were aching. 'Hurry, Ellen. You can do this.'

Ellen climbed out like her sister and scurried down quickly like a little monkey.

'I'll catch you,' Pamela said.

Ellen let go and Rebecca heard her land.

'Now move away.' Rebecca's fall would be farther than the girls. She said a prayer that she not injure herself.

She landed in a bramble bush, the thorns piercing her skin and ripping her dress, but she was able to get to her feet. The rain pelted them like icy shards.

'Where do we go?' Pamela asked. She held her little sister's hand.

There was only one way to go.

If they tried to run for the road, Sir Orin would see them. Even if they managed to slip past him, he'd likely find them eventually. They needed an escape route he could not follow.

'We're going to the lake,' Rebecca said. 'There is a boat there. Hold on to me and to each other.'

It was so dark, Rebecca could only see inches

in front of her. She found the path to the lake by trial and error and by listening to the slapping of the waves against the shore. They slipped and slid down the path, but they reached the jetty. There was enough light to see white caps on the lake and the bobbing of the rowing boat.

Rebecca pulled on the rope that tethered the boat to the post, bringing it close enough to the jetty to grab hold of it. As she reached for it, it dipped away and the memory of being dropped into the rowing boat from the sinking ship made her freeze. She again felt herself seated next to the mother huddled with her two children.

She shook her head.

These two children were her responsibility now. She would not allow them to die like the others.

She caught the boat and held it against the stone jetty. 'Climb in.'

The girls did not hesitate, but they did not know what rough water could do. They climbed in because they trusted her. She climbed in after them and freed the boat from its moorings. She pushed hard against the jetty and the boat floated on to the lake.

The water was rough and the rocking of the boat jabbed Rebecca with memories, but she stayed focused on whatever she must do next. The boat was filled with rain water and they busied themselves bailing out the water with jugs they found in the boat. There were oars, but Rebecca was too weary to try to use them. The wind and the water floated them further and further from shore. They were safe. From Sir Orin, at least.

'Let's huddle together to keep warm,' she said to the girls, wrapping them in an embrace, holding them as close to her body as she could.

'Are we safe?' asked Pamela.

'Yes,' she assured her. 'He cannot reach us on the water.'

'He was a bad man, wasn't he?' Pamela said.

'Yes,' Rebecca agreed. 'A very bad and dangerous man.'

'But Lady Agnes sent us off with him,' Ellen said. 'She said we were going to surprise you.'

'She lied to us.' Pamela huddled closer.

Ellen whimpered.

They clung to each other and Rebecca tried not to think about the rocking of the boat or of how cold it was or of how and when and where they would reach the shore. If they would reach the shore.

Finally Ellen quieted and Rebecca hoped she'd fallen asleep, but her little voice popped up. 'What are we to call you, Miss Tilson?'

She kissed the child's head. 'Call me Rebecca.'

Chapter Twenty-Two

Garret made his way up the road along Lake Windermere from Far Sawrey, looking for the cottage Sir Orin had rented. The rain had stopped at last, but Ben and two of the stablemen who started out with him had been slowed by the mud and rain. Skiddaw, seasoned by years of army life, plodded on and Garret soon was ahead of the others.

There was something about danger that drove away the non-essential clutter of life, leaving a stark clarity of what was important. In the time-consuming effort it took to get this far, Garret became very clear about one thing. Lady Rebecca, Pamela and Ellen were the most important people in his life. He would die to protect them. He did not care what anyone in society or Parliament or even on the throne thought of him. He wanted to share his life with Lady Rebecca and to rear his nieces as if they were his own children.

He'd been this way in battle. Able to see what he

and his soldiers must do to win. And survive. His men had esteemed him and, because he saw himself reflected in their eyes, he'd been secure in believing he was a competent officer.

Now he realised from those first days, he'd seen admiration reflected in Lady Rebecca's eyes. He realised her steadfast support of him helped give him confidence to manage the estate's problems his way. She'd enabled him to put himself back in touch with the people who'd helped forge him as a boy. His workers were his soldiers now and he knew he could bring them through any adversity.

Lady Rebecca had seen him clearly when he'd been unable to see himself. He no longer cared that she'd deceived him as to her name. He, too, had seen her true self clearly.

And now, when he feared losing her, he knew he loved her.

It had taken Garret and his men a long time to reach this road. Lady Agnes did not know all the details, like which cottage Orin had rented. It took time to discover that in Far Sawrey. The darkness thwarted Garret. He feared the cottage would be so obscured by the thick trees and shrubs that he could pass the cottage by.

Up ahead, though, he thought he saw a light

through the trees. A lantern? He urged Skiddaw forward. Yes. There was definitely a light.

Garret came upon a path leading down towards the lake. He dismounted, leaving Skiddaw there, and followed the path. He passed a village cart in a clearing—a villager had seen a man in a village cart. He walked farther and could dimly see the outline of a cottage. Light shone through the windows, but faintly, as if only a candle burned inside. A brighter light was visible in the outbuilding, its roof smashed by a fallen tree. Garret stealthily moved towards it. He peered through a gap in the wall and saw a man trying to free a horse blocked in by rocks and timber. He could not see if it was Sir Orin, but he made his way to the cottage and went inside.

'Lady Rebecca?' he called quietly. 'Pamela? Ellen?'

There was no answer, but he found two teacups and saucers. More than one person had been there.

He entered a second room and found more dishes, a deck of cards and a game of spillikins. On the sofa was the shawl he had purchased for her in Moelfre.

She had been here! The children, too, unless Sir Orin had a fondness for spillikins.

Where were they now? Was he too late?

Garret strode out of the cottage and back to the outbuilding.

He stood in the doorway. 'Sir Orin!'

The man turned and froze for a moment. The light from the lantern shone on his face. It was indeed Sir Orin.

Sir Orin charged at Garret, who deftly stepped aside and caught him by the arm, sending him sprawling. Sir Orin picked up a piece of splintered wood and swung it at Garret, who ducked and seized him from behind.

'Where are they?' Garret snarled.

'I do not know what you are talking about.' Sir Orin struggled to free himself.

'Do not lie to me. I found her shawl in the cottage.'

Sir Orin froze. 'They are gone?'

'Where are they?' Garret roared.

'I rid myself of them!' Sir Orin struggled again, twisting and turning until both men were outside the building.

Garret's foot slipped in the mud, loosening his hold enough for Sir Orin to break free. They scuffled in the mud, but Sir Orin managed to scramble away and run into the trees, quickly disappearing from view.

Garret's heart pounded in fear. Which was true? Sir Orin's surprise they were gone? Or saying he got rid of them?

He picked up the lantern and returned to the cottage. He searched the first room, but there was nowhere they could be hidden. He looked in the second room where he'd found her shawl.

It looked as if they'd just stepped away, but where?

The window was open. Garret walked over to it and leaned out, holding the lantern for light. Could they have climbed out the window? He carried the lantern outside and examined the ground underneath the back window. He found footprints in the mud that led to a jetty.

He walked to the end of it and lifted the lantern high.

The water was choppy, but the wind was blowing the storm clouds away. The moon suddenly shone down on the lake. Garret spied a rowing boat on the water and it looked like someone was in the boat.

Had she escaped with them in a boat? How much courage had that taken?

His heart skittered. 'Rebecca!' he called. 'Rebecca!'

He saw the figure divide into three. There were three of them!

'Rebecca!' he called again. 'It is Garret Brookmore!'

'Garret!' she called back. Using his given name warmed him.

'Uncle Garret! Uncle Garret!' two young voices cried.

He waved the lantern. 'Come in. It is safe. He is gone.'

He watched while she positioned herself with the oars and rowed. Her progress was slow, but she came closer and closer until he finally could reach the boat and pull it to him. He secured the boat to its moorings and held it steady so they could climb out.

Rebecca lifted each girl and handed them to him and finally he reached for her, lifting her out of the boat and into his arms.

He held her against him. 'Thank God you are safe. Thank God you are all safe.'

An hour later Rebecca and the children were in dry clothes and comfortably warm in an inn in Far Sawrey. Rebecca, Garret and the girls were in one room, cosy on one bed. There was no separating them, not after the frightful night they'd had.

Garret's men had reached the cottage by the time they were out of the boat and they wasted no time in finding blankets to warm them. They hitched the horse to the village cart and drove back to the village, to the inn. Garret's men rode on to Brookmore House to inform them that Rebecca and the children were safe and would return the next day.

Rebecca lay in Garret's arms while Pamela and Ellen slept like little angels next to them.

'I am sure we will be the subject of gossip in Far Sawrey tomorrow,' Rebecca murmured.

'I am sure I do not care a whit,' Garret answered. He glanced at Pamela and Ellen. 'Besides, we are well chaperoned.'

'That is not likely to stop talk.'

'Very well.' He placed his lips on the top of her head. 'You will have to marry me then or you will be thought a fallen woman.'

She sat up and looked at him. 'Marry you?'

His mouth widened into a slow smile. 'Marry me.' His expression sobered. 'Marry me.'

Rebecca was afraid to trust in such happiness. 'Are you certain?'

'I am very certain.' He held her gaze.

She looked away. 'I do not know. I have made such a mess of things. I cannot marry you as Claire Tilson. I am not Claire Tilson. But I am not certain I want to be Lady Rebecca either. That brings more trouble, I am afraid.'

He sat up as well and gently moved her face so that she looked at him again. 'I need to know only one thing. Do you love me? Because I now know I have loved you since that first glimpse of you, before you even opened your eyes.'

'You couldn't possibly—' She started to argue with him, but stopped herself.

'Do you love me?' he asked again.

She loved him so much the words would not form in her mouth, but she nodded.

He embraced her again.

'You are the finest man I have ever known.' Her voice worked again. 'I once hoped for a man I could love, but I never imagined there could be a man as principled, kind and generous as you are.'

He hugged her tighter. 'I am not certain I deserve such praise.'

'You do,' she murmured against his chest, relishing the beat of his heart and the warmth of his body. 'But perhaps love does not solve our problems.'

'If you love me,' he said, 'none of the other problems matter.'

She just could not figure it, though. She couldn't have banns read as Claire Tilson and she was not eager for anyone to know Lady Rebecca was still alive. There was no way around it.

'I have an idea,' Garret said.

'Mmm,' she responded.

'We'll go to Gretna Green and marry over the anvil. You marry me with your true name. Then we come back and to everyone you will be Lady Brookmore. To me you will be Rebecca, but we can say that is your middle name or something.'

She sat up again. 'But it is scandalous to elope to Gretna Green.'

He pulled her back into an embrace. 'Pick your scandal, Lady Brookmore.'

She revelled in the comfort of his arms again. 'Did you know that was Sir Orin's plan? To marry me at Gretna Green. As if that would have made me stay with him.'

'Will it make you stay with me?' he asked.

'Absolutely,' she said.

Epilogue

Two weeks later Rebecca and Garret lounged in bed in an inn in Carlisle on their way back from Gretna Green. They were thoroughly man and wife in every way possible. Their breakfast had been sent up to their room and they'd managed to eat it in bed, being loathe to leave its comforts and each other and continue on the road back to Brookmore House. To be close, to be touching each other, was the perfect way to prolong the languid pleasure that came after lovemaking.

The innkeeper sent up newspapers with the meal, the latest local newspaper from Carlisle and a recent paper from London.

Rebecca read the London paper.

'Oh, no!' she cried, bolting out of bed.

'What is it?' Garret put down his paper.

'Listen to this. *"Rescue at sea. Two survivors of the tragic shipwreck of the packet* Dun Aengus *were rescued at sea days after the ship ran aground at Moelfre. Miraculously Lady Rebecca Pierce, sister of the Earl of Keneagle, survived by clinging to debris, along with another passenger, Lucien Roper of Kent. Lady Rebecca convalesced in Dublin until arriving in London one week ago.'"* She looked up at him. 'Claire is alive.'

'Alive?' He left the bed and faced her.

'Who else could it be? That is my name. She didn't use her own, so she must have taken on my identity, as I took on hers.' She covered her face with her hands. 'She is alive. Claire is alive.'

He put an arm around her. 'Then this is good news, is it not?'

'Yes! Wonderful news.' She felt as if she would weep.

'Then why look so distressed? Be happy.' He gently shook her.

She turned and let him enfold her in an embrace. 'Do you not see? I stole her life. She should have met you. She should have been Pamela and Ellen's governess.'

He kissed the top of her head. 'But it is you I love. You must never forget that. I love your courage and independence and forthrightness—everything about you. Claire might look like you, but she could not *be* you, could she? Any more than you could be her.

Besides…' he hugged her closer '…she would not have been at that inn to meet me, so you couldn't have taken a life she never would have had.'

'That is confusing,' she murmured.

He laughed. 'That whole situation is confusing. At least I am sure about one thing.'

'What are you sure of?' When he held her like this, all problems seemed solvable, all obstacles, surmountable, all mistakes, forgiven.

'That I love you.' He leaned down and kissed her.

She wrapped her arms around his neck and lost herself in his kiss.

When he stopped for air, he leaned his forehead against hers. 'I am sure of one other thing.'

She sighed. 'And that is?'

'I would be married to Lady Agnes, if you had not come into my life.'

She smiled. 'Thank God for that shipwreck.'

She'd come to see the shipwreck not as a trauma to be feared, but as a rebirth. The shipwreck had given her a new life, one with everything she'd dreamed of—and more. On the rare occasions the memories returned, she embraced them and promised all those lost that she would appreciate every day of her new life.

'Thank God for that shipwreck,' Garret murmured, capturing her lips once again.

She broke away abruptly. 'Garret, what if Sir Orin reads this newspaper? He will guess Claire is alive, as well. I told him who I am. He will guess that the Lady Rebecca in the newspaper is her.'

Garret looked directly into her eyes. 'We must warn her.'

* * * * *